FACE VALUE

Other books by Catherine Johnson

In Black and White
Hero
Stella

FACE VALUE

Catherine Johnson

OXFORD
UNIVERSITY PRESS

OXFORD
UNIVERSITY PRESS

Great Clarendon Street, Oxford OX2 6DP

Oxford University Press is a department of the University of Oxford.
It furthers the University's objective of excellence in research, scholarship,
and education by publishing worldwide in

Oxford New York
Auckland Cape Town Dar es Salaam Hong Kong Karachi
Kuala Lumpur Madrid Melbourne Mexico City Nairobi
New Delhi Shanghai Taipei Toronto

With offices in
Argentina Austria Brazil Chile Czech Republic France Greece
Guatemala Hungary Italy Japan Poland Portugal Singapore
South Korea Switzerland Thailand Turkey Ukraine Vietnam

Oxford is a registered trade mark of Oxford University Press
in the UK and in certain other countries

British Library Cataloguing in Publication Data
Data available

ISBN-13: 978-0-19-275406-6
ISBN-10: 0-19-275406-8

1 3 5 7 9 10 8 6 4 2

Typeset in Meridien by
Palimpsest Book Production Limited
Polmont, Stirlingshire

Printed in Great Britain by
Cox & Wyman Ltd, Reading, Berkshire

Lauren Now

Lauren Bogle sat in front of the big Paula Rego painting. She was listening to Chloe on the far side of the room talking to Lucy and Natalie from 10 DR. They looked so alike from the back in their school uniforms it was hard to tell them apart. They were talking about Nathan Rogers's party. Who was going. Who wasn't.

'Well done, Lauren.' Ms Thomas had come up behind her. 'Good use of line.'

Lauren tuned out. Chloe had been her best friend since Year 4 at junior school. More than six years of sleep-overs, of not having to think about who would be your partner for school trips or drama lessons, or who to sit next to in class. Six years of shared holidays and all-night conversations. And Lauren just knew it was all unravelling. Chloe wasn't being bitchy; just ever so slowly edging Lauren out. Like this morning on the coach, Chloe had sat across the back with Lucy and Natalie. Three of them, all with nice blonde-to-brown hair, all with the same curve to their eyebrows and all wearing their school kilts hoiked up the same way. Lauren was left to sit with Gail Norman, who liked horses, dried flowers, and Tudor re-enactment.

Lauren knew Chloe didn't have a bad bone in her body. It was just, as Nessa said, the way life goes. People grow up, they change, they want different things. Lauren knew

1

after the coach ride this morning that one of the things she didn't want was Tudor re-enactment.

'Just keep an eye on the way you see the colours, Lauren, and remember, less is more!' Ms Thomas flashed her a smile and moved on.

Lauren stared hard at the picture. It was called 'The Dance', although no one seemed particularly happy. There was a couple in the centre, and three women dancing in a ring; but to the left of the picture, nearest the cliff edge, stood an enormous woman, at least a metre taller than everyone else. Like a giantess.

'I know exactly how you feel,' Lauren mumbled to herself. She was just trying to work out the shape of the clouds when she was aware of someone behind her. Someone watching her. At first she imagined it was Chloe, perhaps, coming to say sorry for leaving her out. But it wasn't. It was a small woman with vivid red-painted lips, dressed entirely in black fitted clothes and the highest, spikiest, heels Lauren had ever seen. She smiled at Lauren, and Lauren half smiled back.

'Excuse me.' The woman talked posher than anyone in Stivenham. She put out a white hand with shiny painted nails. 'Ghislaine Furness,' she said.

Lauren looked around. Ms Thomas was in the next gallery; Lauren could just see her with Sarah and Amy. Chloe and Lucy and Natalie were still deep in conversation. Chloe giggled. The sound bounced off the gallery roof and made Lauren feel incredibly sad.

'I'm sorry?' Lauren stood up; all the better to move away if I need to, she thought. And standing, Lauren was at least twice as tall as this shiny, witchy woman.

The woman looked Lauren up and down, almost measuring her with her eyes. 'Thank you, thank you. I can see now. You're just what we're looking for!' She fished about in her hard black bag and brought out a business card.

'I'm Ghislaine Furness.' She passed Lauren the card. 'From Rain.'

Lauren stared at the little white card. Ghislaine Furness, Rain, International Models. Ghislaine Furness, off the telly, she thought, that show, with models. She looked back to the little woman. Of course! But she looked so much taller on TV!

'Can I ask: how old are you, dear? And what is your name? And you're very tall; how tall would you say? Five eleven, six foot?'

'Fifteen,' Lauren answered. 'Lauren Bogle, fifteen.' She shrugged. 'I don't know exactly, nearly a metre eighty.' Lauren had given up measuring herself years ago. Every time she did she was taller.

Lauren watched the woman write it down in a little notebook next to her name.

'Well, do make sure you talk to your parents first, of course, but please, phone me? Before next week, if possible.' She flashed a last smile and she was gone. Clacking across the stone gallery floor in her killer heels.

Chloe came over, her light brown hair shiny as water.

'You all right? Me and Nat and Luce are going to sneak off shopping in Covent Garden. You can come if you want. Ooh! Your drawing's good! What was that woman after?'

Lauren looked at Chloe and then at Natalie and Lucy, putting on lip gloss in front of a huge Francis Bacon nightmare painting.

'No, 's all right, I want to finish this.'

Chloe looked relieved. 'You won't tell Thomas we've gone?'

'Course not.'

'Thanks, Laur.' Chloe turned to go.

'That woman, she was Ghislaine Furness. She gave me this.'

Chloe didn't hear. She was skipping away with Lucy and Natalie.

Lauren sighed, sat down, and picked up her pencil. How was she going to sell anything that even hinted at modelling to Nessa?

Vanessa Then

Vanessa Harper was wearing her maroon school uniform. It was that livid shade of maroon that manages to reduce all skin shades to deathly and Nessa's summer holiday tan was wearing off. I look gross, she thought to herself and went down to breakfast. On the kitchen table were several prototype perfume bottles with the word 'Hush' written on them in a variety of typefaces. Nessa pushed them on top of the pile of old newspapers and junk mail that sat in the centre of the table.

'Careful, Vanessa, they're for my new fragrance. What on earth are you wearing? Oh! School uniform. I expect they make it that colour on purpose.'

'Is the milk finished, Mum?' Vanessa bent to look into the fridge. This week, she thought, her mother was mostly eating sprouting leaves.

'Haven't we got any cereal?'

'There's some oats in the cupboard, but use water, darling, not milk.' Vanessa's mum, Helena, didn't look up.

'Great,' said Vanessa. 'Porridge with water. Thanks but no thanks.'

'It'd do you the world of good. Flush out all those toxins!'

And so will a fried egg sandwich from the café on the corner; Vanessa didn't say this aloud, she knew Mum would give her an earful about eating healthily and how she needed to lose weight. Vanessa picked up her keys from the hook.

'Oh, and, Nessa darling, remember: tonight I'm having the party. So it will be noisy, and if you think we'll disturb you, maybe you should go and stay with one of your little friends.' Helena Harper smiled, looked at her daughter for a second, and then picked up the phone, stabbing the buttons with her manicured fingers.

Nessa slammed out of the house. It was the only house in the street. Well, it wasn't a house really, it was a ware-house converted into a house. Or as Helena put it, live and work, darling. Helena Harper Designs operated out of the bottom two floors, and they lived in one vast open-plan space on the floor above. Nessa did have her own room, but the walls were thin and Helena Harper was loud.

As her mother was fond of saying, just give it a few years, darling, and this will be *the* place. Nessa looked around. Clockmakers, camera menders, and adult cinema clubs. Clerkenwell, just east of Holborn, didn't feel very happening yet, but what Helena Harper didn't know about trend spotting wasn't worth knowing.

Vanessa wondered sometimes if her mum had been given the wrong baby.

'Course not, Nessa!' Mum would say. 'I had you at home. In the jacuzzi. The obstetrician came over from France specially.'

Little friends! Nessa gritted her teeth. Mum didn't really know anything about her own daughter. Nessa had no friends, little or otherwise. Oh yes, at the start of secondary school everyone had wanted to be Helena Harper's daughter's friend. But it hadn't lasted. At school she was Nessie, the monster of the deep with thighs to match. Nessa pulled her blazer close and hurried on.

When she got home later the place was already full of people, most of them not much older than Nessa. Fashion students, probably; two were lifting a giant palm in a pot up the stairs into the workroom. Nessa looked in. There was what looked like a pond in the centre of the room, and three bored-looking girls were raking yellow sand into dunes.

Helena was in the workroom, talking animatedly into the phone. 'Yes, it's amazing! Ed, Ed McKay's coming. Yes, *the* Ed McKay. And those Irish boys, Sorcha knows them; they're in a band, short name. U2? Yes, something like that.'

Nessa made herself a cup of tea and a mug of hot water for her mum.

'Mum?' Nessa asked when Helena had put down the phone. 'Who's Ed McKay?'

Helena Harper took out a cigarette and lit it.

'Oh, Nessa, you must have heard of Ed McKay! He's in the papers. Well, he's never out of them, actually. Owns a club in Soho and a string of cinemas in the East End. Probably that one around the corner, too. Huge man, massive, built like a barn. The last time he was in the papers they called him the uncrowned King of Hoxton.'

'You mean that Ed McKay? The one that was on trial for robbery when it should have been murder?'

Helena laughed. 'He was cleared, on everything, but there is some edge to the man, yes. A bit of excitement.'

7

'Mum! The man's a violent thug! I read about it; and you've invited him here?'

'Don't be so snooty, Nessa! He's a big sweetie; he let us use one of his cinemas for a shoot. It's going to look great. It was an old music hall he says, or a synagogue, or both. Something like that. Really authentic. And he knows everybody!'

'OK, Mum. If he's such a sweetie, why did they have trouble finding people who would stay alive long enough to sit on the jury! If he's that Ed McKay, the man's killed twice for certain!'

Helena Harper smiled naughtily.

'Come on, Vanessa, they were only other gangsters. He was probably doing the police a favour.'

Nessa sighed and drank her herbal tea. There was no point arguing. Mum had everyone at her parties, famous and infamous, lowlife and highlife. Nessa went through the salon where the students had nearly finished and lifted the lid of the grand piano in the corner. At least while she was playing nothing else mattered.

As soon as people started arriving, Nessa shut herself in her room and got out her homework. It was only four months until her GCSEs, and she had an essay to do. And Nessa had seen enough of her mum's parties. She didn't like the smoke, the noise, and the stick-thin models puking in the loos.

Vanessa opened her books: *Town planning in the Netherlands: The development of the Randstad and its component cities*. Great, thought Nessa.

She had got as far as Den Haag, when there was a noise outside. Nessa opened the door and there was the tallest, skinniest girl she had ever seen. She looked like a little girl made up to look like a woman and then stretched out tall and thin. Her face was, Nessa thought, different; not pretty, more than just pretty. What then? Striking, that was it. Strikingly, almost freakishly, beautiful. Huge wide brown eyes. Large mouth; too big, maybe. Nessa realized she was staring and stopped.

The girl was wearing one of Helena's designs, a slip of a dress that looked as if it was made of liquid gold poured down to the floor. Well, Nessa thought, maybe she would have been beautiful if she hadn't been so out of it. Nessa had seen enough coked-out models before. And this one looked as if she had been crying too. Her eyes were pink rimmed. Her cheeks shone not with shimmery blusher but with tears.

'Can I come in? I need to get away.' The girl looked down the stairs as if someone might be coming after her. She spoke quietly as if she thought someone was listening.

'If you want. Are you all right?'

Nessa realized she was just a girl; younger than herself, she'd put money on it, even if she was twice Nessa's height. The girl sniffed; not a coke user's sniff, but a sob. And Nessa felt bad for thinking she was just some druggy model and let her in.

She wished she hadn't. The girl seemed to make the walls of the room shrink in. She was suddenly aware of the mess, the pair of grubby socks just visible under the bed, her desk, a heap of papers and schoolbooks.

The girl sat down on the only available space, the bed; she was all arms and legs like a baby giraffe. She was still snuffling. Nessa told herself that the girl wasn't looking around and taking anything in at all. She was not interested in Nessa, not the Moomintroll books she had meant to move, nor the piano certificates Helena had insisted on having framed. Nessa thought that this girl probably had the sort of interesting photos of boyfriends you saw in bedrooms in magazines. Nessa felt herself getting cross. The girl would probably look around, re-do her make-up, and tell her mates outside about the sad fat cow she'd found upstairs.

'Look, are you all right? Only Mum doesn't like people coming up here. It is private.'

Nessa heard herself. She sounded priggish and smug, and even if this embryonic airhead was going to slag her off big-time what did it matter? She was upset, really upset, Nessa could see that.

'I'm sorry. Here, have a hanky.' Nessa turned away.

'Helena Harper is your mum?' The girl blew her nose loudly. 'You're so lucky.' The girl sobbed again.

Nessa felt her mouth hanging open. 'I wouldn't say lucky . . .'

She watched the girl wipe her face and take out a small mirror from a tiny matching gold bag. Nessa watched as she re-did her eyelashes then she lifted up the skirt of the dress gingerly and rubbed at a bright purple bruise on the back of her thigh. Nessa couldn't stop herself flinching.

'Ooh, that looks nasty. Do you want some arnica?'

'What d'you say?'

'Arnica. Mum . . . Helena swears by it. You know— homeopathy. It won't kill you but it might not make you any better.' Nessa smiled.

'I didn't know she was old enough to have kids your age.'

'She'd love to hear you say that.' Nessa folded her arms. 'And it's kid, I'm the only one. I think I put her off, didn't quite turn out the way she wanted.'

'She's brilliant, Helena. So kind. So together.' The girl looked away and Nessa thought she was going to start crying again. Nessa thought she must have Helena mixed up with someone else. OK, everyone said she was brilliant, but kind? Helena?

'I better get back. He'll be wondering where I am.' The girl stood up and arranged herself in the mirror on the back of Nessa's door. At the back the dress was cut so low it seemed she was naked underneath it. She arranged the straps, took out a tube of lipstick and re-drew the shine on her lips. Then she pinched at her cheeks.

'Wake myself up, yeah,' she said. She smiled, a half sad, completely beautiful smile and Nessa felt like a rabbit caught in the headlights of a particularly fast car. The girl was stellar, she was the most beautiful girl she had ever seen.

'I wish I could just stay here. You're so lucky!' The girl sighed a long loud sigh and she looked at Nessa sitting at her desk in her maroon school skirt with the waist button undone and Nessa could see she meant it. Really meant it.

Then she had gone. Nessa turned back to her essay but she couldn't concentrate and Randstad Holland looked flatter than ever.

Lauren Now

'So what are you going to do? Haven't you phoned her yet?' Chloe stared hard at the card and tucked some loose hair up behind her ear. 'I can't believe it, Laur! Well, not that I can't believe it, I mean you've always had the height, but you're not what I'd . . . I mean you're more . . .' Lauren smiled, watching Chloe not quite put her foot in it. 'It's not like I don't think you're pretty or . . .'

Lauren laughed. 'No, Chloe, pretty is not the word.'

Chloe laughed too and she settled herself against the wall of Lauren's bedroom, sprawled on the big blue beanbag where she always sat. Lauren's room was tiny, squashed up under the roof of the cottage she shared with Nessa. Through the window Lauren could just see the sea, big and grey and reassuring, filling the silence with a kind of rushing white noise. For a while she felt it might almost be like old times.

'But, no, I haven't called yet, not called properly.'

'What do you mean?'

'Well, I dialled the number yesterday and let it ring, and then this morning before school it was an answer-machine—"This is Rain London."' Lauren did a squeaky New York voice.

'Not like that, not really?'

13

'Honest!'

They laughed some more.

'So she was the real thing, then, not some weirdo?'

'I think so. It's not just that, though, it's Nessa. She'd freak seriously if I said it was modelling. You've heard her. Remember that time your mum got tickets for the Clothes Show and she never wanted me to go. She says it's all shallow and surface. Says it ruined Paula.'

'Yeah, well, that was years ago, wasn't it? It's different now. And you're not Paula.'

Downstairs a door banged and the girls heard Chloe's little brother, Jack, coming up the stairs two at a time.

'Look, Laur, he's finished his lesson now, I gotta go. If you phone that woman and she does want you, I'll come with you, up to London, if you want. It'd be a laugh.'

'Really?' Lauren tried not to sound too pleased.

Chloe stood up, and Jack burst in waving his piano book.

'Hi, Lauren. Are you coming round to stay over tomorrow? I like you better than Lucy . . .' Chloe twisted his arm. 'Chloe, get off!'

Chloe reddened. 'Sorry, Laur, I never asked, I just thought you might be, you know, doing something else . . .' Chloe couldn't even look at her; she stared at the carpet and Lauren felt her stomach turn over. She swallowed, told herself to stay cool.

'Yeah, well, as it happens, I am.' Lauren stood up too. 'And don't worry about London. I'll be fine on my own, OK?' Lauren tried to smile but her mouth was set in a straight line.

'See you then.' Chloe pulled Jack away from Lauren's

desk and they hurried downstairs, shouting goodbye to Nessa as they left.

Downstairs Nessa had started playing; Lauren thought she recognized it: Sibelius, one of Nessa's favourites, slow and sad. Lauren pushed open her bedroom door and listened for a while, then tiptoed across the landing and sat down on Nessa's bed. She picked up the phone. The bedside clock read 5.30. The office could be shut, Friday night, everyone gone home. Lauren hesitated; next to Nessa's bed was a little collection of photos. Nessa as a baby dressed in some freaky Babygro with wings. Lauren on the beach as a toddler. Nessa and Lauren's mum in a photo booth, just like her and Chloe. Two girls. Best friends. Lauren sighed: she didn't have anyone now.

Lauren looked at her face reflected in the glass of the bedroom window. She looked like the ghost of her mother; paler, skinnier, with eyes like the holes in a skull, and a bigger nose. Did Ghislaine Whatsit really think she'd make a model? She looked back at her mum and Nessa in the photo. Mum had done it. Brown skin, full lips, long legs. Lauren wondered sometimes if that really was her mother, her own skin was so pale, paler than Chloe's. She looked down at her forearm where the white of her skin was almost translucent. Her veins were visible, like underground rivers or motorways on a road map. It was worse on her breasts, it made her feel like the Visible Woman they used to have in primary school. A see-through plastic diagram of a person. She had to look away. Unhealthy.

She couldn't really be a model, could she? I mean, it wasn't anything she'd ever thought about, no one ever said she was pretty, no one had ever asked her out or even danced close at a party. She rolled over on to her back. She was too tall, her mouth and nose were both far too big to be pretty and there wasn't a bra on earth made small enough for her to fill. She thought of Chloe and Lucy comparing cup sizes.

Chloe wasn't her friend any more. Chloe wanted something else. To wear the same clothes as Lucy and Nat and get invited to the parties and meet boys who wouldn't look at Lauren because she was taller than they were. Lauren sighed and sat up. She reached for the phone and dialled.

Nessa Then

The whole building reeked of the party. Old beer and wine and dead, damp cigarette butts. When Nessa's alarm bleeped on she had already been awake for half an hour with the duvet pulled up over her head to cut out the stink, trying to will herself back to sleep. She was used to sleeping through music, raving, noise; she had been all her life. But smells were something else. Nessa knew Mum wouldn't be awake for hours.

She dressed and got her things together for school at the last minute. Scooping the books off her desk and into her huge bag, she saw something. A flash of gold, like the dress that girl had been wearing. She bent down to where it had fallen off the end of the bed and onto the floor. It was a bag. A tiny useless sort of bag as big as the palm of Nessa's hand and with a tiny gold clasp.

Nessa checked her watch. She was late. She stuffed the bag into her blazer pocket and set off to school.

She didn't get round to checking the bag until first break in the library. It contained three things. A red Christian Dior lipstick, an old-fashioned green one pound note, and a black and white photo of a black woman and a white man smiling. Nothing else. Nessa shook it, it was perfectly empty. 'Stupid! Stupid!' she told herself. As if anyone would go out to a party and drag along a bag with their own name written inside. 'What am I thinking?'

'You muttering about something, Nessie?' Elaine Schaller walked up to the desk. Vanessa hid the bag as quickly as she could. 'First sign of madness, I heard.'

'Push off, Elaine.' Vanessa tried to sound exasperated and cool.

Elaine sat herself down on the corner of the desk and bent over Vanessa. 'I can't believe that woman's your mother. Or did the genes skip a generation?'

Vanessa picked up a book from the shelf and started reading.

'Her party was in the papers. I expect she shuts you up out of the way. Like the mad woman in the attic.' Vanessa ignored her. 'Scared you'll frighten off all the beautiful people.'

On the way home Nessa bought an evening newspaper from the man outside Farringdon tube station. It was fat and heavy and difficult to hold, and a wind was blowing up. She flicked through quickly. There it was: *Out and About. Fashion guru Helena Harper held her launch for London Fashion Week in her out-of-the-way Clerkenwell warehouse. A converted clock makers' factory had been transformed into a desert oasis under a starry velvet sky where Helena and friends celebrated her most extravagant and eye-popping collection to date. We at Out and About can't wait for Christmas when Helena will be launching HUSH! her new signature scent. Sure to be a not-to-miss event!*

Nessa moved on and read the captions under the photos. She skimmed across rock stars and models and there: Ed

McKay and his companion, new face Paula B. There she was: the girl in the gold dress. Ed McKay's companion? The thought made a shiver of disgust run down Nessa's spine. He was so old! One of two women draped around either side of him, making the bad man look badder. Nessa looked hard at Ed McKay. He *looked* old, too, his dark hair creeping back from his forehead. Forty-five, fifty maybe? He didn't look like a rent-a-thug, the suit was too expensive. He didn't look evil, but then Nessa told herself she'd never seen a murderer except pictures of some woman who killed children or the Yorkshire Ripper. She tried to get a good look at his eyes. Murderers always had evil staring eyes, didn't they? But his eyes were too small to check.

It was like a photograph of beauties and the beast. But the truly amazing thing was the way the girl looked. She didn't look anything like the little-girl-lost Nessa remembered in her room. The camera had transformed her. The girl in the gold dress was beautiful, tall, staring professionally bored into the distance. Half waif, half Amazon.

Lauren Now

It was the last Saturday of the spring half-term. It had been one of the most boring half-terms Lauren could remember. The wind that blew in off the North Sea tore at your face when you opened the front door. Through the window Lauren saw Mrs Pridmore from the bed and breakfast stepping out in matching rain hat and plastic overshoes. Lauren stayed indoors watching videos and pretending she wasn't in when Gail Norman came round.

At least, she told herself, she had the trip to London to look forward to. But she alternated between excitement and nerves. She was, as Chloe had reminded her, not pretty. She was skinny, like someone had rolled her out length-ways overnight but her body had never snapped back to normal size.

Lauren had traced the route in Nessa's tatty *A–Z* so she wouldn't look too much like a tourist. She checked herself one last time in the mirror. Pale skin, whiter than Nessa, dark brown eyebrows like two thick straight lines, dark brown hair. She liked her hair; it was sort of curly and shiny. Her head, though, looked enormous. 'Why the long face?' she said to her reflection. She had avoided looking at herself sideways since Year Five when she realized her nose was almost the same shape as a set square stuck on to the front of her face.

Nessa was getting ready to go out too, some music thing over in Aldeburgh with Ian. Nessa hadn't said she was going with Ian, but Lauren knew just by the lipstick that Nessa wasn't going on her own.

'And, Lauren, keep your mobile on, but please don't wave it about.'

'No, Nessa.'

'And give my love to Chloe.' Nessa turned and smiled at Lauren. 'I'm so glad you two have made it up. I know it's hard. God! I wouldn't be fifteen again for anything. I'd never really had any mates until I met Paula and it was awful, so lonely.' She stared out of the window as if she was remembering. 'You need your mates. Here.' She fished a twenty pound note out of her pocket. 'In case you see something nice.'

'Thanks, Nessa.' Lauren kissed her on the cheek and felt guilty she had told Nessa she was shopping in Cambridge with Chloe. Still, it did make life a whole lot easier. I mean, Lauren told herself, the shoot could be a disaster, and Nessa need never know. If they did want to sign her up, then she'd have to cross that bridge when she came to it. She sighed, pulled her scarf closer, and set off for the station. She'd spent most of last night trying to figure out what to wear. Most of Lauren's clothes were built for comfort rather than glamour. She'd pulled on her favourite jeans, the ones so loose you could imagine her legs were more shapely than stick-like. And the jumper she always wore, the one Nessa had made for her birthday last year. It was big, floppy, all enveloping, and Lauren's favourite shade of emerald green.

'And take a jacket!' Nessa called after her. 'It's colder than you think.'

22

Lauren had never been to London on her own. Come to think of it, she thought, the furthest she'd ever been alone was to the specialist art shop in Cambridge. She'd been to London with Nessa, but Nessa always said she hated the city. She said she hated the crowds and the traffic, but Lauren thought she just said it to try and make it true.

Every time they went, and they went usually once or twice a year, Nessa found incredible places to take her. They walked along the riverside and past the Globe Theatre, and to Borough Market for a fry up in a greasy spoon. Last summer, when the local beach filled with holiday-makers, they'd taken the train the other way and had a picnic on Hampstead Heath and gone swimming in the ponds. Nessa seemed to enjoy London but told herself and everyone else that it was dirty and noisy and dangerous.

Lauren came out of the station; the air was different here, you could almost taste the traffic in it. She crossed the road from Liverpool Street station and bought herself a coffee from a Starbucks. She smiled. The buildings were huge, the sky glittered blue, and she was going for a photo test. She caught her reflection in a glass door. Her hair was blowing all over the place. She looked ordinary, she thought, not starry or modelly or like the girls you see in magazines. She took the card out of her pocket again. It wasn't a mistake; it was her they wanted, wasn't it?

There was so much to look at. The bloke walking in front of her had a bullet hole tattooed into his neck. It was fascinating and hideous at the same time. So hideous that Lauren forgot to check her step and felt her shin burn as it hit a stack of books on the pavement. She rocked for

23

a second holding the coffee like the Cat in the Hat just before he falls. Then the coffee sort of leapt up and out of the polystyrene cup and down her front. Lauren gasped with shock; the coffee was hot and she felt her chest burning. The mug slipped out of her hand. The bookshop door swung open and Lauren was still frozen.

'Are you all right?' The voice wasn't English.

Lauren nodded yes. Then feeling the hot coffee turn freezing cold and damp against her front shook her head no. She could almost feel her bottom lip quivering so she pinched her wrist and breathed deeply. She tried to look the man in the face and be together. But when she did look him in the face she fell apart again.

'Come in, we've got a heater.' The man smiled and Lauren felt her insides froth up and boil over like hot milk. She had never believed in the stuff you read in books where people fell in love at first sight. She had never had crushes the way Chloe had, crushes that turned the boy from the garage you saw every day into some mysterious brooding object of lust overnight.

But this man was different. It was, she thought afterwards, that combination of voice and skin and eyes. Deep dark skin, smooth and not quite shiny; she had to stop herself reaching out and touching him. He stood up and shook some coffee off a comic. He was tall. Standing next to him Lauren felt normal sized. She shook the thoughts away; she was dripping with coffee and globs of fluffy milk. He must think she looked like some kind of idiot. And how could she turn up at the photographer's like some walking cappuccino? He held up the comic.

'I don't think we can save her.'

A lighter-skinned boy came out; he was younger, too, about the same age as Lauren. He shook his long, not-quite-Afro curls.

'Don't worry, man, I think these have had it.' They were saturated. The younger boy smiled at her. The most beautiful man in the world shook his head. His T-shirt read *Finer Books—Another World* in black letters. His trainers kicked against the coffee cup; it leaked a brown river on to the side of a box of comics.

'I'm so sorry.' Lauren bent down to pick up the cup. 'Your comics! They're ruined.' Lauren fished around for the twenty pound note. 'I'll pay for them, honest.'

'Forget it. 'S only *Mutant Planet Girl*. Dad keeps buying boxfuls at conventions but we never sell them. He's the original geek, my dad. Mum'll think you've done him a favour.' The boy picked one up. '"Mutant Girl Lives! Loves! Destroys!" See, her problem is, anyone she touches she can't help reading their minds. Everything they've done she feels. So she wears these anti-psy mittens. Only they look more like those oven gloves.'

Lauren held her top away from her front.

'Jesus, you're soaked. Look, come in. It's only a book-shop but at least you can get dry.'

Lauren hesitated. The most beautiful man spoke; his accent seemed to trigger the release of butterflies around her middle. 'You must come in, you must be dry.'

Lauren couldn't meet his eyes without feeling that she would blush volcanically.

She went into the shop, a cave of books; it smelt of old damp paper and the paraffin heater.

'I'm Luke,' the younger boy said. 'This is my dad's

shop. It's not me with the lycra-suit fixation, honest. The heater's by the counter. And this is Thierry, he's helping out.'

Thierry held out his hand and Lauren shook it. 'Thierry,' she said back. 'You're French?'

'Ah yes, but not, unfortunately, a footballer.'

Lauren looked down at herself. Her jumper was wet through, and she stank of coffee. She had to think. Be sensible. What would Nessa do? It wasn't the end of the world. They would probably only be photographing her face.

'Are you sure you're OK? Sit down if you like, there's a chair behind there.'

Lauren sat down as close to the fire as she could. Luke smiled. She smiled back hoping Thierry was smiling too.

'You are soaked, I think,' Thierry said.

'Just a bit.' Lauren looked at her watch. She had ten minutes. She ought to get her top off and just wear the jacket. Or perhaps she could buy herself a T-shirt from somewhere.

'You in a hurry?' Luke said. 'I'll put the kettle on, if you like. It's like a morgue in here on Saturday; the market's shut, see. I could do with a customer, just for the company.' He was trying to cheer her up; she could hear that in his voice. Perhaps she looked really grim.

'I have to go, I'm late already, but thanks, yeah.' She looked around the shop: books everywhere, children's books, a Moomintroll original Nessa would kill for, face out, high up. On the opposite wall local history and crime took up most of the space. The little paraffin fire glowed red. Maybe she could just get dry.

'Look, I'm no kind of nutter, all right? But if you like you could use one of these.' Luke held out the front of his shirt. 'Mum designed them, see. Thought we'd sell them, not many takers though.'

Luke fished about in the space under the till which was overflowing with bits of paper and plastic carrier bags.

'Here.' He held out a *Finer Books* T-shirt. 'It's not been worn.'

Lauren offered him her note but he wouldn't take it.

'No one will notice it's gone.'

'I think we are the only—what's the word?—mugs who wear them.' Thierry smiled at her. He smiled at her and her insides rocketed. Lauren changed in the tiny lavatory behind the local history and East End Crime section. She peeled off the jumper and put on the shirt. It was small, a large child's size maybe, but it was clean and dry and had long sleeves. In the square mirror above the sink she splashed her face with cold water. She'd have to do.

She checked her watch again. She said thank you over and over and thought that if the shoot didn't take long she'd come back. Buy them both a coffee, maybe. That's what people do. She started a scenario in her head where Luke had gone—home or wherever, it didn't matter—and Thierry was alone at the counter flicking through some French novel. She would come in fresh from her make-over; he wouldn't recognize her—'You look so chic, so modern.'—and they'd spend the rest of the evening sitting outside one of the bars in Hoxton wearing interesting clothes and people walking past would stare at them because they looked so cool.

She looked back quickly at the shop and saw Luke

outside stacking up comics. He waved at her and she shouted thanks back. She hurried on and turned the corner into Fournier Street.

Nessa Then

The address was west London. Nessa had sneaked into Helena's office and copied it out of her contacts Filofax on the desk. She looked it up: Fredericks Mews, just round the corner from Marble Arch, right in the centre of town. The road was so tiny it disappeared down a crack in the *A–Z*.

At first Nessa thought she'd just phone her up. There was a number, after all; but Nessa was intrigued. She wasn't the usual kind of model, the ones that never look down and notice I'm here, Nessa thought. She was more like a kid, dressing up. Nessa was sure the girl was younger than her, no more than 15. And if so, what was she doing with that thug McKay? Nessa felt responsible for the girl. She hadn't spent long in her bedroom but it was long enough for Nessa to know there was something a bit special about her. She'd been around her mother's world long enough to have seen creepy old men hanging round young models, but this girl was different. This one was *so* young. And Ed McKay? A murderer? It was almost unfathomable. Something had been up that night at the party and it wasn't just too much coke. Had he hit Paula? He was a thug, wasn't he? Creeped her out? Nessa wanted to find out for herself. She would go straight after school on the tube.

The street was cobbled and the tiny houses were all painted seaside colours, blue and yellow and pink and white. It was hardly real; like Toy Town full size. Nessa checked twice to make sure she had the right address and pressed the bell.

Paula B answered the door in jeans and a white T-shirt; she looked like an advert for stunning. She had sunglasses tipped on the top of her head squashing down her black curls. She stared at Nessa for a long minute. Then looked down the little street both ways.

'Do I know you? Ed's not here, you know.'

'No.' Nessa held out the gold bag. 'You left this, at my mum's, Helena Harper?' Standing in front of Paula made Nessa feel shorter and dumpier than ever. Paula looked at the bag and her face lit up with a smile.

'Jeesus, yes!' She took it as if she had just remembered how important it was, unzipped it and rifled through it. Nessa watched Paula's face relax with relief as she realized everything was all there. Paula kissed the photo and beamed at Nessa.

'You saved my life! For real.' Paula swooped down and kissed Nessa. 'What's your name again? Come in, it's bloody freezing!'

Nessa stepped onto the thick white carpet and closed the door behind her. Inside, the door opened straight into a sitting room with a metal spiral staircase. It was all one space with kitchen stuff against the far wall, everything small and dinky and fitted and sparkly white or chrome. Like a space-age Wendy house.

'Vanessa.' She held out her hand for Paula to shake. 'I mean, Nessa Harper.' Nessa, seeing Paula stifle a laugh, flushed bright red and put her hand in her pocket. 'Sorry, sorry.'

'You don't go in for the air-kissing, then? Like most of them?'

'When I was nine I fell against some pop star and bit him on the cheek by accident. Mum was mortified. So I stick to hand shaking. It's safer.'

Paula burst out laughing. 'You never!'

There was a loud clicking in the corner of the room and the telephone answer-machine clicked on. The message played and Paula grabbed Nessa's arm and put her finger to her lips. It was a man's voice, loud and deep. It was him.

'Paula? Where are you? Spending my money, I bet. Listen, tonight's off. Something's come up. Get yourself a takeaway or something.' In the background the girls could hear voices. 'Gotta go.' And it clicked off.

Paula sat herself down on the white leather sofa.

'Thank Gawd for that. I didn't fancy hanging out with him and his old man mates. They treat me like I'm not there. It's like work: you wear the dress, you walk around, you're just this smiling thing with tits. Or in my case hardly any tits.' She hugged a cushion to her middle. Nessa thought this was the place where she should be asking questions but Paula didn't stop. 'Jeez, don't listen to me. It's not that bad. 'S better than working in McDonald's. Have you seen the size of this TV?'

It was the biggest TV Nessa had ever seen, huge and boxy and shiny. Paula clicked it on and it was the news. She made a face and clicked it off.

Nessa looked around. On the walls were loads of photos in clip frames. Not of Paula but of Ed McKay. Ed McKay with some boxers, holding up a trophy and smiling. Ed

McKay with some singers Nessa had seen on the telly. Ed McKay with royalty. He didn't look like a man who had famously nailed someone's hand to a bar counter in Bethnal Green. Nessa looked at Paula. Did she know about him? She must do. Had he ever admitted anything to her? Had he really killed those people? Did he talk in his sleep? Did Paula sleep with him? Did she like him? Love him?

'Oh, God, yeah, he loves himself doesn't he . . .' Paula got up and looked closer at the photo Nessa was studying. 'He's got this career plan, right. Ends up with him hosting his own late night chat show in 1995. Providing no one locks him up beforehand.'

'Do you think they would?'

'Depends.' Paula shrugged 'They can't get him for that stuff he did years ago, the famous stuff, 'cause of—what's he call it?—double jeopardy, innit. Where they can't do you for the same thing twice. But if he gets his hands dirty again, you never know.'

'So he did do it? Really kill that man, Pete Farrer?'

'Believe me, Ed did *everything*!' Paula smiled and Nessa was torn between asking more and shutting up. She caught her reflection in the TV. Her mouth was hanging open.

'Jesus, I rattle round this place, I really do. Tell you what though! If you fancy a pizza we could phone out and get one. There's a place round the corner that delivers them! You don't have to get up off your arse! And I owe you for the other night.' She looked serious. 'More than you know. Come on! Watch a video with me, he's got loads of videos.' Paula took Nessa's hand and dragged her towards a bookcase full to the ceiling with videotapes.

'What d'you reckon, *The Thing*? *Driller Killer*? *Night of the Living Dead*? Or my favourite, *Breakfast at Tiffany's*!'

Nessa had the best night out she'd had for ages. They didn't talk about homework or Helena Harper, or Ed McKay. They ordered two pizzas, super family size, special delivery. Nessa thought Paula must have hollow legs because she ate one and a half.

'Yeah, well, there's a lot of me,' Paula said, pulling off a strand of melty cheese.

'Vertically, there's a lot of you,' Nessa said.

'You what?'

They watched *Breakfast at Tiffany's* first, then *Meet Me in St Louis* which Paula had never seen, but loved, and *Night of the Living Dead*. Well, the start of *Night of the Living Dead*. Nessa looked up at the clock just as the first load of zombies pushed up out of the earth. She jumped, it was ten thirty and a school night.

'I've got to go home. Helena'll kill me. Do you mind, can I use your phone? I better call a cab.'

'Course! I'm not paying.' Paula smiled.

'I've had a lovely time.' Nessa stood up. She meant it.

'You make me laugh, you do! You sound so unreal! I couldn't make you up if I tried. Look, would you come again sometime maybe? If you've got nothing to do? I don't fancy watching the rest of the zombies on my own. Reminds me too much of Ed!'

'Yeah.' Nessa smiled. 'I'd love to.'

Lauren Now

Lauren didn't know what she had been expecting. Possibly something like *Pop Idol*, only with models. She'd seen that once on the telly, a room full of girls with shiny faces and too much mascara. Lauren had decided not to wear any make-up at all. That way, she reckoned, she wouldn't get it all over her face by accident when she rubbed her eyes, and it would make her look I-don't-care cool. At least, that had been the idea. She reached the address and searched the bank of buzzers for the photographer's name. Jamie Holdsworth. She pressed it and there was a woman's voice. 'Come up, we're on the third floor.'

It didn't seem upmarket at all. More like a warehouse with white paint on the walls, and the lift didn't work so Lauren climbed the stairs. Chloe would have hated it. The whole building seemed virtually empty and smelt of wood-dust and glue. By the time she reached the third floor she was out of breath. The door said HOLDSWORTH in capital letters. Lauren pushed it with her fingertips and, like in the stupidest horror films, it swung open.

Lauren relaxed. There was a smell of coffee and a tape playing. She recognized it: Nessa had a soft spot for Studio One. There was a youngish man with a close crop and a small young woman with bunches and a T-shirt that read 'Fake'.

'Lauren Bogle?' The woman looked her up and down; Lauren looked hard back at her. She was older than she looked, twenties perhaps. Lauren guessed that she would have to get used to being stared at.

The woman smiled. 'I'm Jamie, that's Carl.' The man grunted hello.

'Oh, Jamie, right.' Lauren tried to look as if she'd been expecting Jamie Holdsworth to be a woman.

'Do me a favour?' Jamie asked, looking hard at Lauren. 'Move your hair back from your face a minute, yep, that's it, yeah. And don't be afraid to stand up straight. That's it, as tall as you can. Yeah! Oh, and relax!'

Lauren stretched up. Nessa always said she hunched. *'You talk to Chloe and you're permanently stooping. If I was as tall as you I'd make the most of it.'*

Jamie didn't take her eyes off Lauren for a second. Lauren held her hair up and stared out of the window. A pigeon flew past and she could see a church steeple, white with a weather vane.

'Listen, we won't take long. Just a couple of Polaroids and then some photos so they can see if they like you. Is that OK?'

Lauren nodded. She put both hands in her back pockets and watched Carl pulling down a giant roll of paper against the wall. What on earth was she doing here? She could have been back at home stroking the cat. Yes, she told herself, and tying herself up in knots over Chloe, which was sadder than sad. It wasn't as if Chloe was her boyfriend, so why did she feel so bad? Maybe she was a lesbian? No, she'd never fancied Chloe, had she? Well, she'd never had any boyfriends either. Was that why she felt so bad now?

What about Thierry? That proved she wasn't a lesbian, didn't it? She would love to tell Chloe all about him, but to be honest there wasn't anything to tell.

Chloe wasn't upset about anything, so why should she be? She could make other friends. There were other people at school, six hundred others, what was her problem?

Lauren looked across at the photographer. She was studying the Polaroids she'd already taken and smiling.

'Great face! So strong!'

Lauren smiled back. She had a great face.

'You know, if you had a crop you'd be stunning. Those bones!'

So maybe it was just her bones that were great. She imagined peeling off her skin and posing. Posing. That's what Paula had done. This. The same. Her mum. She suddenly felt close to the woman in the photographs at home. That woman who never seemed real even when Nessa talked her up in stories, even though she'd seen the pictures. Nessa and Paula, best mates for ever. The story of Paula, the first black woman on the cover of *Marie Claire*, the story of how she and Nessa went on the run from Paula's creepy boyfriend in his Bentley, the story of Lauren being born. She felt like Paula.

The thought made Lauren's throat thicken and the hot feeling of tears come behind her eyes, so she concentrated hard on a plant she could see growing out of a building opposite. It was thin and wiry with no flowers but it had cracked right through the concrete wall.

Lauren hadn't realized the woman had already taken five or six more Polaroids. She'd stuck them in a row on the wall and she and Carl were examining them.

'Look at this one.' Jamie waved Lauren over. It was a perfectly square photo and her face loomed out of the smudgy out-of-focus background. The girl in the photo had her hands in her back pockets and her hips pushed out. The girl's arms and legs seemed impossibly long and giraffe-like. Not a girl but a drawing of a girl, like a fashion illustration, all angles and corners. And the girl in the picture looked distant and cool, almost sad; no, sophisticated. Even her features looked as if they belonged on her face, rather than collaged together. Lauren couldn't believe it was her.

'Right,' Jamie said. 'Let's see what you do with some light.'

Jamie Holdsworth spent about an hour carefully arranging the lights and trying not to arrange Lauren too much. Lauren lost count of the number of times she was told not to try too hard, or to stand up straight, or to relax. But Jamie was kind and funny, and Lauren enjoyed herself. Lauren had thought she'd have to be made-up or dressed-up, but no, she spent the whole afternoon in the book-shop T-shirt and jeans. Carl went out for sandwiches and Jamie asked her about school and friends and Lauren wound up telling her about Chloe.

'You're how old? Fifteen? Won't do you any good me telling you this but what you need are new friends. Get yourself a boyfriend, if you want one. Why aren't they falling over you?'

'I think it's me that does the falling over, actually. I still haven't figured my legs out. And where I'm from I'm too tall. And not . . . I don't know, whatever it is I'm not it.'

Jamie laughed. 'I was always too small. And I looked

38

twelve until I was twenty-five. Anyway, you can never be too tall for this job. And you scrape ceilings. Still growing, I bet.'

'Yeah, but I don't know; it's not me, is it, this?' Lauren pointed at the Polaroids. 'It's what I look like sometimes.'

'Well, make the most of it for a change! You've got a chance loads of girls would kill for. Look, Ghislaine is hardly ever wrong. Scratch that: never wrong. She's been around so long she's practically the Bible. If she thinks you can make it, well . . . I expect she'll call you when we get these pictures done. And promise me you'll tell your mum.' Jamie looked at her seriously. 'Otherwise this has all been a waste of time.'

Lauren floated out of the studio trying to walk as tall as she could. Jamie had let her keep one of the Polaroids, a close-up of her face. And she looked . . . well . . . if not exactly pretty then definitely interesting. In the slightly fuzzy square her eyes were huge and dark, her skin was ghost white, and her mouth, instead of looking just big, looked almost sexy.

Lauren smiled. 'Hello, Horseface.' She saw herself in the shop windows and stopped to check herself. Yeah, she was the tallest girl she'd ever seen, but so what. She walked with her hips out in front of her like Jamie had said and her reflection looked more like a praying mantis than a girl and she giggled. When she stopped to cross the street some men in a car looked at her. Instead of shrivelling up and pretending to be somewhere else, Lauren held herself tall and looked at them down her nose as if they smelt of cat poo. The lights changed and the men laughed. Maybe, Lauren told herself, she hadn't got the look quite right.

She walked to the station past the bookshop. She rehearsed walking tall through the door and offering to buy Thierry a thank-you coffee. She would be cool this time, not flustered, but sophisticated. After all, he could only say no. But the pavement outside the shop was empty and when she leant against the shop door it was locked shut. She peered inside through the posters for *The Jack the Ripper Walk* and *In the Footsteps of the Krays* walks. There was a girl sitting inside at the till holding a book. She had wiry curls and dark brown skin and she was laughing at something, someone. Thierry came out of the back room and Lauren jumped out of sight. She wasn't a stalker. She could hear him now, talking close, quietly, and whatever he was saying the girl thought it was very funny. She sneaked another look, almost expecting to see them kissing. They weren't. The girl was leaning across the counter though, definitely interested. Lauren shrugged; the scene in her head evaporated. Oh well, she told herself, nothing's perfect.

Lauren was home early. Nessa hadn't returned from her concert and the house was empty. Saturday night, Lauren thought, and I'm on my own. She wanted to tell someone about what had happened, about the photos and the studio and the boy from the bookshop. It almost felt that if she didn't tell someone then maybe none of it had happened. Chloe would have wanted to know. Lauren could have told her the exact colour of Thierry's eyes and the length of his legs. She could have told her how the Polaroids had looked and what Jamie had said and that would have fixed it all, like varnish. Her hand went to the phone and she had dialled the first half of Chloe's number before she stopped herself. It was Nathan Rogers's party tonight. She wouldn't be in.

Lauren went up to her room and turned over the pages of her purple starry address book; Chloe Bradfield, Louise Shaw—she'd left school last year and moved to Peterborough. Gail Norman had written in her e-mail address, otherwise it was empty. Back in the sitting room she turned the telly on and flicked through the channels. In the kitchen she opened the fridge door and ate half a yoghurt but it tasted of nothing.

Lauren was half asleep on the sofa when Nessa came in. She heard Ian kiss her goodnight and their voices sounded muffled and faraway.

'Hello, love.' Nessa came in. Although the make-up had worn off hours ago she was, Lauren thought, glowing.

'You had a good time?' Lauren stretched herself awake.

'Yeah,' Nessa nodded, 'we did.'

'You should have invited him in. I'm not that scary, am I?'

'No, it's not that.' Nessa sat down on the sofa next to Lauren. On the TV two plain-clothes policemen were wrestling another man to the ground and handcuffing him. 'I like him, really. A lot.'

'It's fairly obvious, Nessa.'

'Yeah, but you get to my age, you're used to things the way they are. I tell you, Lauren, it's not waking up with him I worry about. It's him in the kitchen making tea. Or wandering around our house in his underpants . . .'

'Ian. Underpants. No, that is far too much information, Ness. I'm going to bed.' Lauren yawned and stood up.

'Did you have a good day with Chloe? I am glad it's all right with you two. Don't say anything! I know a rocky patch when I see one. But I'm glad you're still mates. You know, when I was your age I don't know what I'd have done without Paula.' Nessa yawned. 'Did you see anything nice? Oh, new shirt!'

Lauren looked down. *Finer Books—Another World*, it said. Lauren felt herself redden.

'Oh, this, I borrowed it . . . off Chloe. Yes, today was fine.' Lauren started up the stairs. She never lied to Nessa. Well, only stupid tiny lies about homework. And now it was just more and more lies on top of each other. Little ones, she told herself, not really big ones, not life or death ones. Nothing might come of it and Nessa would never have to know. On the other hand, if she did have a future as a model she would have to come completely clean. Maybe if Nessa was really happy with Ian she'd be able to slip her the news easily.

Lauren shivered. She was doing *Macbeth* at school. Look where lying got you. Ghosts coming out of the woodwork, blood and death and madness. Tears before bedtime.

Lauren brushed her teeth and stared at herself in the mirror. She pushed the hair up and away from her face. Would she look better with a haircut? She was so huge she thought she'd be taken for a boy with short hair. A giant twelve-year-old boy with skinny arms. Her mouth foamed white with toothpaste and a blob fell down onto the front of the T-shirt.

Then she remembered she'd left her favourite jumper back in the bookshop.

42

Nessa Then

Nessa didn't realize how much hard work it was having a best friend. Especially one like Paula who seemed to live in another universe where school had stopped somewhere back when she was twelve and you did what you liked. She phoned Nessa up at all hours, once at three o'clock in the morning, wanting to talk for hours. Not about Ed. About how she'd started getting some real modelling work, doing her first catwalk show in Paris. Maybe even a magazine cover. About how she would name her son Fred or Gene and her daughter would be Audrey or Lauren.

'You're not pregnant, are you?' Nessa said, suddenly wide awake.

'Nah, I've got it all worked out, see. I marry this bloke, a bit like the guy who works in Maroush Juice; you know, the caff on the Edgware Road, nice bum, gorgeous.'

'Not Ed, then?'

'Definitely not Ed. Yeah, and we have two kids, one of each.'

'Yeah, and you live happily ever after.'

'Yeah.'

'Go to sleep, Paula.'

'I can't, Nessa. I've got a job in Paris doing a show! On a catwalk! Ed's livid, says he can't be without me. It's just all starting, Ness. Real work! I'm so wired, Ness!'

'You shouldn't do that stuff, Paula, you'll only have a headache tomorrow.'

'But I can't sleep anyway. Not now. Ed's coming round in a bit.' She sighed. Nessa forced herself to speak.

'It's great news, Paula, the cover, and Paris. But you've got to look after yourself.'

'If I had a mum she'd be just like you.'

'Go to sleep, Paula.'

Another time Paula showed up outside school one lunch-time, leaning against the gates sucking a Chupa Chup and wearing very tight jeans and a baggy T-shirt tied at her hips. Nessa saw her from the library window and ran downstairs to talk to her through the wire fence.

'Come shopping! I thought we'd go up west. Ed's left me some cash, look! Loadsamoney!' Paula waved a bundle of notes. 'An' I've got to be fitted for this super posh frock for some première thingy I'm going to with Ed. Come on, Ness. Please? It'll be fun; we'll get something for you, I promise!'

'I hate shopping.'

'Come off it! No one hates shopping for new stuff!'

'No, it's OK for you, anything looks fantastic on you. Me, I look like a dumpy short-arse whatever I wear.'

'Look, you help me choose, yeah, then we do whatever you want. Deal?'

Nessa looked up at school, she thought of double PE and Elaine Schaller sniping at her. The electric bell for lessons whirred and Nessa ran inside, grabbed her bag and her heavy maroon blazer and ran back out through the side entrance.

'You know, I've never bunked off in my life. Ever. You are such a bad influence, Paula.'

'I don't believe it, Ness, come off it. You can't get to our age and never have bunked off. It's impossible.'

Nessa shrugged: 'School's just something you do, like piano and extra music. I drew the line at ballet, though, I was rubbish at that.'

'I bet you had horse riding an' all. Horse riding and your own pony if you'd have wanted.'

'Yeah, I did actually. And fencing.'

'Fencing?'

'With swords, you know. But I was seriously crap.'

Paula looked blank. 'Swords? Bloody hell, Ness, you fell on your feet. Anything you want you can just have. You really don't know you're born!'

The girls walked down towards the Strand. Nessa noticed that walking with Paula everyone did double-takes, men and women, tourists and delivery boys. As if she was an alien, only a beautiful alien with incredibly long legs.

'Do you know how many people have stared at you in the last five minutes?'

'Nah, I switch off. If anyone looks too long, though, I smash 'em.'

'You wouldn't?'

'I did once, these lads from school.'

'I thought you said you never went to school.'

'This was when I was fostered with this number one bitch, over Plaistow, it was. She tried to make me go, every bloody day. Anyway, these lads from the estate opposite, they'd always arks me stuff, calling out to me an' this an' that. I got so sick of the big one, Martin Michaels he was,

45

I got him with his baby brother's activity centre right across the face. That stopped him.' Paula turned and smiled at Nessa, a completely angelic butter-wouldn't-melt smile, and Nessa couldn't stop herself laughing.

Paula took Nessa to Bond Street.

They went in and out of several shops, the sort with buzzers you had to press before you were let in. One shop didn't let them in at all and Paula swore heavy curses into the intercom. The shop assistants in Ralph Lauren gave the girls withering looks, which Paula returned like an expert. In Lacroix Paula was recognized and the shop girls fawned all over her. Nessa sat on a gold-painted chair in her school uniform and watched. She'd seen it at home, her mother gushing over clients in almost the same way, and normally she switched off. The models never took any notice of her, but Paula did.

'What d'you reckon?' Paula made a face at her reflection in a red satin dress that was split up to the thigh. Nessa shook her head: the dress was the colour of a just-sucked boiled sweet.

Paula looked at Nessa in the mirror. 'Yeah, you're right, I dunno, it's . . .'

'Cheap,' Nessa said. The shop girl folded her arms, but Paula nodded.

'Yeah,' she agreed. 'Tarty. Ed doesn't like me tarty.'

There were more dresses and three pairs of shoes, a pile of bags and costume jewellery. Paula sent the girl away for something else and Nessa came over and looked through the stuff with her.

'See anything you like?'

'Dunno, I fancied something like a goddess, one of them

Greek ones, you know, long and white and my hair up like this.' Paula pulled her black curls up on top of her head. 'Classy, you know.'

There was a bracelet on a tray. An oversize charm bracelet with coloured enamel charms; a bright red heart, a tiny blue fish, a pearly, iridescent seashell, and a blue glass eye to ward off evil. Paula wrinkled her nose.

'That's weird!'

'No, they have stuff like that in churches, in Greece and Spain. We went to Greece last year. You get a bad leg so you buy a little metal pretend leg and say a prayer and pin it up in church. It's gorgeous. It's for good luck.'

'I thought you were lucky enough, Ness.'

The girl came back with a white pleated dress. Paula put it on and looked stunning. Nessa couldn't help being impressed. The neckline plunged in a deep V to Paula's waist and the white silk shone against her brown skin.

'I'll need some of that tit tape. Look!' Paula leant forward and the whole dress fell open. Nessa thought she saw a yellow bruise on Paula's middle and winced. Paula was bright.

'Fell on a door—got me right there!'

The shop assistant grimaced in sympathy, and the bruise was forgotten.

'So,' the assistant said, looking at Paula in the mirror. 'We'll sort that out for you, and . . . um . . . take it in at the waist?'

Paula looked at Nessa. Nessa nodded. Paula looked, as her mother would say, divine.

The shop girl fussed and pinned and promised they'd do all the alterations. Paula chose some matching shoes and a bag and stalked out of the shop reminding them to have the dress sorted by next week. 'And it better be perfect.' Paula had her own clothes back on again and the transformation from goddess to fifteen year old with a big mouth was instant.

Nessa was quiet. She caught her own dumpy maroon reflection in a shop window. She knew she'd never look the way Paula looked and there was no point in even thinking about it.

They'd only walked around the corner when Paula stopped. She looked down the street behind her and put her bag down on the pavement. 'Nessa, look. For you. For trailing round the shops with me. Your face in that chair! It's for putting up with me.' She put her hand in her trouser pocket and pulled out the charm bracelet. It still had the hand-written price tag on it. It was nearly £300.

Nessa gasped. 'Did you nick that?'

'No, it jumped into my hand. What do you think?'

'But you had money! Ed's money.' Nessa was shocked.

'Yeah, but this is a present. From me, not Ed. And it's more special if I nicked it.'

Nessa didn't say anything.

'Don't you want it? Ain't you never nicked anything?'

'Paperclips. Some socks once, never something like this. I never even saw you do it!'

Paula rolled her eyes. 'That's the idea. I thought you said you liked it.'

'I love it, but . . .'

'But nothing. Here.' Paula helped fasten it on to Nessa's wrist. 'It's lucky. I can tell. And if it's not it doesn't matter, 'cause you were born lucky, yeah?'

'It's gorgeous.'

'It doesn't feel like shopping if you don't nick something,' Paula said.

'If I'd known what you were doing I'd have been terrified.'

'That's why I never said nothing, innit?'

'Three hundred pounds, though! Won't they know it was you? What if they catch you?'

'Paula B? Girlfriend of Mr Ed McKay? They can always have a word with Ed if they've got a problem with me. He'd sort them out! Anyway, serves them right. I know what they're thinking, the way they look at us. They think we're shit. Well, anyway, they think I'm shit. Just shit with money and they want some of that. Serves them right.'

Nessa thought she had a point. 'Thank you, Paula, it's beautiful.' Nessa held her arm out and looked at the bracelet hanging on her wrist and smiled. 'You know what? You deserve cake!'

Nessa took her to Patisserie Valerie, a French cake shop in Soho. When she was little Helena would take her there for treats. They'd sit together at a table and Helena would talk to her. But that had been a long time ago, Nessa thought, seven years at least.

'Oh, my God, Ness, have you seen this!' Paula was rapturous over a cake covered in a mound of curls of white chocolate; they shared a slice and Paula bought a whole one in a box to take home. 'This place is amazing!'

Nessa felt good. Paula was happy and it made her happy that this beautiful, funny girl was her friend. Paula paid with Ed's money.

'That's what it's for, keeping me happy.'

Nessa tried to work out how much money was there. It looked like nearly £400.

'Did he really just give you that?'

Paula nodded. 'That's what he's for, innit, really, give me money. 'S not like I never earn it.'

'Earn it? Modelling? You never give him your money?'

'He looks after me.' Paula pulled a face. 'And I only just started earning properly, like. And I'm useless with sums and maths. He looks after me.' Paula looked away.

Nessa rolled her eyes. It was like a soap. 'Hasn't he got a wife and kids somewhere? In Essex?'

Paula forked up a large amount of cake and shrugged. 'Don't bother me.'

'Don't you, you know, love him?'

Paula stared for a long second, her huge eyes round. Then she laughed. She laughed so long Nessa thought she was choking and the waitress brought a cup of water over.

'But then, don't you hate him near you?'

Paula said nothing while she ate some cake.

'I've had worse. I just think of something else. There's worse things than an old bloke, believe me!'

'I thought you'd have to love him or something. Does he hurt you?'

'What, you mean he forces me to stay in my very own mews flat, and take me to parties in thousand pound dresses and that.' Paula scraped up the last of the cream, and looked past the chiller cabinet full of chocolate éclairs and marzipan animals. She sucked the last of the cream off the fork.

Nessa thought she looked so young. 'But you're fifteen!'

'I know, but I've got old bones.' Paula laughed. 'No, it's

50

you that's different, really different. I never known someone like you. You're so, I dunno, straight. But you're all right. And you've got things. I never had anything, sometimes nowhere to live, and he's a laugh, Ness, honest, sometimes. The first time I went out with him,' Paula sighed remembering, 'it was brilliant. He knew everyone, I really was like the queen or something, like a lady. *"May I take your coat, Miss?"* We went to this hotel, the Dorchester, serviettes like tablecloths! You know what I mean. I bet you went there every week for Sunday dinner. And the dress he bought me for that date! I'll show it you. Unbelievable.' Paula carefully brushed the crumbs off her lap. She licked the fork again just in case she'd missed anything, then she pointed it at Nessa. 'And I don't see him that much, Ness, he only stays over once a month. Most of the time he just shows me off, you know? Like Audrey Hepburn in *Breakfast at Tiffany's* where she's in love with George Peppard, but she has to marry the other guy, the rich guy.'

Paula looked out of the window; a crush of art students wearing home-made clothes were reading the menu. Paula's face looked blank, as if she was outside too, looking in at herself. She sighed. 'It's not like I have to kiss him all the time. I hate kissing him. I used to smoke before Ed, you know. Then I saw his teeth, Jee-sus! I gave up straight-away then. You know, the only thing I don't really like is the hair. It's all on his front and on his back. He's really hairy, like some kind of ape. He thinks it's, like, sexy.' Paula shivered. 'God, don't make me bring up my cake!'

They walked down to Trafalgar Square. Nessa looked up at the clock on St Martin-in-the-Fields. They'd all be coming out of school round about now, but she didn't want to go home, not yet.

The charm bracelet rattled happily on her wrist. It was the nicest thing anyone had ever given her. Mum used to buy her things all the time. Expensive bits and pieces from all over the world: Japanese T-shirts that no one had in Britain yet, but didn't fit her; trainers from New York that made her feet look huge; earrings from Southern India when she'd never had her ears pierced. But nothing she'd ever asked for. Nothing she ever really wanted.

'I tell you what I want to do, Paula, I want to go and see a film.'

'We could take the cake home and get a video.'

'No, a proper film. In a cinema.'

Nessa walked her across the footbridge over the Thames and headed for the National Film Theatre. Helena had been a member forever and Nessa remembered the brochure that had come in the post last week. *The Golden Age of the American Musical*, it said.

They saw *Oklahoma!* Paula opened the cake box on her lap and they ate a good half of it. There was nearly two hours of Technicolor cowboys singing and farm girls dancing. They both agreed the modern ballet bit went on too long but Paula cried at the happy end, wiping her tears away with sticky white-chocolate fingers.

They walked home across the river; it was dark now and the city lights reflected yellow and orange shapes on the black water. Paula handed the cake box to Nessa and danced all the way over the footbridge. She swung the carrier bag and sang, *'I'm just a girl who can't say no.'*

Lauren Now

Lauren leant against the netball post with her arms folded and shut her eyes. The wind whipped around her legs and she burrowed her hands in her armpits to keep warm. The week was nearly over and no one had called. And now it was double PE. Year 10 A team against the Bs. And Lauren was in the Bs. She was no good at running, jumping, catching, or throwing. Her arms and legs seemed to end so far away from her body there seemed to be a kind of communication breakdown en route. The ball was far up the other end of the court. She let her mind drift.

Thierry had got out of a car in the middle of Stivenham; he had unfolded his legs and he stood like a god by the post office, waiting for her to come by after school. She would acknowledge him casually, Thierry would walk across and drape his long arm around her shoulder, and they would walk somewhere, the beach maybe, a foot taller and a mile more in love than anyone else.

'Goalkeeper! Wake up!' Lauren snapped into the present. Miss Gifford was shouting at her but before she had time to react the other team had scored. Lucy Marsham had scored. Lucy smiled and wiped her brow with a pale pink sweatband. Lauren thought she'd never hate a game as much as she hated netball.

Chloe had talked to her yesterday. Sat down next to her at lunch and asked her how it had gone at the weekend. Lauren tried to be cool, but Lucy was with her and Lucy had modelled for a hairdresser in Ipswich and knew everything there was to know.

'Was it a go-see? Do you have a portfolio? I got my cousin Sean to do mine so he did it for nothing. I could show you if you like. You've seen it, Chlo, haven't you?' Lucy swished her hair over to one side and smoothed it down all in one seamless move.

'Yeah,' Chloe said ''S great.'

Lauren opened a packet of crisps. 'No, it was Polaroids, mostly.'

'Oh. Polaroids. Like instant pictures? Are you sure it was Rain? That was what you said, wasn't it, Chlo?'

Chloe nodded. Lauren noticed she had new shoes. The same ones that Lucy wore.

'Yes.' Lauren sighed. 'It was Rain. It was OK, Chloe, thanks for asking.' Chloe looked embarrassed. Lucy wouldn't shut up.

'*The* Rain International? Are you sure? It might have been a rip off. How much did you have to pay? Did they put the pictures on the net?'

'I never paid anything! Look, they haven't said for definite yet, they said they'll let me know.' Lauren was trying to stay calm.

'Well, Hair Port phoned me up straightaway the day after. I was in the *Gazette* and I did a show for them in the Sports Centre, before Christmas, remember? And I'm with this agency firstmodels.com and they've got all my pictures.'

Lauren remembered. Lucy had come in with the printouts for weeks afterwards. *Lucy Marsham 5ft 4ins. Dress size: 10, eyes: blue, hair: blonde. Hair, hands, feet, catwalk.* Lauren hadn't said anything at the time but she'd thought it was all horribly tacky. *Buy me*, it said, *I'll do anything.* Perhaps Nessa had it right about modelling.

'Well, tell us, yeah?' Chloe said. 'If anything happens?'

Lauren nodded.

'Yes, *if* anything happens.' Lucy swished away and Chloe smiled apologetically.

Lauren consoled herself with fantasies that involved tripping Lucy up as she shot for goal, or smashing her hard across the face with a rounders bat, in slow motion, of course, watching the trail of blood and teeth arc out in mid-air as Lucy's face whiplashed back. The thought was very satisfying. Perhaps she was her mother's daughter, after all. Not an Our Lady's girl, not a Stivenham girl. Something else.

When Lauren came home there was a letter addressed to her on the doormat. The envelope was thick white cartridge paper, slightly textured and expensive. Lauren let her heavy schoolbag slide to the floor and picked the letter up. She looked at the handwriting on the front: scratchy, blue-black lines, postmarked London WC1. She turned it over. It was from them, no question.

Outside Nessa pulled up in her blue hatchback. She finished early at the music library three times a week when she gave lessons at home. Lauren shoved the letter in her skirt pocket and went up to the loo.

She didn't open it at first, just sat there on the flipped

down seat. She'd read about Schrodinger's Cat, the one in the box that may or may not be dead until you looked at it. Lauren reckoned if she didn't open it, then if it was bad news she'd never know. Downstairs she heard Nessa shout hello; Lauren called back. She patted the envelope; the letter was thin. That was bad, wasn't it? Or was it? What could they say that would take up more than one piece of paper?

She stopped on the landing. In a small wooden photo frame on the wall there was a faded colour photo of herself as a baby. Nessa had told her it was taken just after she was born. Nessa said that the midwife had said that Lauren was the longest baby she'd ever seen. In the photo Lauren waved starfish hands with long pointy fingers. All you could see of Paula was a large brown hand holding the baby Lauren tight in what looked like a towel. Lauren's eyes were screwed shut and her mouth twisted in mid cry. Lauren opened the letter and read.

Downstairs, Nessa had clicked the kettle on and was leafing through a pile of sheet music that was stacked in a box by the piano. Lauren came down the stairs, slowly letting her feet slide over the steps, the letter in her hand.

'Hello, love.' Nessa didn't look up. Lauren hovered in the doorway, one leg wound around the other. 'School OK?'

'Mm.'

'Do us a favour and put a teabag in a mug, the lemon and ginger, I've got Katie Hargreaves in five minutes.'

'Sure.'

Lauren went into the kitchen and fished out the teabags. The kettle boiled and as she poured the hot water out she re-read the letter.

Hi, Lauren,

The pictures are wonderful; we'd love to put you on our books. Could you call or e-mail and we'll arrange a meet in our offices? Please let your mother know—this is vital. You're still only fifteen and there is a limit on the work that you'll be able to do and of course we wouldn't want to get in the way of any exams.

We look forward to seeing you in London,

Ghislaine Furness

There was a colour photocopy of some of the pictures. Lauren looked long and slim and pale and interesting. She smiled at the girl in the pictures; she looked a world away from Lauren Bogle, the titless, horse-faced giant of Stivenham. What could Nessa possibly say? She was bound to be pleased for her, eventually.

'What's happened with the tea?'

'Oh!' Lauren lost her grip on the suddenly slippery letter and the photocopy fluttered down to the floor colour side up.

'What's that?' Nessa bent down. 'It's you!' She paled. 'God, I thought it was Paula.'

'No. It's me.'

'They're very . . . um . . . professional.'

'I was going to talk to you.'

Nessa's face was whiter than Lauren's, a flat china-plate whiteness.

'They've scouted you, haven't they? Some agency? I knew this would happen, I knew it. Was it in Cambridge with Chloe? Or at Southwold in the autumn?'

'No, Ness, it's fine, really. They're not cowboys, they're really nice.'

'They always are.'

'It's Rain, you know. *The* Rain International.'

Nessa put her hand up to her mouth and laughed a crazy-woman laugh. 'Straight to the top, eh?'

'Ness, look, it's a really good chance—'

'For what, Lauren? A chance for what? To forget school? To be exploited?'

The doorbell rang hard and loud and Katie Hargreaves, glasses and bunches, was on the doorstep clutching her copy of Grade 2 studies and arpeggios.

Lauren left them to it. She could hear the edge in Nessa's voice from the kitchen so she went upstairs. She couldn't imagine anyone else's parent going so completely over-board. Most mothers would be delighted. Chloe's mum would have gone with her to London, helped her, bought her clothes. Some parents paid for pictures, that's what Lucy had said. She knew it was to do with Paula, but that was the past. Before she was born.

Jack, Chloe's little brother, was next. He came with Chloe's mum in their people carrier. Lauren looked out of her bedroom window and saw Chloe in the car too. She was on her mobile phone, admiring her newly plucked eyebrows in the rear-view mirror.

When he had finished, Lauren was ready. She knew what she was going to say: only a bit of work before her GCSEs next year and no going crazy, absolutely not. The money would be useful—Nessa was always going on about university fees. And, most importantly, she was not Paula. Whatever had happened with her, Lauren was different.

Lauren wasn't going to end up banged-up or dead by sixteen. How many models end up in prison anyway? Lauren breathed deeply, picked up the letter and went downstairs.

Nessa was putting sheet music away, her face hard. Lauren sat down on the arm of the sofa.

'Nessa, I know you're not happy, but listen to me, please. I am sorry I never told you about the photos. I meant to. I was going to. I thought if they didn't want me then no one would ever know.'

'No, Lauren, *I'm* sorry.' Nessa pushed the hair away from her face. 'I knew someone would sign you up, sometime. I mean, you're your mother's daughter. Legs like yours don't come along every day.' Nessa smiled a tired smile. 'But these people, these agencies, they're not in it for you. I know it sounds pathetic but they'll just exploit you. You're just a thing, a bit of meat, and that's all they want. They want you to be a thing. And it's not real. It's all just pretend.'

'I know that!'

'I'm trying to protect you!' Nessa sighed. 'It's going to happen anyway, I'm not stupid. The way you look. But not now. I know what happens if you mess up your exams. Look at me. 32 and doing a part-time degree! I don't want that for you.'

Lauren had stopped listening. Nessa had said she knew it would happen, *the way you look*. She caught sight of herself in the mirror. She was angry and she looked great. Her cheekbones were sharp as knives and her eyes were fierce. She looked like the girl in the Polaroids. Like a model.

'Well, maybe I want it. I won't stop school. Look in the letter, they don't want to get in the way of my exams.

See?' Lauren stood tall, no slouching, and waved the letter under Nessa's nose.

Nessa was a foot smaller than her. Another species with a snouty pudgy nose and a squeaky voice. Lauren looked at her. Maybe Nessa was jealous. She was only 32 and already she dressed like a forty-year-old home counties matron. Bad, no-nonsense jumpers and corduroy trousers that were too tight across her thighs. She had piggy little squinty hazel eyes and a tendency to spots, even at her age. What did she know about modelling or fashion? She bought her clothes by mail order, only ever wore flat shoes. Nessa's arms were folded under her bust. Lauren could see she wasn't going to move an inch.

'You know what, Nessa. I was thinking, upstairs. Chloe's mum, anyone else at school, they'd be really pleased. This is something about me, not you, about me. You don't see it, do you? It'd be good for my confidence and I'd be earning so much!'

Nessa stifled a laugh. 'Self-confidence! Models don't have egos. They are employed to be things, Lauren, things that just are!'

'Well, maybe I'd like to *just be*! Maybe I don't want a degree or a poxy job. I could do this. Look, they think I can do this!'

Nessa turned away. She muttered very quietly but Lauren heard.

'Your mother thought she could do it, too. Look what it did to her.'

'Come off it, Ness. It wasn't just modelling Paula had to deal with, was it? Was it? I'm not like her, I'm starting from somewhere else, not like Paula!'

'No, I suppose not,' Nessa said in a tight voice.

'Anyway, Ness, when it comes to it you're not my mother, are you? You can't tell me not to do this! You know what I reckon? I reckon you're jealous! I've never seen myself like this. I never thought I could look like this!'

Lauren slammed the door on the way out.

Nessa Then

'I'll get Hannah to drop the pieces they need, is that OK?' Helena Harper looked up at the kitchen clock. 'And I'll be along later, around six maybe? No, not any earlier, I've got to meet East End Ed.' She made a face into the phone. 'I know! Yes! The man thinks he's my best friend. Wants me to invest in one of his flats, *duplex apartment*, he says! I know! In Wapping. Wapping; you know, by the river. He's letting us do the shoot for the City Shifts range there so I have to play grateful. Yes. Yes. *No!* No, all right, I'll be there. Yes, fine.'

Helena clicked the phone off and lit a cigarette. Nessa took the Rice Crispies from the cupboard and poured out the last of the milk, letting it drip into the bowl. She sat down at the table and took a book out of her dressing gown pocket. It was a second-hand paperback she'd bought in a junk shop in Exmouth Market *The London I Know* by Ed McKay. It was old and worn and soft as corduroy. The photo on the back was one of Ed McKay in 1978 by his pool in 'his luxury villa on the sunny Spanish Costa del Sol'. He had sculpted seventies hat hair and a huge shiny medallion hung against the forest of his chest.

Nessa had nearly finished it. She'd read about his early life in Hoxton bought up by Nanny Sherman. She'd read about his boxing career and the knife fights he blamed on 'youthful bravado and high spirits'. She had read the chapter where he talked about the killing of Pete 'Fat' Farrer in his pub in Shoreditch. Ed didn't exactly admit it, but he didn't deny it either. There was a joke about his old mate Stanley Sanders who was left-handed so having his right hand nailed to a bar wasn't *so* much of a hardship. He talked about the armed robbery the police tried to pin on him in 1977 and how he was now *'in early retirement in Spain with his wife Lorraine and their lovely son Ashley'*.

Nessa bent the spine of her book open at her place.

'Vanessa! Oh, my God! It's ten o'clock! Don't you have school?'

Nessa pulled her dressing gown close. She'd stayed out at Paula's till late. And bunking off had become normal now. Why should she have to deal with Elaine Schaller or double physics if she didn't want to? ''S Founder's Day.' It was a lame excuse but she knew her mother was too busy to care.

'Oh. Right. Well, make sure you do some revision or something. Haven't you got exams soon?'

'Five weeks.' Nessa didn't look up. She'd revise later. They didn't care and she didn't care. Her mother was rich, why should she bother? Paula was right about that.

The phone went again.

'Ed? Hello!' Helena's voice smiled even if her face didn't. Nessa sat up, closed her book, listened.

'Yes, I know. Haven't forgotten. We'll find it, I'm sure. No, you don't have to send anyone. I said I'll be there.' She put the phone down.

'Jesus! Remind me never to work with Ed McKay again.'

'That was him now?'

64

'He thinks he's some kind of minor god because he's in the background of a few photos.' Nessa slid the book back into her pocket. 'Are you listening to me, Vanessa? Sometimes I don't know why I scrape together your school fees, I really don't. He's not in the good ones, the David Bailey ones, though, is he? I can't stand the man.' She screwed the cigarette into an ashtray with FRED'S in big letters all the way round the edge. 'Unreconstructed egomaniac.'

Nessa looked at Helena and bit her lip.

'I have never met such a thoroughly oleaginous man. Don't think much of his air of menace—the man wears too much aftershave. Love his girlfriend, though, now she is *simply* gorgeous, sort of damaged goods. She's doing the pictures for the City Shifts range; if she looks right I'll think about her for the Hush launch. Trouble is, the City Shifts clothes are supposed to be mainstream. We can't risk just a black face, even if she is brown; we've got Anna Maven as well, you know the one. She's so white she's practically blue.'

Nessa was used to her mother talking about models like this. That girl's too short (5ft 7ins), or too fat (when you could see the bones in her chest), or too old or too common or, worst of all, too last year. Just so much meat. And Paula was just the same, meat or damaged goods or anything else, but that didn't matter at all to Helena.

'I thought you were a fashion designer, not a social engineer.'

'Don't hit me with the big words, darling, it doesn't suit you.'

Nessa smiled at her mother, showing a mouthful of Rice Crispies.

'Do you have to do that? Anyway, that girl of Ed's is a one-off. She's so fresh, so different, so . . .'

'Exotic? Is that fashionese for not white?'

'Vanessa, why are you being so confrontational? What is wrong with you? You're so bitter! It's not right at your age.' Helena picked up the phone again.

Nessa finished her breakfast.

'So, Mum. Can I come? To the shoot?'

Helena stopped dialling and looked at her daughter. 'Provided your attitude changes. Positivity, Vanessa! Honestly!'

Nessa went in the cab with Helena and her PA, Jevonka. Through corridors of damp-stained flat blocks and under railway viaducts. Over a tiny iron bridge where the light suddenly changed and the world seemed to open up in the reflected silver water of the empty docks. There was a class of children in canoes, Lego coloured, under the suddenly wide sky. Then the taxi twisted again down a road lined with close high brick walls and they were in a canyon of warehouses. Tall, black-brick warehouses with folded-back cranes and archways through to the river.

'Smashing!' Helena, occasionally stuck for words, reached back into the seventies. 'I was here you know,' she said to Jevonka, 'in '75; Derek Jarman had a party right here!'

Jevonka, who was super efficient and a Yale graduate, looked at Nessa for help. 'Who is Derek Jarman?'

'He made gay films in Latin,' Nessa pointed out. She'd only seen a bit of *Sebastiane*; Helena had thought she might find it useful for her Latin exam but it had subtitles and the young men were so beautiful Nessa had found it hard to concentrate.

As the taxi pulled in Nessa noticed a row of three cars. Two shiny black saloon cars with darkened glass and one beautiful, pale sky-blue antique car. A man was getting out of it, a big man with dark receding hair slicked back. As he stood up Nessa realized he wasn't that tall, it was that he was broad, almost square. It seemed unbelievable that he fitted into the low, sleek blue car. There were others getting out of the black cars. Nessa, who knew a bit about good cloth, could see their suits weren't half as expensive as blue-car-man's.

'Helena!' He shouted across and took off his gold-rimmed dark glasses and folded them into his top pocket. As he came closer Nessa smelt the aftershave her mother had warned her about coming out in a wave. She almost looked away but she wanted to look at him. He had big features, like a child's idea of a man. He was pale, and his eyes glittered blue. She'd read in the book he'd had his nose fixed in South Africa. It looked slightly weird although she had to admit it wasn't as mashed-up or as big as '70s Ed on the book cover. He seemed bigger than the street, too; it wasn't just him and his henchmen or whoever they were, you couldn't help looking at him.

'Helena!' He bent down and kissed her on the cheek. 'Look at this!' He looked up at the building. 'Nineteenth century, bloody beautiful! Don't make them like this any more!'

Nessa noticed how close he stood to her mother, towered over her, filled any space around her. That was scary. He was talking softly as he led her through a wooden door into a narrow cobbled arch and up some steps. Nessa could feel Helena's discomfort. His hand on the small of her back was huge, like a white, black-haired spade, and the nails were bitten down so low and so raw it turned Nessa's stomach.

'My daughter Vanessa,' said Helena. And he suddenly turned round and noticed her, as if he hadn't before. Nessa could see he was scanning her, head to toe. She saw herself as he saw her. Short, fat, sullen. Not interesting. He dismissed her in seconds and turned back to Helena.

Nessa thought then he could kill anyone he wanted, if he wanted. No problem at all.

The warehouse was falling down. The stairwell smelt of wee and oil paint. There was a dull thudding from below that sounded like a band rehearsing.

They walked up and up. The lower floors were all occupied by artists. 'Squatters,' Ed said. 'Bloody soap dodgers, if you ask me. They won't stick around once they know what's good for them.'

As they neared the top it started getting lighter. The top floor was enormous; huge and open at one end where the roof and walls had been glazed like a massive ramshackle conservatory. The view was breathtaking. Vanessa could see all of London spread out to the west and the flat, dull, metal river cutting the city in two.

Wooden pillars, pale with age and pockmarked by woodworm, held up the roof. And when she leant against one Nessa could smell, not linseed oil or damp, she was sure she wasn't imagining it, a deep dark tobacco smell from all the sacks they'd ever stored here for nearly three hundred years.

The space was massive. Two indoor tennis courts it looked like. Nessa was used to converted warehouses but this was different. The glass wall and roof at one end looked home-made. It was like the rooftop laboratory of a Frankenstein waiting for a thunderbolt. In the original part of the building there were rows of tiny squares of barred window and huge dark wooden doors in the wall, secured with ratchets, and heavy chains that swung outwards like cuckoo clock doors over the river. It looked as if the whole lot was about to fall down. Nessa moved as close as she dared to the glass. Down below was a tiny pebble beach lapped by the Thames.

'Vanessa!' It was Helena. Nessa smiled. Helena was terrified of heights. She was terrified for Nessa.

'It's OK.' Nessa turned round; Helena had paled.

'Your mother's quite right, love. Could have a nasty accident there, couldn't ya?' Ed smiled and Nessa imagined a body head down on the beach and stepped away, suddenly cold.

At the far end of the space under the glass roof the photographer was setting up. They were photographing stuff from Helena's City Shifts collection. Nessa had no idea why anyone thought these clothes were wearable, glamorous, or stylish, but someone must. 'Greed is Good,' Nessa muttered to herself. The clothes were like deconstructed suits: uber shoulder pads, lapels flying off, pockets inside out, red braces translated into shiny ribbons. Nessa had hated the drawings. They looked less like clothes and more like modern architecture.

She looked for Paula. She could see Anna Maven, the blue-white woman, in a bowler hat and red-ribboned bodice. Then Paula stepped out from behind a screen. She had a bowler hat too and her curls exploded out from underneath it. She was wearing one of the pin-striped skirts that buckled up vaguely bondage-wise and a red-ribboned corset. Both models had spidery false eyelashes on one eye. They looked terrifying.

'Good, isn't it!' The photographer was schmoozing up Helena. 'Sort of *Clockwork Orange*. With girls. And bondage. But *so* feminine!'

Normally talk like that made Nessa cringe. But Paula looked magnificent. Anyone else would have looked entirely ridiculous, but these two looked like beautiful aliens. Or elves. Bondage thug elves, Nessa reckoned. Or something.

Both models huddled around a giant industrial blow heater, which rushed and roared like a fairytale ogre. So it had to be changelings. Both girls were definitely not of this world. Then Paula looked up and saw Nessa and smiled. Nessa smiled back and then she realized that maybe Paula wasn't smiling at her but at Ed standing behind her.

Ed walked straight up to Paula and held her tight around the waist as if he thought she'd blow away. The ribbon corset puckered up round her middle and Nessa could see Paula's discomfort. She was subtly trying to wriggle out of his grip. His corpse-white, bitten-nailed hand moved up under Paula's skirt and Nessa looked away.

Lauren Now

'Well, you should thank Ian really,' Nessa said, shutting the piano lid.

'I will, Ness, promise. I'll thank him big time. And I'll be really good and wash up and clean upstairs and the bathroom—for the rest of the year—and all course-work will be in absolutely on time!'

'I know you think I'm being selfish. And over-reacting. But I'm not, honestly. Oh, God, let's not start again. Why shouldn't you screw all the money you can out of them, eh? Oh, I didn't mean that, I just don't think modelling's the barrel of glamorous fun it's cracked up to be!' Nessa smiled but Lauren could tell she wasn't as convinced as she was trying to look. Nessa went on, 'Just any time, love, any time you want to stop, just say, OK? I'm only trying to . . .' Nessa sighed, 'oh, you know, Lauren, I'm trying to protect you. I can't help looking at you sometimes and seeing your mother.'

'I know, Ness. But it's like Ian said, I'm not her, am I? And things have changed. I know the photographers will treat me like meat and I'll have to get used to rejection and people looking at me like I've got no feelings. But I'll be fine, Nessa, really. It sounds exactly like school.'

Ian's car horn sounded outside and Lauren watched Nessa touch up her make-up in the hall mirror. She had her dark grey interview-and-funerals suit on and the only pair of heels she owned. Lauren hugged her.

'I'm sorry about the mother business, Ness, really. I wouldn't want anything else. Anyone else.'

Nessa looked at Lauren, licked her finger and brushed Lauren's eyebrows into place. Lauren smoothed the dust off Nessa's lapel.

'It's not like we have a choice, Lauren.'

Ghislaine Furness had an office on the back floor of the building that looked out onto a narrow roofscape. It was totally quiet, any noise soaked up by the thick dark carpet and double-glazed windows. Lauren and Nessa had been shown in by a tiny blonde girl.

'Hi, I'm Minty. Tea? Coffee? Water?'

Lauren felt her mouth so dry she couldn't speak. On the walls were two huge photographs of the supermodel Nina Holland looking bored and exclusive. Spread on Ghislaine's desk were the photos Jamie Holdsworth had taken a few weeks ago.

Nessa's face set hard. Lauren thought she looked really sharp. She squeezed her hand.

'Good morning.' Ghislaine was purring, her red mouth like a drawn-on smile. 'Sit down. Please. You wouldn't *believe* the interest we've had with these.'

She leant across the desk and shook Nessa's hand. 'And you are?'

'Vanessa, Vanessa Harper, I'm Lauren's guardian.'

Ghislaine looked hard at Nessa as if she might have recognized her. Lauren tried not to laugh. Maybe she was about to offer Nessa some job modelling suits for old ladies.

'Your mother wasn't Helena Harper, by any chance, was she?'

Nessa nodded. The atmosphere changed. 'Interesting.' Ghislaine Furness smiled a thin red smile. 'Well then, I think we both know what we're dealing with here.' Nessa nodded and Lauren realized they were talking about her. Ghislaine continued, 'She has the capacity to do very well indeed; not in the regular magazines, not in any kind of juvenile backwater.' She waved her manicured hand. 'Does she move well?'

Lauren felt more and more like a prize cow. Nessa just nodded and sipped her water.

'Absolutely.'

'Did you have any ballet training, dear?'

Lauren blinked. 'Um . . . not since I was little.' She flashed back to the church hall at Stivenham and saw herself head and shoulders above the other pink-clad fairy girls like Gulliver in Lilliput.

Ghislaine scribbled something into a black leather-bound notebook. Nessa always said clumsy was her middle name. She crossed her legs so that no one would notice her scabby knee from where she'd fallen over outside the language block last week.

'Well, you realize a lot of our favourite photographers have been extremely interested in working with Lauren. We'd like her to spend a couple of weekends in London, finding her way, trying things out, getting a really good set together. We'll sort out a flat for Lauren; you can accompany her, of course.'

Nessa leaned forward. 'I hope you understand, Lauren is still at school; we wouldn't be in the position to come to London until the Easter holidays at least.'

'Of course.' Ghislaine nodded.

Lauren had to shut her mouth to stop her jaw hitting the desk. This wasn't Nessa Harper: music librarian to the fens. Nessa seemed to have hardened into the suit.

On the wall, Nina Holland stared out from the photos with that mixture of disdain and otherworldliness culti-vated by supermodels. Lauren wondered if that's what she was really like, hard and cold and shiny, or if that was just how the photographer had asked her to look. Or maybe that's how the jacket she was wearing was supposed to look. Or perhaps Nina Holland had spent the whole day waiting for the photographer to sort out the lights and she was bored stiff. Or in fact she was being utterly exploited and her soul had been captured in a photograph long ago and now she never, ever aged.

Then her mind floated off again. Thierry had seen her photograph and written to her; his handwriting was long and spiky and the blue of his pen was perceptibly French. He wanted to meet her; he'd never forgotten her. She sighed to herself and imagined she felt Thierry's breath hot on the back of her neck.

'So that's settled, then.' Ghislaine Furness stood up.

Lauren realized Nessa and Ghislaine were shaking hands; she must have missed something. Nessa stood up, so Lauren did too, suddenly pushing her chair back from the desk with a little too much force. Nessa's glass of water spilled over the desktop.

'Oops!'

So much for moving well, Lauren thought.

Out in the street Lauren found her voice. 'Nessa, thank you.' Bent down and kissed her on the cheek. 'I won't make you regret this, I promise.'

'Better not, girl. That's all I can say.'

'And you were brilliant in there, really.'

Nessa smiled. 'You know, I quite enjoyed it in the end. Maybe I should have become some CEO instead of a music librarian. Oh, Lauren, I'd forgotten how seductive this whole business is, and they all want you so badly! It's obscene.'

'Isn't that good?'

'Depends, I suppose. Lauren, whatever you do please don't forget there's more to you than your bones and your face. And don't get a swollen head, OK? If you do I'll disown you.'

'Yeah, and if I do I'll never get any work.'

'Very funny. Come on, we've got serious business now.'

'I know. And I promise, Ness, I'll keep up with everything at school. Honest.'

'You've said that about ten times! And don't hold your breath, Lauren. Even if every photographer in London is very interested in you, it could still all turn to ashes. Nothing's certain. Don't go chicken-counting, all right?'

'All right.'

They took a black taxi across town to see Paula and Helena.

'This is it!' Nessa took a deep breath. Lauren could tell she felt guilty.

'I haven't been here for years.' Lauren squeezed her arm, but Nessa stopped suddenly just inside the white sculpted gates.

'Flowers! Oh my God, Helena needs flowers!'

There was a shop opposite. The flowers cost ten times what they would have in the Flower Pot opposite the bus stop in Stivenham. But they were beautiful. White lilies, big and showy and heavy with scent.

'These are for Helena,' Nessa said and she picked up a bunch of freesias. Tiny, perfect, purple, yellow, and dark pinky red. 'For Paula, she loved these.' She handed them to Lauren and then they crossed the road back to the cemetery.

'You know when Paula died?'

'Yeah?'

'Did you never think of giving me up? I mean, you were only young, sixteen, seventeen?'

Nessa shook her head. 'I promised Paula, I promised her.' She turned and faced Lauren. 'After Helena died, she always said we were family. I don't know, it was a bit like that. Neither of us had anyone else. I couldn't let her down.'

The cemetery was one of the big old inner London ones. Helena had bought herself a plot years before she died. The newer graves were tucked away from the centre, around the southern gates away from the road. Lauren gripped Nessa tightly. The place was full of knots of school-boys smoking cigarettes and old men drinking bottles of cider. They seemed to walk for ages. Past enormous pyr-amids of marble and what almost seemed like stone houses with railings.

'Here.' Nessa left the path and up against the wall there was a modest black granite stone. *'Helena Harper'* was carved into the stone very discreetly, *'Designer 1945–1989.'* That was all. To the left a white marble heart. *Paula Bogle*

76

Much loved, much missed, 1974–1989. It looked like the grave of a little child, Lauren thought.

Nessa had already started clearing the graves, brushing the stones down with her hanky. Lauren could see her eyes were red and puffy. Paula Bogle. Her mum. Lauren didn't really feel anything and took the cellophane off the flowers. I should do, she told herself, that's my mother. But she'd never known her. Sometimes she'd lie in bed and try to remember being a baby. Being in prison, being held by Paula and not Nessa. But she couldn't. She stuffed the flowers into the holder and realized Nessa had gone to fetch some water.

There was Nessa's mum next to hers. What a family. Half dead. She thought of Paula's long bones under the ground, and touched Paula's gold-leafed name.

'Right.' Nessa was in a calmer mood when they left, less wired. As if she had made some kind of peace. 'I'm off to Boosey and Hawkes; I need some music for my Grade Twos. Are you coming? Topshop's just around the corner.'

Lauren wanted to get the jumper back and maybe Thierry would be there. She shook her head.

''S OK. I'll meet you at Liverpool Street, for the train,' Lauren said. Nessa didn't look convinced.

'Where are you off to then?'

'I want to go to this bookshop. I saw it last time.' She was thinking of the Moomintroll book; Nessa would love it. 'I thought I'd get Ian something, you know, a thank-you. He likes books. As well as trees.' Ian was a tree surgeon. Lauren liked the job title. 'And I've got my phone.'

'OK, if you're sure. But don't mess me around, Lauren.

Please. Liverpool Street half past five or you're worse than dead!'

Lauren ran round the corner of Brushfield Street towards the market. It was busier than the weekend when she'd been here last. The Starbucks full of office workers, the market hung with hand-made clothes and soap made out of dried flower heads and coloured lard. There was the bookshop with boxes of books and comics out on the street, so they were open. She slowed down. Tried to rehearse what she was going to say. OK, maybe Thierry had a girlfriend; Lauren didn't want to make a total fool of herself. But then what if they'd thrown her jumper away? Perhaps Luke's dad, cross when he realized the jumper belonged to the idiot that had ruined his—what was it—*Extinct Planet Girl*? No, *Mutant Planet Girl*. Lauren bit her lip and walked into the shop.

'Can I help?' A huge man was sitting inside reading a comic. He was dark brown and big featured, well-fed like an American. Lauren had expected a black version of that comic-book guy from *The Simpsons*, pot-belly and ponytail. But this man was slightly greying and more dignified and his eyes were dark and kind. He folded the comic on the counter shut.

'I'm looking for my jumper . . . um . . . I left it here. Once.' God she sounded thick.

The man said nothing at first. Perhaps super-psychic girl had stolen his brain through the pages of the comic with her psy-mitts. Perhaps she had imagined what had happened with Thierry. Lauren read the posters on the wall behind his

78

head. Second-Hand Comic Convention, Manchester; Spital-fields by Night Walk; The Streets of London's Gangland. Lauren was just thinking she should leave when the man spoke.

'You're Lauren!' She could see the wave of recognition. 'The jumper's at home, Judy put it through the wash. I told Luke, I said you'd be back, home-made jumper like that.'

'Oh, thank you!'

'I'm Clive.' He held out an enormous hand. 'Look, it's at home, around the corner. Puma Court, do you know it? Someone's in. There's always someone in. It's in a Marks bag, somewhere.' He looked at his watch. 'I'll be there in fifteen minutes myself. Not exactly overrun, am I?'

Lauren bought the Moomintroll book for Nessa and a guide to trees of England for Ian before she left.

Puma Court was a thin, dark alley of old, thin, dark houses. She imagined this was first stop on any Jack the Ripper Walk. It looked like a film set and it smelt of wee and old beer. Nowhere smelt of anything in Stivenham; the wind scoured everything away and salted what was left.

The house had an old-fashioned bell that you pulled. It sounded loud, the ringing bouncing off the dark brick. Lauren stood tall. She half expected the door to creak open and reveal the Addams family. Instead a small woman in a tracksuit and a paint-stained apron opened the door.

'Hello, dear, are you a friend of Clare's?' She wasn't really looking at Lauren; she turned and yelled up the stairs.

'Clare! It's for you. Come on in, love.'

Lauren stepped into the house and the door shut behind

her. It smelt wonderful, of warmth and paint with a back-note of damp, curling paper and hot dinners. The walls were dark red and the floor was bare wood.

'I'm not really a friend,' Lauren had started but the woman had already disappeared. A few moments later there was the sound of someone coming downstairs lazily, like a slow canter. Bare brown feet and a long denim skirt. It was the girl she'd seen in the shop with Thierry.

'Look, I'm sorry, I tried to tell her.'

'Mum, yeah! She's always a bit preoccupied. Are you a mate of Luke's? Have I seen you around?' She looked Lauren up and down.

'Lauren. Not really. I ruined *Mutant Planet Girl* and I left my jumper. I just came for that, really.'

The girl smiled. 'It was you, was it? Come in, you did us all a favour. If you want to go back to the shop and get rid of the rest of them you're welcome. Look, come up, Luke's not back for ten minutes but you might as well wait upstairs.'

Lauren followed her upstairs. The house seemed to go on for miles, up and up and up. Piles of books and keys and clean washing rested on every step. It smelt of coffee and paper and oil paint. There was music coming from the top floor. Clare pushed open the door and Thierry was sitting on the bed playing the guitar.

'This is Thierry, our lodger—he's at uni in town.'

Lauren felt her face getting hotter.

He looked up. 'We've met. At the shop. Lauren, isn't it?'

She thought of all the things she'd imagined doing with him and concentrated on not blushing.

Clare sat down next to him and Lauren tried to keep smiling. The room was tucked under the top of the house. The sloping low roof reminded her of home, but the room was bigger and the windows were longer. She tried not to look at Clare or Thierry at all. The books on the shelf were a mix of old children's stories, *Orlando the Marmalade Cat*, and psychology text books. There was a double bed.

'Um . . . it's just my jumper, really. I think I probably ought to go.'

'Ah yes.' Thierry put the guitar down. 'Luke brought it home, he knows where it is.'

'Yeah, 's cool.' Clare was leaning over a roll-up she was building on her lap.

Lauren wished she was somewhere else. It was almost as if Thierry could see inside her head and read all the stupid fantasies she had allowed herself. It felt like torture. Thierry put the guitar down and ran his hand down Clare's back. Lauren picked up *Orlando Takes a Holiday* and stared very hard at the pictures.

'There you are!' Luke put his head around the door. He held out a Marks bag and Lauren could see the familiar green jumper inside. 'You lot stopping for lunch? Mum says it's on.'

Thierry and Clare were going out. Somehow Luke persuaded Lauren to stay. Downstairs a space had been cleared in the middle of the table, newspapers and a fruit bowl pushed back into a wobbly heap. Lauren sat down and she felt the chair wobbling underneath her. Luke leant over and whispered.

'Everything's like that round here. It's like they've never heard of furniture or shops. Except book shops.'

'Luke found your jumper then.' Clive sat down opposite Lauren. 'He said your name was Lauren—not Bacall, surely.' Clive laughed. Judy rolled her eyes.

'No, Bogle. Lauren Bogle.'

'Bogle?' Luke's dad looked up, grinning, 'Bet your dad's called Paul.'

'It was my mother's name, yeah, and she was Paula. How did you know that?'

'Don't tell me you never heard of Paul Bogle?'

Lauren shook her head. Luke rolled his eyes.

'Oh no, here comes the history lesson.'

'No, come on, Luke, it's interesting.' Luke's dad sat back.

'Well, it depends whose history you're talking about, then, doesn't it. You say Paul Bogle was a revolutionary, a hero.' Judy buttered the bread on her plate and didn't look up. She was smiling.

'Absolutely!'

'But what about the people he killed, Clive?'

'He never killed anyone. And it was all overreaction! The governor of Jamaica coming over all SAS. It's only the British establishment that saw him as a murderer.'

'So murderers can be heroes then; so the Krays were heroes too?'

'Paul Bogle was no murderer, he wasn't a criminal at all. You cannot compare Paul Bogle, who stood up for his fellow men, with the Kray twins who ran a crime empire enforced by torture and murder. It's totally different.' Luke's dad folded his arms.

'Yeah, Mum, he's right, you know. Totally different.'

Luke's mum pushed her glasses up her nose. 'I'm only winding him up, love. Devil's advocate.' She turned back to her husband. 'His followers had machetes though, they killed people!'

'Jude, the British had guns, I bet. Did they have guns then, Luke?'

'Course they had guns. Anyway, the only reason Mum's like this is she's pissed off with you taking all that gangster stuff in the shop.'

'I wouldn't do it if I didn't have to! You know that! But Paul Bogle was different; we were slaves, Jude! Slaves!' He brought his coffee cup down hard on the table. Jude smiled and wiped her hands on her apron.

'The poor are always oppressed, love, one way or another.'

'But colour is different, Jude. You can't hide it, ever!'

'I bet, Clive, if I suggested selling books that glorified black on black violence you'd really have a go. What's the difference between Yardies and the Krays? Or Jack the Ripper! For God's sake, Clive, can't you make those stupid murder tourists and walkers go somewhere else?'

'Oh, Jude, the shop needs the money!'

Luke mouthed 'Let's go' at Lauren and they left Judy and Clive arguing about revolutionaries, race, Robin Hood, and the Krays.

'They are like that all the time,' Luke said. 'On and on. If it's not race or crime or exploitation of women it's the annihilation of indigenous Americans. Or Aborigines. And of course Mum thinks Dad shouldn't talk up the crime thing at all. The tourists love it, though.'

'Well, I think they're lovely, your parents.'

'You don't live with them.'

Luke lived at the top of the house in the room opposite

Clare's. The ceiling was low, like Lauren's room at home, but not so low she had to duck.

From Luke's windows a sea of rooftops and chimney pots lapped the oversized tower blocks of the city. The noise was constant, too, but it wasn't the come and go of the sea, it was a soup of traffic, car alarms, sirens.

There was a desk piled with stuff: books, school worksheets, the usual rubbish. But on the wall behind the desk was a patchwork of drawings, pencil and colour. Lauren recognized Clare and Thierry lying in a heap in one of them.

'These are gorgeous! Did you do them?'

Luke took a CD from a shelf and slotted it in. 'It's the only thing I'm any good at apart from sleeping.'

Lauren didn't recognize the music, but she liked it.

'I'll let you borrow it, if you like.'

'Thanks, but I'm never in London. Well, that's not true, but you'd probably never get it back. I live in Stivenham; it's like The Land Time Forgot.'

'Look, take it, leave me your number and I can harass you when I want it back.' He smiled.

She looked at her watch. 'I've got to go.' She picked up the bag with her jumper and put the Moomin book she'd bought for Nessa and the trees of Britain handbook she'd got for Ian inside.

Luke handed her the CD. 'My e-mail's on it,' he said casually. 'If you want.' And he walked downstairs behind her.

'Thanks, then, for looking after this.'

'No problem.'

Lauren looked round and saw herself and Luke in the large hall mirror.

'So your mum was black—or mixed, yeah?' Luke said to her reflection. 'I thought you weren't just white.'

'What do you mean?'

'From your features. You know, you're not just a regular English country rose, are you.'

Lauren blushed.

'Look at us.' Luke pointed at the reflections. 'I'm technically a mulatto. You know, when they used to breed slaves.'

'That's horrible!'

'Yeah, people are horrible. But it's only horrible if you let it be horrible. It's like reclaiming words, you know, like queers or niggers. You're a what, quadroon? Octoroon maybe?'

'You what?'

'It's to do with how white you are. Or how black you are. Stupid, really, like we're cattle or something. Quadroon is three quarters white, octoroon is one eighth black.'

'But that's daft. How white is white? No one's really completely anything. People always think I'm white. They don't want to believe me. They want me to be what they want me to be. Not what I am.'

'I know, I know. It's how people look at you, what they think. I'm always Brazilian or Mediterranean. But I'm saying this, I'm saying it's what you want, how you think of yourself, and saying I don't care which box you put me in. I want to go in any box I like. So, what about you?'

Lauren thought. 'Quadroon. Yeah, I'm that.'

'Say it loud, you're beige and you're proud!'

* * *

85

Lauren spotted Nessa at the station, with armfuls of shopping bags. For someone who hated London she seemed in a very good mood. 'Look! I got an ironing board cover and the music for Katie Hargreaves's Grade 2 and, plus, at last I got some decent shoes.'

'Ness,' Lauren asked, 'have you ever heard of Paul Bogle?'

Nessa Then

Helena was shouting. Nessa forced her eyes open and Helena was standing over her shouting about school. She rubbed her eyes and pulled the sheets up. Slowly Helena sharpened into focus. Nessa could see she was furious. Nessa shut her eyes tight and rolled over to face the wall.

'Don't you turn away from me, Vanessa! I don't know what you think you are doing but let me tell you, you are ruining your life! It's not a dress rehearsal, darling, this is it. You want to know what life's like? You want to try the real world? Fine! Get yourself a job! Do you know how much that school costs me? Honestly, Nessa, if there's something wrong in your life then why won't you talk to me?'

Nessa opened her eyes a fraction. The white-painted wall had a tiny crack like an imaginary river flowing down from the ceiling. She tried to tune Helena out but it wasn't working. Her stomach felt so knotted she thought she was going to retch. She had missed her first two GCSEs, English Lit I and Chemistry. Helena must have found out.

'For pity's sake, Nessa!'

Nessa slowly twisted round. Helena's face was red and puffy. Had she been crying? No, she was just upset about paying out for five years of secondary education. Nessa blinked and that seemed to send Helena off into more of a rage.

'The school phoned me. Just now. God, I'm not dressed! That foul woman who sits in the office with bad make-up and Terylene blouses! She said to me, did I not realize you'd missed your exams? Do I not know where my daughter is? Vanessa, you made me look like such a fool!'

Nessa thought to herself that Helena spent her career making other women look foolish all the time but she didn't say anything. She knew this had been coming from the moment she had missed that first exam. But she found the fear ebbing away. She wasn't scared of Helena, she just wanted her to go away.

'I've called a taxi, Vanessa. If you get dressed now you'll catch your Physics exam. Come on, darling, I don't want any more arguments, all right? You do these exams and then if you want to leave school, get a job, whatever, we can talk about it.' She sighed and sat down on the bed as if all the air and anger had been puffed out of her. She looked old and tired. 'Vanessa, darling, I just don't understand. Was there a problem, at school, with the teachers? With the girls? You can always talk to me, you know.' She pushed her hair back from her face. 'But this isn't the time to fall apart, darling. Not now.'

Nessa said nothing. Helena tried staring hard at her, looking somewhere between tortured and angry. Nessa had to stop herself laughing; Helena didn't seem fierce any more. She wasn't scared of her at all. That had to be Paula's work.

A plane flew across the square of sky beyond her window. Paula would be back from Paris by now. Even

though she'd only been away six days Nessa had been surprised how much she missed her. The phone calls, the
evenings in front of the telly. She'd go round there today;
at least there'd be someone who was pleased to see her.
Nessa sat up and rubbed her eyes. One thing she would
not be doing was talking to Helena.

'Mum, OK, I'm getting dressed. All right?'

'Good.' Helena smiled a tight little smile. 'I'll take this
afternoon off and we'll talk, darling. OK?'

Now that, thought Nessa, is scary. She said nothing,
though, and when the taxi came Nessa told the driver to
take her to Fredericks Mews. No way was she going to
school. She'd get yelled at some more and then spend all
morning in the hall looking at a piece of paper she didn't
understand. Missing school had become normal. And
physics. I mean, Nessa could not imagine a time in her
life when she would need to discuss gravity or electricity
or anything like that. Paula was right, it was a total waste
of time. She settled back in the taxi. Holborn sped by, and
then Shaftesbury Avenue. She didn't know what she
wanted to do with her life, but like Paula said, Helena was
rich, so why should she bother. She twizzled the lucky eye
charm on her wrist. It was like Paula said, she was lucky.

Nessa got the driver to let her out at Marble Arch. There
was one of those day and night food shops that sold stuff
you couldn't get anywhere else, American sweets and
Arabian pastries and Betty Crocker cake mixes. Nessa
bought the one that promised a pure white cake, not yellow
but white, 'gleaming snow-white sponge and matching
ready-made frosting to pour 'n' sculpt'. The list of chem-
icals on the side ran to three columns.

Nessa walked through the arch of Fredericks Mews and down the cobbled street. The sunshine bounced off the seaside-coloured houses and just over the wall she could hear the nuns in the Tyburn Convent skipping and playing catch. She looked at her watch. It was only nine thirty; Paula might have come in late last night and not be up yet. Perhaps she should have phoned first to check. No, Paula wouldn't mind. Paula was her friend.

She was almost at the end of the mews when a large maroon car coasted down the cobbles and pulled up outside Paula's. The passenger door opened and a man got out. He was old, his bald head liver-spotted, and he was small, not much taller than Nessa. She slowed her pace. There was no one else in the mews. The sun shone and even with the noise of the nuns playing the air seemed still. The man spoke to the driver and shut the door. He looked as if he knew where he was going. And then he rang Paula's bell.

Nessa wasn't sure what to do. Something told her Paula wouldn't thank her if she waved and shouted. She stared at the man. He was smartly dressed: shiny shoes and a suit that reflected the light. He turned and looked right through Nessa, smoothed what was left of his short grey hair, and licked his lips. Nessa heard Paula open the door. She heard her laugh too loudly when the old man mumbled something. And then he'd gone in.

Nessa went and sat in Hyde Park. He must have been something to do with Ed, she thought. Had to be. Old bloke like that in a shiny suit. Maybe Ed had stayed over and the old man had come to see Ed. That had to be it. She'd go round later. Phone her first from the phone box on the corner of the Edgware Road. She checked her watch, back at school they would have started the physics paper.

The park was full of tiny posh kids in smocked summer dresses and Mary Jane shoes with their nannies. Knots of women veiled head to toe in black threw bread to the ducks on the Serpentine. Nessa thought they reminded her of Hattifatteners in the Moomin books. The sun went in and the sky clouded over with vicious yellow-grey storm clouds. The nannies headed home but the Hattifatteners stayed, throwing endless armfuls of what looked like Weetabix towards grateful ducks. After an hour and a half had crawled by in the park, Nessa tried the phone.

'Nessa! Great! Come over.'

'You sure? Ed's not in, is he? I'll only be two minutes— I'm just around the corner. I've got a Betty Crocker. A white one.'

'Great, and there's no Ed. I'll see you in a bit, yeah. I've got some great news.'

The storm broke as Nessa turned into the Edgware Road; she pulled her blazer up over her head and ran.

When Paula answered the door she was in her fluffy white dressing gown and her hair was dripping wet.

'You got me out of the shower!' She was smiling.

Nessa was going to say something about the man she'd seen, but Paula was so pleased with the Betty Crocker mix that she took it straight into the kitchen and made it up there and then. Thirty minutes later they had huge slabs of warm glo-white cake for lunch.

'Ooh, Ness, look at this.' Paula sat on the edge of the white leather sofa and passed an envelope to Nessa. Inside were photos. It was Paula, wearing an Italian designer; Romeo Gigli, she said.

'These pictures are great!' Nessa tried not to spray them with flecks of white sponge cake.

''S good, innit. Don't say anything yet, Ness, but this is gonna be an ad. An advert! Full page. In *Vogue*, you know. *Vogue*!' Paula giggled.

'Bloody hell, Paula!'

'I know. And doing the catwalk stuff was excellent. I was dead nervous. But I loved it, Ness! And I was good. This photographer I did the ads with says I should get a proper agent, you know.'

Nessa looked up from the photos. 'What do you mean?'

'I've only done bits and that. Ed handles it all. And I'm not supposed to be working too much, innit, not till September, after I'm 16.'

'Oh, Paula these photos . . .' The dresses looked as if they'd been designed just for her. Long, high waisted, classical; Paula looked cool and expensive. 'You look so . . . brilliant.'

'I thought you, or your mum, you might, you know, know something. About agencies and that.'

'Honestly, Paula, you don't need help! I mean you're already working. You've already got loads of work. Agencies will be falling over themselves to sign you up. In fact, just ask Ed who he's been sending your stuff to, you know. You must be earning loads already.'

Paula said nothing. Nessa didn't notice at first but she'd stopped eating her cake.

'What's up? Tastes OK to me.'

'Here, you have mine. I'm not hungry.' Paula flicked on the telly and they watched some World War Two romance set in a Japanese internment camp. Nessa didn't feel hungry then, either. She had wanted to tell Paula about the row with Helena, about heroically missing her GCSEs, about sneaking out this morning. But Paula was staring fixedly at the TV, chewing the end of her fluffy white dressing gown.

'D'you want to go shopping. Or something?' Nessa asked, shifting herself on the leather sofa.

''S all right. I'm knackered. Been busy.' She flashed a sudden brittle smile. Nessa felt as if she didn't know Paula at all. 'Anyway,' Paula stood up and stretched, 'haven't you got school to go to or something, didn't you say you had exams to pass?'

'No, well . . . um . . .' The cake felt like sawdust in her mouth and she felt her insides fluttering and swooping. She looked at Paula, who looked completely cool. She held her dressing gown tight and ran her hand through her clean hair.

'There was this geezer on the plane. He was going on about his daughter, *Same age as you*, *darling*, he goes, *she's doing very well*. He put his hand on my leg.' Paula shivered, but didn't look at Nessa. Nessa felt indignant on Paula's behalf.

'That's horrible.'

'Men are horrible. I should've given him a slap. Creep! I said to him, I said, does your daughter like being pawed by old pervs? Should've seen his face! Made me think, though. You know, she's probably just like you, his daughter. Even if she falls it's like there's a big cushion of money, making it all good. You know what that's like, don't you? You don't have to do nothing and everything works out just fine.'

'What?

Paula was staring at Nessa now, and Nessa, who had seen Paula lay into shop assistants and other people, shifted in her seat.

'You've never had to do anything you don't want to do, have you?'

'That's *so* not true!'

Paula smiled. 'Yeah, yeah. What did Helena ever do to you? Send you to school? Hold you down and force-feed you cake? Poor little Nessa! You don't know you're born, you're like a baby, a fat know-nothing baby! I don't know why you're here, I really don't. Oh, hang on, I remember. You don't have any friends, do you!'

Nessa felt shaky. 'Paula?'

Paula stared into the TV. The phone rang. Paula sighed and went to pick it up. Nessa saw her own reflection in the mirror over the minimalist fireplace. She was a dumpy schoolgirl with dirty blonde hair. Whatever made her think someone like Paula would be interested in having her as a friend?

Paula took the phone into the kitchen. Nessa could hear her laughing. She took her damp school blazer from the hook in the hall and shut the door behind her quietly.

Lauren Now

Monday morning was freezing cold. It was supposed to be spring but the wind was blowing
sideways with an edge like a knife, cutting off
the new blossom and turning petals into snowflakes. Lauren
kept quiet about the weekend. Apart from the fact that she
had no one to tell, when she thought about it what *had*
happened? She was signed on to the books of Rain and
she'd seen Thierry again. She felt herself warm up just
thinking about him. But what was there to warm up about?
He had a girlfriend, he slept in a double bed with her, and
he was twenty-one. It was a waste of time.

'What are you looking so glum about?' Chloe was asking,
wide-eyed. They were in the corridor outside the music
room; Chloe lowered her voice. 'Didn't they take you on?
At Rain, you know?'

Lauren nodded. 'Look, Chloe, don't tell Lucy, but yeah, they
did. But it's not as if I've got any jobs lined up or anything.'

'No, I won't say anything, but it's great, Laur, really.
You deserve it.'

Lauren shrugged. She didn't think deserving came into
it. It was a fluke, a genetic accident that she looked the
way she did. Luck with a capital L.

'I'll catch you later,' Chloe said hoisting her schoolbag
up onto her shoulder.

'Later,' Lauren answered watching her go. When she thought about it at the end of the day she realized that was the only time anyone apart from a teacher had spoken to her at all. Even Gail Norman had given up.

During break Lauren went to the library and found herself looking up Paul Bogle in an encyclopaedia, but he wasn't there. She asked the librarian if they had any books on the history of the West Indies but it was so general it told her nothing she didn't know already.

She booked net space at lunchtime and there he was, just like Luke's dad had said. He was a Jamaican national hero. Stood up for workers' rights, got himself killed for his trouble. Lauren pressed print and smiled. *Say it loud, I'm beige and I'm proud.*

On the way home it started raining. Lauren was lucky, she didn't have to pile on a bus, school was just a walk away. But everywhere she went in Stivenham now, she was on her own. She could feel the cold seeping into her bones and seizing up her joints. When she got home she turned the heating up to high and sat shivering in her room, almost willing the walls to close in on her. She went downstairs, flicked on the computer and shut it down again. She wanted to talk to real people, not strings of words on a screen. Lauren felt as if she was marooned at the edge of the world.

Outside, the trees on the street bent under the rain and Nessa's little blue car pulled up in the drive.

'God, remind me to leave my brain at home when I go to work!' She clicked on the kettle. 'That job is doing my head in completely. If I have to tell another first-year not to scribble notes in the margins again I'll . . .'

'I'll make the tea, Ness. If it's any consolation, I've had a cacky day too.'

'Our Lady's not a barrel of laughs either?'

Lauren nodded.

'Well, I tell you what, Laur.' Nessa looked at her watch. 'Katie'll be here any minute, but why don't you go over to Chloe's and tell her mum I'll have to see Jack another time. I think I'd shut the piano lid on his hands, the mood I'm in.'

'Can't I just phone?' Lauren said quickly. 'Have you seen the rain?'

'Don't you think I tried? It was engaged non-stop; I bet Chloe's online. And her mum's mobile's switched off. Oh, go on, love, and you can talk to Chloe. I'm sure she'll be pleased to see you. I know what you girls are like.'

Nessa rolled her eyes. Lauren almost said something, but she could see if she tried any harder to get out of it Nessa would just ask more questions.

The doorbell rang and Lauren let Katie Hargreaves in and herself out. The rain looked worse than it was. She tucked her hands under her arms and sped up, turning the corner into the estate of new brick houses where Chloe lived.

She rang the bell. Through the glass she could see that it was Chloe's mum in the hall. She could pass the message on and go.

'Lauren! Come in, quick, before the rain gets in the porch.'

'I won't be a minute, it's about Jack's piano lesson.'

'No, please! You can't have been round for ages! It's lovely to see you.'

Lauren smiled back. Chloe's mum, Chris, had always been good to her. 'OK, Chris, just for a minute.' She stepped inside. It had been a long time since she'd been in Chloe's. The house even smelt familiar.

'Come on in! Look, Graham's finished the kitchen, you haven't seen it, have you? Chloe's not in, I think she's at Lucy's, but you must come and have a look. It's just how I wanted it.'

Lauren relaxed. It was nice to be back. Jack even looked up from his computer game for long enough to say hello, and when Chris offered her a coffee she said yes.

'Look at this, mess all over the kitchen table!' She swept some leaflets into a pile. Lauren looked around. It was very flash. Lots of granite surfaces and a huge square shiny sink. Chris was beaming. Lauren couldn't help smiling too. Is this what it was like being an adult? Getting excited over a kitchen?

'Yes, it's lovely,' Lauren said.

Chris flicked on the kettle. 'Help yourself to biscuits, I've got those brazil nut ones you like. Well, I like them too. Chloe never eats them any more, so you'll do me a favour if you get rid of some.'

'Thanks.' Lauren reached for the biscuit tin. Although the kitchen had been made over the tin was in the same cupboard as it always was. She took two and sat back down at the golden yellow table.

Then the phone rang in the hall and Chris went to answer it. Lauren ate tiny nibbles off her biscuits, trying to save them until the coffee came. But they were her favourites—the really thick ones with liberal sprinklings of broken nuts, so it was very difficult to stop. She looked around. On the big American-style fridge she recognized letters from Our Lady's and several well-done school certificates for Jack. There was a magazine on the table under the leaflets. Lauren pulled it out. *Hello!* Nessa never bought magazines like this and Lauren had a soft spot for them. Then one of the leaflets caught her eye. Lauren had assumed it would be about dog fouling or bridleways or something like that. Chloe's mum was always very involved. Lauren pushed *Hello!* back and re-read the words.

WORRIED ABOUT THE ASYLUM RECEPTION CENTRE PROPOSED FOR HISTORIC STIVENHAM? WE WILL NOT BE A DUMPING GROUND FOR TERRORISTS AND UNDESIRABLES! STIVENHAM COULD NOT COPE WITH EXTRA PRESSURE ON OUR SCHOOLS, OUR DOCTORS. WE DO NOT WANT THESE ECO-NOMIC MIGRANTS HERE!

Lauren scanned the rest quickly; the poster promised asylum seekers would bring crime, tuberculosis, and Aids. There was a petition and signatures. Lauren recognized the names: Mrs Mullan who lived next door, Terry and Barbara who ran the little café, Mrs Pridmore who ran a bed-and-breakfast. Loads of people.

Chris came in from the other room with the phone under her chin; she was talking loudly.

'Yes, and it looks like the whole village is going to the meeting. It'll be marvellous, real people power. I know, I know! And next to a school! I don't see how they can get away with it. I mean, I know I'm not alone, but plenty of us who moved to Stivenham came precisely to get away from people like that! I know! It'll be just like London, before we know it. People have been phoning all afternoon, it's non-stop. Yes, yes I will. We'll talk before then, yes. Bye.' She put the phone down and beamed at Lauren. 'I see you've found our leaflets. Take one, tell Nessa, won't you. Right, coffee! One sugar, plenty of milk?'

'Yes! Um . . . no! I have to go! Nessa will be thinking I've missed you. Or something.'

'If you're sure? Well, do me a favour, love, and take a handful of these.' She pushed some of the leaflets at Lauren. 'I'm sure Vanessa can take some to the library.'

Lauren left as quickly as she could.

She dumped all the leaflets in the bin outside Historic Stivenham's best known and most famous fish and chip shop. Lauren pushed them well down and covered them with old chip paper, just in case. Then she walked home.

Lauren couldn't stop thinking. She had known Chris, Chloe's mum, all her life. She'd been to Cornwall with them last summer; she'd always been so kind, hadn't she? She knew Chloe hadn't been born in Stivenham; well, of course, neither had she. But what was it her mother had said? *They'd moved here to get away from people like that.* Even Lauren knew what that meant. And did Nessa feel the same? Is that why Nessa had never wanted to go back to London, is that why she hated the place? It's full of people like that. People like me, she thought.

Inside, Katie Hargreaves was playing the Grade Two pieces from her new book. She stumbled over the notes again and again. Lauren went upstairs. Outside the rain had stopped and some boys had got a football out on the green. The mobile library van was parked outside the pub and the awning on the shop cracked in the wind. Lauren lay down on her bed and shut her eyes.

Nessa Then

Nessa had missed physics and Helena knew. When she got home she found Helena incandescent with rage. Nessa sat still and quiet while Helena shouted around her. She picked the skin at the side of her thumb until it bled and the pain was tiny and far away: Nessa thought it didn't really feel like her. She wasn't really listening either. It was a re-run of this morning, only with more gnashing of teeth and anguish and self-pity as to what—in heaven's name—Helena had done to deserve a daughter like this.

Nessa sat still in the kitchen chair and waited until Helena had finished, then she went to her room and lay down. The sound of the city traffic outside sounded thick as summer insects buzzing and she couldn't rest even though she felt incredibly tired and drained. Helena had pinned an exam timetable above her desk and Nessa could see that tomorrow was geography. But nothing seemed to matter.

Some time later she opened her eyes and it was dark, but she was still lying on her bed dressed in her school uniform. She got up without turning the light on. Her head was thumping and she'd had nothing to eat all day but half a slice of chemical whiteness. She pushed open her bedroom door but the rest of the flat was in darkness too. Helena must have gone out. She opened the fridge but shut it again quickly—the light from inside seemed much too bright.

The clock on the oven glowed for 11.00 p.m. Helena must have been seriously cross not to leave a note, Nessa thought. The idea was like a slap in the face. It just wasn't like Helena at all. She always left a student working away downstairs in the studio if she was out at night and she always, always, left a note. Nessa heard the silence all around. The fridge hummed, outside a bus pulled away from a stop. A man was thrown out of the Willow adult cinema down the road and Nessa could hear him swearing as he walked down the road to the station. She couldn't hear any noise from the workroom below, no late night radio, no students talking. Nothing at all. She felt very uncomfortable.

Nessa tried to shake the uneasy thoughts away. She poured herself a glass of water and took it back to her room. She flicked on her bedside lamp and the exam timetable seemed to jump out at her. Tuesday the 14th, it said, geography. Geography wasn't so bad. She'd never had any problems with geography exams because they always gave you a map to look at. If you could read a map you could usually work out the answers. It was all common sense: rivers flow downhill, heat goes up making clouds, rain falls down, rocks dissolve or wear away. Nothing stays the same. She took down her textbook. Maybe she'd surprise Helena by not being scared and by walking into school tomorrow and doing geography. She took a sip of water and opened the book. She shut out the empty building and the quiet dark all around and concentrated on hanging valleys and oxbow lakes instead.

*　　*　　*

The light on her face woke her up. That and the pain in her cheek where she'd fallen asleep on a double page spread of the Santorini Caldera. She'd had a dream about Paula. Paula had been dancing through the Amazon rainforest protesting about damage to the soil caused by international logging conglomerates. Nessa smiled first, imagining telling Paula about it, then stopped when she remembered what had happened at her house yesterday.

The clock at her bedside winked 8.30 a.m. She had half an hour before the exam began. Nessa had never got dressed so quickly in her life, but she remembered the charm bracelet for luck, tucking it up her shirt sleeve so she wouldn't get told off. Then she hurried out of the house and into the street and it wasn't until she reached school that she realized she hadn't looked in on Helena.

The exam wasn't too bad. Actually Nessa was pleased at the amount of questions she thought she might have right. She didn't hang around, though. She didn't want to bump into the headmistress or, marginally worse, Elaine Schaller. Nessa hurried home; although she didn't admit it to herself, she wanted to check on Helena.

Nessa turned the corner and knew immediately the warehouse was empty. It looked like a big empty shell, the daylight-blue neon strip lights Helena had on the first floor were off and sitting on the doorstep thumbing through a brick-sized Filofax was Jevonka. She was wearing one of Helena's war-correspondent-style waistcoats and looking faintly ridiculous in an ordinary street. Nessa relaxed; even though Jevonka looked anxious it was a relief to see her. It meant that things really were normal.

'Vanessa! Where is everyone? I've been here for an

hour. Fabien and Sandra haven't come by and where is Helena? Is she sleeping something off?'

'Jevonka, Helena hasn't drunk alcohol since 1977. Haven't you heard that story? She was on some boat going up the Thames for the queen's Silver Jubilee with some band and one of them was sick on her original bondage trousers and she didn't notice.'

Jevonka looked at Nessa amazed.

'Unbelievable! Helena had original Vivienne Westwood bondages?'

Nessa unlocked the door and they went in.

Nessa didn't say anything but inside it felt still and strange, like the accounts she'd read of sailors coming across the abandoned *Mary Celeste*. There was a half-finished sandwich in the workroom and two half-full mugs of cold coffee. Jevonka was matter-of-fact.

'Fabien is such a slob!' Jevonka said, sitting herself down at her desk and clicking on the answer-machine.

'Hi, Jevonka, people! This is Fab! I'm so-o sorry, I just can't crawl in today, last night was just too much of a nightmare . . .'

Nessa smiled and went upstairs. It was nothing freaky, just Fabien out all night and Helena probably over at some friend or other's moaning about Nessa and sorting out the Hush launch. Yes, that had to be it. They had been arguing over the shape of the bottle and whether the letter Hs of Hush should be silver or pale green. There would be a message upstairs scrawled in pink on a piece of newspaper on the kitchen table, or the answer-machine would be winking fit to explode with messages from her apologizing for sloping off like that.

Nessa relaxed. She had been stupid to get so wound up.

She put her keys down on the kitchen table and flicked on the kettle. There was no note. She walked across to the answer-machine which was on a low table by a large square window; the LCD display flashed 8 on and off. Eight messages. She sat down and clicked the machine on, shook the charm bracelet down onto her wrist and fiddled with the lucky blue eye as she listened.

'Helena, darling, it's Susannah, it's umm, nearly ten o'clock and I can't move on the Italian order. I tried the office and there's not a soul, hope you haven't had some kind of disaster. Anyway, can you call me back as soon as poss? So much to sort out!'

There were three more almost the same and one from the council: *'Ms Helena Harper? This is Colin Nelson, remember? From the Council? You called about the Willow adult cinema? Well, you were right, their licence is due for renewal. Call me back if you want to go ahead with a formal complaint, my extension is 667.'* Nessa smiled. Good for you, Mum, she thought.

The next message stopped her in her tracks. It was unmistakable. Paula's voice sounded far away. Nessa froze. Paula, voice fuzzy on the answer-machine tape, coughed.

'This is Paula, Paula Bogle. It's a message for Vanessa.' In the background of the tape a lorry rattled past. It sounded as if she was in a phone booth rather than at home in Fredericks Mews.

'Nessa? Look, it's me. I'm sorry. I am really, really, sorry.' She sounded close to tears; somewhere close by a pelican crossing bleeped into life. *'I was out of order. Totally. I'm sorry for being such a bitch, I reckon it must have been jet lag. No, that's a lie, it wasn't jet lag at all. I'll explain, honest. Can I come round maybe? Or talk? Maybe we could meet up. Not at Fredericks Mews, something's happened. I'll tell you when I see*

105

you. I'll phone again. OK, Ness? I'm sorry, all right. Honest. You didn't deserve that. Thing is, I'm really not a nice person and you so don't deserve me. Sorry.' Paula's message stopped and Nessa replayed it again, making herself tea as she listened. And then the doorbell sounded downstairs. Nessa ran down the stairs; she knew it was Paula before she opened the door.

Outside, a group of men coming out of the Willow cinema were shouting at Paula. She was wearing a tiny denim skirt and her legs were bare and brown and long. Her arms were crossed around her and she wore huge brown sunglasses. She was carrying an overstuffed tatty sports holdall. It wasn't until the girls stopped hugging and Nessa saw Paula's face that she realized there was something wrong.

Paula reached up and took off her sunglasses. She had two technicolour black eyes that shaded from red to purple then to yellow and brown. 'Paula! My God! What happened?' Nessa had never seen any black eyes close up.

'Have you got some twenties or tens? I haven't got any change,' Paula started, but the crack in her voice made her gasp for breath and Nessa thought she was going to cry. 'For the meter.' She gestured down the road where Nessa saw Ed McKay's shiny blue convertible parked half up on the pavement outside the Willow cinema.

Lauren Now

Lauren didn't say anything to Nessa about the leaflets. She told herself she didn't want any kind of row, but she was more than a little scared. What if Nessa agreed with it all? Nessa always said that they lived in Stivenham because it was safe. That she'd hated London. Maybe Nessa had signed up to the petition as well.

Downstairs Katie Hargreaves banged out of the house and Lauren snapped herself awake as she heard Nessa calling up the stairs. 'Lauren! It's happened.' Nessa sounded resigned. It must be Rain, Lauren thought, and tried not to get too excited.

Nessa was in the kitchen putting some water on for pasta. 'There was a call while I was teaching. They're not letting any grass grow.'

Lauren pressed play.

'Hi, Lauren! This is Minty at Rain, we've got a couple of go-sees for you. We can fit them in next weekend if that's any good with you. Our flat's sort of empty so it's a good one for us. Call me back when you can. Bye.'

Lauren forgot about asylum seekers and petitions. She went upstairs to the bedroom phone and called back immediately, even though Nessa said it was better to make them wait.

'I can't, Ness, I'll never eat anything until I know.'

So she did. Minty was breathless, gushy, could Lauren come down next weekend? Could she and Nessa come on Friday, there was a lot to do, if that was all right. The flat was empty. Oh, there was another girl but she was going on Saturday morning.

Lauren was already agreeing when she remembered she'd have to check with Nessa.

'We can't have you on your own, I'm afraid. You're fifteen, you see, you need a chaperone,' Minty breathed. Lauren promised to call back.

Downstairs Nessa was dishing up something that approximated to spaghetti carbonara.

'Go on then, what did they want?'

Lauren looked Nessa directly in the eye. 'They want us to stay in their flat this weekend. They want me on Friday for hairdressers, then two appointments on Saturday. I'd miss school on Friday afternoon but it's only PSE and I already know what to do if someone offers me drugs or makes me join a religious cult against my will. Please?'

'Oh, really? And what did you say?'

'I said I had to check with you.'

Nessa smiled. 'Thanks, Lauren, I appreciate it. How does it feel, then, all this? You're not too excited, are you; you do know they could make a pig's ear of your hair and make you wear all sorts?'

'I know, Ness, fur bikinis in February. No, not really. She never said that, it's just go-sees. Can we go? Please? I promise not to get swollen headed. Promise, promise, promise. We'll have a flat, and maybe there's something on at the Wigmore Hall you could take Ian to. It's two bedroomed. He could stay over Saturday night. If you like.'

'Lauren, I'm sure Rain's flat isn't some upmarket knocking shop for past-it ladies from the shires.' She smiled as she grated Parmesan over the steaming pasta. 'But then again, you never know.'

At school the next day Lauren sat herself next to Chloe at lunchtime. Force of habit, she told herself, but really she just wanted to tell her everything. Lauren slid her school dinner tray down and swung her legs under the table. Chloe looked pleased to see her.

'Hi, Chloe. How's stuff?'

'OK, and you? I heard Mum roped you into the full kitchen tour experience.'

'Just a bit, yeah.'

'She wants the bathroom done now, keeps sidling up to Dad with paint charts. The only good thing about this campaign she's worked herself up into is that the bathroom business is on the back burner.'

'I saw the leaflets.' Lauren kept her voice cool. How did Chloe feel?

'You know, she wanted *me* to go with her last weekend up to the shops in town and stand around collecting signatures.'

'Did you go?'

'No way! I told her there's no way I'm making a fool of myself, standing in the middle of town with a clipboard!'

'So you're not with her on this one?'

Chloe shrugged. 'I don't care really. I mean, this place they want to build is over by Garswick. I don't see how it'll affect us. I should think it'd be worse for them, the refugees. I mean, imagine you trek halfway across the world and hang on to the bottom of a train, or nearly suffocate in some lorry, then the police get you and you fetch up in those old army camp huts with the wind coming at you straight from Siberia! I'd be gutted. Can you imagine anyone escaping to Stivenham? I mean, if I had any choice I'd be out of here on the double.'

Lauren agreed and relaxed. Chloe was still Chloe.

'Hi, Chlo, Lauren. Where are you going then?' Lucy Marsham sat down next to Lauren. On her tray was a bottle of water, a Diet Coke, and two packets of low-fat crisps.

'Oh, nowhere as usual,' Chloe said. 'I was just saying if I wanted to run away I wouldn't run here, that's all.'

'Me neither. Los Angeles, London, maybe. When I leave school Dad says he'll help me with a deposit on my own place. I said I'd rather travel—America, or work over the summer in Spain, you know.'

Lauren stood up. Lucy was starting on *What I'll do with my life*. It involved plenty of plastic surgery, hair extensions, a boyfriend with a convertible, and a lot of clubbing. Lauren couldn't resist saying something.

'I'm off to London. At the weekend. Rain are putting me and Nessa up in their flat.'

Lucy did her best but Lauren could see her eyes widening.

'You mean Rain signed you up. You!' Lucy looked as if she had a crisp stuck in her throat.

Lauren felt bad for a fraction of an instant. Nessa had told her on no account was she to act brat-like or show off, but she couldn't help it, the look on Lucy's face made

110

it so worthwhile. She nodded as meekly as she could but it was an effort. She wanted to go on about the hairdressers and the appointments lined up for Saturday. Maybe find out if Lucy had heard of the designer she was seeing.

'Really?' Lucy slurped up her Coke, trying desperately to feign cool. Lauren had to bite her lip. It really wasn't fair at all that she should go on about it; after all if she talked it up now then there was more chance of everything going wrong. But it felt so good.

'I'll see you in English.'

'Yeah, see you, Lauren.'

Lauren felt better for two reasons that afternoon. Just knowing Chloe was not her mother's daughter was a big relief, and the look on Lucy's face had been priceless. All through RE she let herself dream about returning to school on Monday morning as some kind of shiny new demigoddess. Heads turning as she passed, the boys from St Bonaventure's looking twice because she was gorgeous, not because she'd fallen over, and not shouting freak or giraffe-head like they usually did.

But even if she came out of the hairdresser's, or the stylist's, or whatever as an impossibly sophisticated sexy young woman (as opposed to skinny schoolgirl) Thierry really was a lost cause. It was harder to see herself walking through Stivenham turning heads with him these days. She closed her eyes and he was in the bed with Clare. And she didn't want to think about that at all.

Lauren wanted to e-mail Luke too: *I'll be in London, on Saturday*, something short, easy and simple. Not demanding, no subtext. He was a mate and she liked his family; apart from the heartache of seeing Thierry and Clare, she liked

Clive and Judy and Luke. He talked. Lauren didn't know many boys who chatted and looked you in the eye at the same time. She booked a computer at school but then almost chickened out at the last minute. She let her finger pause over the mouse, and then before she could think herself out of it she clicked on send. Gone.

Done.

Nessa picked her up at school on Friday after lunch and they got to London just as the city was emptying for the weekend. Nessa moaned about the traffic, the congestion charge, and the dirt.

'It's in Hoxton, Minty said.'

'I know what she said,' Nessa snapped back. 'Hoxton's a nightmare. I got lost there once with your mother. Never again. I thought they'd have a flat in Chelsea or somewhere smart.'

'I'm sure it'll be fine, Ness.' Lauren was feeling worried. She had checked the school computer last thing and she hadn't heard back from Luke. And Nessa was in a foul mood.

They pulled into a tiny cobbled side-street. 'Absolutely nowhere to park! My God, this town is hell on a stick.'

In the back of her mind Lauren had been half hoping for a top floor modern warehouse with wooden floors like on the telly. Acres of space and a huge American fridge. At street level a café spilled tables onto the street. Nessa, still bad-tempered, rang the bell.

Minty let them in, kissing them both twice. Lauren almost laughed when she tried to kiss Nessa. Nessa never kissed.

'Come up, *so* good to see you.'

There was a girl in the flat already. 'This is Eda. Her English isn't very good, is it, darling.' Minty said it loudly as if the girl was completely insensitive and deaf.

She sat at the kitchen bar and her hair was the hair that Lucy and Chloe would have killed for: long, straight, and shiny and fluid as Lucozade. She was like the perfect idea of a sixteen year old, how everyone she knew aspired to look, all legs and bony hips and tiny breasts like orange halves that sat high on her chest and pointed skywards. She looked so perfect Lauren thought she might be American. When she smiled her mouth was big and generous and Lauren thought she'd never seen eyes so green. Except the time Lucy had worn those contact lenses.

Minty went on, 'Eda's just staying over tonight, and she'll be at the first go-see you've got tomorrow, OK? Fine. Good.' Eda put out her hand graciously and Nessa shook it. 'Eda's from Kosovo, aren't you, Eda? Now I'll just leave you a minute to settle down and then,' she looked at her watch, 'I'll be back with a cab for the hairdresser's. Great.'

It wasn't until Minty left that Eda spoke.

'Your English isn't that bad.' Nessa was encouraging.

'I know, I am sorry. It is Minty, she babies me. I speak not perfect English, but enough. I am not Kosovan, I'm Albanian. My family escaped from Kosovo, I live in Welwyn Garden City.'

Nessa Then

Nessa patted her skirt pocket and handed over a couple of twenty pence pieces. She stood in the doorway as Paula fed the meter. What was Paula doing with Ed's car? Was Ed around? He wouldn't let Paula drive his car, would he? Paula was still only fifteen. Nessa looked up and down the street. From behind her she heard the phone ring in the workroom. Jevonka sounded harassed.

Paula walked back. She looked hunted, scared. Nessa could hear Jevonka behind her taking the call.

'Hello? Yes? No, this is the office. Vanessa? She was upstairs a minute ago. You want to speak to her, yes? Well, I'll give her a shout, who is it, please? Mr McKay. OK.'

Nessa fiddled with the charm bracelet. Ed McKay wanted her. She didn't know that Ed McKay knew her name. Her heart had speeded up and she stepped out of the house into the street. Jevonka was calling her, shouting her name into the house.

'Paula, Paula.' Nessa realized she was whispering. She took Paula by the elbow and steered her back towards the car.

'We have to go, he knows you're here.'

'What?' Paula met her gaze.

'Ed.'

Paula blanched and both of them ran to the car. Nessa

got into the passenger seat; the car smelt expensive, of leather and polish. Paula fumbled with the keys and crunched the gears as she reversed.

'Can you drive?' Nessa remembered Paula was younger than her.

'Sort of.' Paula pushed her sunglasses up her nose and steered the car into the street. 'I made it here, didn't I?'

Nessa gripped the side of her seat as Paula steered the car through the narrow side streets and onto the main road. The top was down and the wind blew the words out of Nessa's mouth.

'This is Ed's car! What's happened? Did he do that to your face?'

Paula stepped suddenly on the brake as a pelican crossing shrieked into life.

'Ness, I need your help. I don't know what I'm doing. You don't know what's happened.' Paula's knuckles were white as teeth clamped on the steering wheel. A car behind hooted and Paula made the car jump forward then stall. 'I don't know where I'm going. Where can I go, Ness?'

Nessa could hear the catch in her voice. The cars behind were hooting louder. One man was shouting. Paula turned the key and the engine turned over, once, twice then revved into life.

'He's gonna kill me, Ness, I know it.'

Nessa put her hand on Paula's shoulder. The car lurched forward into the traffic. Nessa was quiet. What could she say? Ed had killed people. She'd read the book; that Pete Farrer was a definite, and there were others. She looked at Paula, her face wet with tears and screwed up with the effort of driving.

'Is there anywhere you could go? Anywhere you want to go?' Nessa asked.

'Far away. Anywhere.'

Nessa thought of her grandmother's house in Stivenham, empty since the winter when she had died. Helena hated it there and Nessa knew she hadn't bothered to clean the place out.

'OK, I know somewhere, he'll never find us.' Ness looked at the street sign. They were coming up to a roundabout, *Ring Road, A10, The East*, it said.

'Take the next left. We'll be all right, Paula, I promise.'

Nessa thought she might regret that promise. She patted her blazer pockets; she had two pounds fifty and a bus pass, no change of clothes. She had the charm bracelet, though. She thought she could sell that if she really had to.

Paula slowed for some traffic lights. A council pick-up pulled up alongside. The man in the passenger seat grinned at Paula. 'Nice car, nice legs! Give us a ride, love!'

Paula spat at him and sped away. 'Bastards.'

They were almost at the edge of London. Allotments and low-rise warehousing and furniture superstores gave way to the endless trees of Epping Forest.

Nessa tried to imagine what Paula had done. Maybe there had been someone else. That was it. What if he'd found out about the man who had visited Fredericks Mews? In the autobiography Nessa remembered him saying that he was a jealous guy. That he'd punched the lights out of someone or other who'd looked too long at Mrs Ed.

Nessa looked at Paula. The old guy? The one even older than Ed. She didn't believe it. She was on the verge of asking. Worked herself up to phrase the question just right when Paula swore.

'What is it?'

'Police.'

For a split second Nessa froze. The policeman would look at Paula and they'd be carted off to be arrested or whatever. She turned to Paula. You couldn't see any sign of her black eyes. Her cheeks were dry and she still had a smudge of lipstick. Nessa thought about the way those men in the pick-up truck had looked at Paula. Nessa thought she felt seasick, as if she could feel the world turning underneath her. Paula pulled over and turned the engine off.

'Listen.' Nessa felt her thoughts and her heart racing. She had to hold herself together. If Paula opened her mouth or took off the sunglasses they were in shit. She turned to Paula. Behind them the police car had stopped and a tall young policeman was striding towards them.

'Paula!' Nessa whispered. 'Listen, just smile, I'll think of something. Look sexy, say nothing.'

'Story of my life,' Paula muttered.

The policeman bent down to the car and Nessa closed up her face and buried all her fear. She smoothed her school skirt and breathed in. She turned in her seat and smiled at the policeman. Holding herself still. She wished she'd paid more attention in drama lessons. Posh, sound posh, she told herself, not too posh, just firm. Just like Helena in meetings.

'Officer?'

'Ladies!'

'I'm afraid Annazorah doesn't speak English. She's my au pair, you see, from Colombia.'

Paula bit her lip to hold in a smile and crossed her legs. Her skirt slid up a centimetre. Her face was cool and blank.

'You do know,' the policeman leant against the car, 'you took the last left without indicating?'

Nessa changed her tone. 'Annazorah! How many times has Daddy told you! I'm Vanessa, Vanessa Forest. We live in Epping, near the Country Club, I'll give you the address.'

The policeman didn't take his eyes off Paula's legs. Nessa wittered on in her best public school voice about her orthodontist appointment in Theydon Bois. She could hardly believe it when the policeman waved them on. Paula held her face frozen until the police car had turned off and burst out laughing.

'Annazorah! Where did that come from? Bloody hell, Ness! Even I believed you. Jesus, you're good!' Paula looked at Nessa and beamed. Nessa felt her head swimming; with every bend of the road her stomach lurched. The dark trees of the forest cut the sunshine into knives. 'You're white as a sheet, Ness. Are you OK?'

'I think I'm going to be sick.' Nessa could feel her forehead slick with sweat.

Paula pulled over and Nessa opened the door and bent out of the car and vomited. It seemed as if she was vomiting forever; the waves of sick, no sound but the birds and the cars passing, and the retching. Paula was rubbing her back and when she sat up she felt clean, she felt better.

'Sorry, Paul.' Nessa tilted her head back. 'Oh my God, I needed that.'

'You need a hanky, you've got sick on your chin.'

'I could do with a drink as well. There isn't any water?' Nessa opened the glove compartment and rooted around,

119

it went down deep, and right at the bottom there was what looked like an Argyll sock stuffed with something hard. Nessa felt the bile rising up again as her hand closed around it. She could feel its shape through the fabric. It was a gun.

'Paula, what the hell have you done?'

Lauren Now

L auren had forgotten she hated hairdressers. The last time had been with Chloe. They'd paid for cut-price sessions so students could practise on them. It had taken all day and when the girl had finished with her Lauren thought she looked like the pictures of Nessa's mother, hair stiff with products and highly flammable. The minute she walked into the salon the smell brought it all back.

But it was better this time. Not much, though. Lauren still hated the feeling of sitting with her head bent back over a sink, even though the towels were infinitely fluffier than those at Hair Supreme in Stivenham. She shut her eyes, listening to the assistant's fingers squeak through her hair. She worried about the horribly ripe spot that had come up on her hairline which she'd been covering up all week. She tried to think of something else.

'Well, we won't colour it, exactly, just give you a rinse, deepen the tones, what do you think?' Lauren didn't know what she thought so she said nothing. 'But Rain said you're keen for a crop?' The hairdresser lifted Lauren's hair off her face. 'Yes?' Lauren knew she should have said no but her mouth seemed to have stopped working.

It was dark outside when they had finished.

'There!' the hairdresser said behind her. 'Sultana of Chic, though I say it myself!'

Lauren looked. The hair around her on the floor had been swept up. The hair that was left on her head was very short. Like a cap. She put her hand up to feel it. The back of her neck felt like brand new skin. The spot seemed to have receded. Her eyes looked huge. She smiled. The Lauren in the mirror smiled back.

The taxi was late. Lauren waited in the salon doorway to escape the hair smells. She caught herself checking herself in the big glass window of the shop next door. Her neck looked impossibly long and almost elegant. She caught a boy across the street doing a double take and smiling. She stretched as if she wasn't being watched, making herself longer and leaner; he was still looking. Then the taxi drew up and Lauren stepped inside; the boy was still looking as it pulled away.

She stopped smiling when she got back to the flat. Eda and Nessa were watching *EastEnders*, eating a takeaway pizza.

Nessa dropped her food. 'Lauren, you've had a number 2!' And although she followed this immediately with, 'You look great, fabulous!' in those few seconds Lauren realized what the reaction in Stivenham would be and ran into her room and shut the door. There was no escape there. One wall had a huge dressing table mirror that seemed to be angled straight at her.

She looked like a freak show. Fine for walking round London or for someone on the telly but Chloe would look at her and say nothing. Lucy would laugh and the boys at the bus stop would shout foulness rather than be struck dumb by her heart-stopping good looks. The haircut exaggerated everything she had spent the past four years trying to disguise. Her angular face, her big features—the girl in the mirror had a mouth like two Cumberland sausages taking a nap, and a nose like a vegetable. A very large vegetable. The darkness of her hair made the pallor of her skin more near-death than anything else and her freckles were like liver spots.

Thierry and Clare laughing in bed popped up into her head. She had to stop herself crying. She could imagine Nessa coming in saying, *Told you so*, so she sniffed back the tears. But when she went into the living room Nessa had gone out.

'She said to say she was getting you another pizza, and she will not be very long.' Eda sat on the sofa eating ice cream straight out of the tub. 'Don't worry, Lauren. You do look fabulous.'

Lauren said nothing. She sat still, passing her hand over her hair, feeling the shortness.

Eda sucked her spoon. 'You know you have to be brave with hair like that or it doesn't work.'

'I don't know if I am.'

'Pretend, then. And after a while it's just what you do. That's what I do; you will too, that's our job. For instance, today they looked at me for a catalogue, good money if I get it! But you know how they see me, All-American Girl! All Albanian, I think. Hah! It's a joke!'

'But what do they think I am? Sexless thing with no hair? Camp survivor?'

'Don't joke about it! Your hair is far too shiny for that! Have some ice cream. It'll give you an appetite for pizza.'

Lauren sat down next to Eda. 'How long have you been doing this?'

'Three years, since I was fourteen.'

'Do you like it?'

Eda shrugged. 'There's much harder ways to earn money. I'm saving up. I'm buying my family their own house soon, and it's not so bad. I started doing those magazines when I was young, you know, *Heaven* and *Girl*, and now it's a little bit of advertising, mostly editorial.' Eda shrugged. 'I look the way they pay me to look.'

'Yeah, but you look like a model looks. Well, you know, people don't laugh at you, do they?'

'Where do they laugh at you? That is just so stupid! No, listen, you are not thinking. Look at yourself, and look at me. See? They've got something in mind for you, someone or something. You look different. That's what you have. You know what I do most? I do catalogues and catalogues and catalogues. It's not my life. I smile and take the money. It is just pretend. They don't want me, they want what they make me. With you, it's you they want.' Eda pointed her spoon at Lauren. 'You will see.'

Nessa came back with another Margherita with extra onions: 'Like you like it.'

'I saw it in your eyes, Ness, I saw you hate the hair. And how can I walk down to the shops like this? I'll get put away!'

'I'm sorry, Lauren. You look so different. Good different. Really. I wish we were back at home; there's a picture I want to show you, of your mum, hair all scraped back. Or wet or something. You're the spit.'

'Yeah, yeah. She never looked like this, she had hair. And her nose never looked like a vegetable. I'll get myself a hat tomorrow. Maybe two hats.'

'Lauren, you can still walk away, you know.'

Lauren pretended she was absorbed in the telly. She couldn't go back to school on Monday saying she'd wimped out over a hairdo. She folded her arms.

'I told her, Vanessa,' Eda said. 'I said she has to be brave, not care what people think.'

Lauren ate the crust off her pizza. Brave. Easier said than done.

Nessa Then

'I never knew it was in there, honest!' Paula looked almost as shocked as Nessa. They'd driven onto a side turning, a small road that went into the heart of the forest. Paula had pulled over onto the verge. Nessa had shut the gun away quickly in the glove compartment.

'I have to go home.' Nessa opened the door and stepped out. 'I can't do this any more.' She began walking into the trees.

'Ness, wait!' Paula loped after her and caught her arm. 'Wait! Where are you going, we're in the middle of nowhere!'

Nessa stopped. She looked up at Paula who looked just as lost and confused as she felt. There were trees all around them and it was quiet. Nessa wanted to stop and cry and rewind to yesterday or the day before.

'You've got to help me, Nessa, I haven't got anyone else.' Nessa thought Paula must have read her mind.

'What are you doing with a bloody gun? Paula, are you mad?'

'It's not mine.'

'I never said it was!'

'I never knew it was there! I never looked in the car, I just took it! I just got in it and went, OK? The man was gonna kill me, he'd just smashed my face up and my body.

Look.' Paula lifted her shirt up. Nessa had to look away, she'd never seen anything like it, Paula's brown body was multi-coloured, red and blue. Nessa thought she would cry. She put her hand to her mouth. Paula went on.

'I had to get away, Ness. I had to. I just took the keys! He never said he had a gun, all right? OK?'

Nessa whispered, 'Sorry, Paula.'

They were quiet. There was birdsong and the slight riffling of wind through the treetops.

After a long second Paula spoke. 'There is something, though.'

'What? Don't tell me. Ed McKay with his head smashed in curled up in the boot.'

Paula said nothing.

Nessa walked back to the car. She took the key from the ignition and opened the boot. It was empty.

'Not there.' Paula had followed her. She picked up the holdall that was on the back seat and unzipped it. It was full of bundles of brown notes. 'I don't know how much. I know it's his, but believe me, Ness, he owes me so much.' Paula sounded hard and bitter. 'What are we going to do?'

Nessa said nothing for a long time. She had never seen so much money in her life. She picked out a bundle expecting it to be mostly newspaper like on TV. But it was money. All the way through.

'What did he do, Paula? Tell me now. Tell me everything.'

Paula sighed and leant against the car. 'He wanted to stop me working. Well, working for anyone but him.'

'I didn't think you worked for him. I thought you were, like, a sort of girlfriend?'

Paula smiled sarcastically. 'Joke. I did hospitality.'

'What?'

'I looked after his clients, men he did business with, when they were in town. Only the extra special clients.' She shivered. 'Horrible old men who liked nice young girls. Well, less of the nice, really.'

Nessa's jaw opened as the penny dropped. It made sense.

'Paula, it's horrible. Why didn't you just stop?'

'Yeah, and end up like this? He used to make sure I knew what was coming. And most of the time it weren't him who dished it up. This was special. And yeah, what if I'd put my hand up, 'scuse me, Ed, I've had enough. What would have happened? He'd have kicked me out. Lose my nice house and my clothes and my life? I'd never had that stuff without Ed. I'm not lucky, like you.' Nessa felt as if the wind had been knocked out of her.

Paula sat down carefully. 'It wasn't every day, you know. And it's not like I'd never done tricks before. I used to tom with my mate Lisa when I lived out in Swanley. Sometimes. Not all the time. But I'd done it for money before. If we needed fags, or to get in a club. I did it for this jacket once, a leather one. Funny thing, once I got it, the jacket, I never wore it. I gave it to Lisa.' Paula smiled. Nessa didn't know what to say.

'It wasn't the worst thing, sex. There's worse, believe me. But you saw, I'd got a chance to do legit stuff, to do modelling. They wanted me for proper jobs, they said I had potential; your mum wanted me to be the face of Hush! He went mad. Said I was too busy, said he never knew when he needed me.'

'You could have said something!'

'You've got no idea, have you? That's why I let rip the

other day. I just saw it. The way you have everything and you don't know, you don't care. Jeesus, if I had a mum like that.' Paula shook her head. Nessa almost spoke but Paula stopped her. 'I'm sorry. I know, I know, I tried. In the end I got your mum to talk to him.'

'Helena?'

'Yeah, she's been great.'

'She knew?'

'Only when I told her, only since yesterday, no, the day before. She said she'd sort it. "Leave it to me," she goes then next thing I know Ed comes round to Fredericks Mews and threatens to break my legs if I leave. This was him.' She pointed to the black eyes. 'I couldn't stay, Nessa, you can see that.'

Nessa nodded. 'I didn't know. You could have talked to me, you know, you could have said something. We're friends.'

'Yeah right, Ness. Hi, Ness! It's me, Paula, I'm a tart who sucks off old men for a couple of frocks and a warm house, d'you want to come over and watch *My Fair Lady*? You'd have had me down as some coke-headed slapper.'

'No I wouldn't! I would have helped! I know you!' Nessa felt hurt.

'Yeah, well you didn't always know me. You wouldn't have liked me either. That was what it was about the other day, when I bad-mouthed you. You've got everything. You've never had to do nothing you don't want to, except exams. People care about you. Not what you look like or what you're wearing. Not how much money you can make for them. I was jealous. I felt like shit next to you. A piece of dirt. I'd never had a friend like you. So straight! I loved

130

that, Ness. Honest. I thought you'd drop me. So I dropped you first. There. Now you know me. That's what I'm like. A nasty piece of work. Everything you ever heard about me was true. You ask any of the house mothers, any of my teachers. Anybody.' Paula's voice was cracking. Her knuckles on the steering wheel looked skinless.

Nessa reached over and put her hand on top of Paula's. She coughed before she spoke. She wasn't going to cry.

'Don't be stupid, Paula. I know you. I know you're not that. I don't think like that.'

'So help me *now*. Ed won't let this go, he's not like that. Well, maybe he'd have let it go but I took his car. And I never knew there was so much money. I just wanted a bit. I reckon he owed me some of that.'

Nessa composed herself. She had to think and be sensible. She could do that. At least the money would make it easier.

'We lose the car.' Nessa leant over and reached into the glove compartment. 'And we take this.'

'I thought it made you sick.'

'It does. But you never know. Do you really think he'll come after you? Stupid, of course he will.' Nessa remembered the book. Ed had prided himself that no one ever got away with putting one over on him. The Franks gang in Stoke Newington lost two of their members three years after the war between them and McKay's men was supposed to be over.

She put the gun in her inside blazer pocket. Even though it was quite small it felt heavy and cold, even through the sock. It made a lump against her chest.

'Do you think the cash is real?' she asked Paula.

Paula shrugged. 'Looks good enough to me.'

'Right. We get a lift to somewhere with a station, get ourselves some new clothes, and we go to Stivenham.'

'Where's that?'

'Suffolk, by the sea. It's where my grandmother lived. We've still got the house. It's only a small town, not more than a village. There's a key with the neighbours. He'll not find us there.'

'I just hope you're right, Nessa.'

Lauren Now

Lauren woke up and she was sure her head felt less heavy than normal. Less hair, she told herself. She could feel a spot coming on her chin, one of the big red unhideable ones. Why was she doing this? Didn't Nessa say it skewed your head? The most important thing in the world was not the length of her hair or the size of a spot. She picked up her mobile from the bedside table. No one had texted her. In the other room she could hear someone already up: Nessa, she thought, but it was Eda eating yoghurt and watching Saturday morning TV.

'You're coming to the go-see at Julien's?' Eda said through a mouthful of yoghurt. 'Minty says the taxi will be here in an hour.'

Lauren put on her green jumper and jeans. Nessa sat in the taxi doing the crossword with Eda who had been to around a hundred of these things and acted as if she didn't care.

'You mustn't worry, Lauren. These people talk like you're not there but that's what they do. I don't listen. I have shutters in my ears. I think of the car I'm getting next month and whether to have it black or silver.'

'Black,' Nessa said and Eda nodded.

They were dropped off outside a shop in the West End. It was in a parade of shops that sold carpets and giant

133

oriental pots. Nessa smiled at the jacket on display approvingly. 'Julien Isaacs. Not bad.' Lauren thought it just looked like a jacket. Although she knew she'd read the name somewhere before she couldn't put her finger on it. Nessa as usual knew a lot more than she ever let on. Lauren riffled her hand through her hair and rubbed her ears, which now felt the cold.

It wasn't anything like the time at Jamie Holdsworth's. They went through the shop and up a spiral staircase to a white-painted workspace. It was newly painted but old, the floors sloped to join the window. A workbench ran along one wall, with telephones and cloth samples. There was a rail of clothes. Lauren couldn't see any bikinis, which had to be a good sign. She didn't fancy dazzling any potential employers with the glaring whiteness of her skin.

No one spoke to her apart from Minty and Eda. Nessa sat in a corner with a huge paper cup of coffee and her headphones. In the middle of the room, Lauren stood around with Eda and a couple more freaks of nature, stringbean girls, like pictures of girls, ready to be given the once over and hired or fired. Lauren remembered Nessa saying that there were places in London where young men stood around on street corners waiting for other men in vans to take them off to building sites for work.

'What do we do now?' Lauren whispered to Eda.

'I think I go back to Welwyn Garden City. Look at the others. I am like a munchkin compared to the girls here. I think this call is for people like you. I will talk to Minty and get the train home.'

Eda kissed her twice on the cheek before she left. Lauren

was sad to see her go, the other girls all seemed older, cooler, and moved like cats. Two of them carried folders, portfolios . . . no, books, they called them, Lauren thought. She didn't even have one of those yet. She sat down on a plastic chair next to Nessa. She imagined being at school and trying to put some kind of positive spin on this for Chloe. Nessa had finished the crossword and was deep into a fat Sarah Waters novel. Lauren wished she had a book. A reading book. She had started *To Kill a Mockingbird* and remembered it was at home by her bed.

'There she is!' Minty was arm in arm with a short dark-skinned black man dressed in an over-large check suit and hard black-framed glasses. They stood in front of Lauren and Lauren felt Nessa elbow her in the side. She jumped up. She regretted it instantly. The man seemed even smaller standing up, like a perfectly turned out gnome.

But the man seemed immune to Minty's enthusiasm. He looked Lauren over carefully. Lauren tried to flick the switch inside her head so that she wasn't there but it was hard. She concentrated on the windows high up in the walls instead.

'What's your name, babe?' His voice was a soft-but-hard London voice, it made her relax. She looked down at him.

'Lauren, Lauren Bogle.'

'Lovely, babe, lovely. Listen,' He talked quietly and she found herself bending down slightly. 'I've brought a suit over, it's down in the shop, would you be a darling and put it on?'

Lauren nodded and moved a hand up to tuck her hair behind her ear before she remembered she didn't have that much hair any more. Lauren looked to Minty who nodded and she went back down the spiral staircase into the white-and-beige painted shop.

There was a girl in similar check trousers sorting through paperwork at a desk. She looked up and smiled at Lauren, looking her up and down too. 'You've come for this?' and handed Lauren a suit. It wasn't checked, it was a very dark, intense navy blue, and the fabric was so subtle and beautiful it felt like soft water against her skin.

Lauren put on the suit. She'd never worn anything like it in her life. It was long enough in all the right places. She looked at herself in the changing room mirror. She stood as tall as she could. The trousers sat on her hips snugly, the jacket closed at her waist. Even with her grey T-shirt underneath suddenly the haircut made sense. She walked upstairs—all the other girls had gone. Nessa looked up from Sarah Waters and held her breath. The small man looked critically at her.

'Would you take the shirt off, babe?'

'Sorry?'

There was nowhere up here to change. Suddenly Lauren had this vision of herself standing naked in front of all these people. The man must have seen it too because he was trying not to laugh. He came close and took her by the arm.

'Don't worry, Lauren, isn't it? Go downstairs, come up again as if nothing has happened. You look fabulous, babe.'

Lauren did as she was told. But she felt a strange mix of emotions. She could see that in the trouser suit she'd changed from being a gawky schoolgirl into something else, but she wasn't sure what. It was a very strange experience watching Minty and Julien Isaacs and the shop girls

136

watching her. Lauren walked the way the suit made her feel like walking and she felt as if the real Lauren had somehow floated out of her head and was hovering under the ceiling trying not to laugh.

They were at the shop until nearly five. Minty had gone into such raptures that Lauren had had to wait, standing up in the suit so as not to crease it, while she phoned a photographer. They took pictures of her shoeless, shirtless but jacketed, sitting, standing. Julien Isaacs told a joke about two skinheads and a politician and Lauren laughed so much and the photographer kept going while Lauren tipped over into a chair with her mouth open.

On the way back to the flat Nessa leaned over in the cab and kissed her as if she was five.

'Well done, Lauren.' She shook her head. 'I'd never have believed you could work a trouser suit like that!'

'What do you mean?'

'Come off it, you looked like a pro! Your mum would have been proud.'

'You think so?' Lauren couldn't help thinking how far Nessa had changed her tune. 'I thought you'd prefer it if I didn't get the job.'

'Maybe. If you'd asked me this morning. But you're a natural, it's like you put on that suit and I was watching someone else. And you got the booking! I mean, do you know who that guy is?'

'Julien Isaacs? He was all right actually.'

'Best young British designer of the twenty-first century. That's what the Sundays said last year.'

'Vanessa Harper, you are such a hypocrite! You make out like fashion is such a big nothing and not interesting and you only ever wear comfy shoes but you know everything!'

Nessa smiled and looked out of the taxi window as London went by.

Even so, Saturday night seemed a kind of anti-climax. Nessa had a date with Ian at the Wigmore Hall.

'Are you sure you don't want to come, Lauren? I know it's not your thing but it's got to be better than sitting around on your own here.' Lauren shrugged and pulled the arms of her jumper down over her knuckles.

'I'll be OK, early night. I am knackered. I've got to have my photo taken again tomorrow, haven't I?'

'Yeah, not till eleven though, love.'

''S OK, I'll just watch the telly.'

Lauren looked out of the window as Nessa left. The street was full of bars and restaurants, young people with haircuts that made her own look no more than average. She waved at Nessa as she got into Ian's car and blew her a kiss. Then she shuffled across to the fridge in her socks and took out a pot of yoghurt. Flicked on the telly and tucked her feet under her. *Casualty* put her off her yoghurt so she flicked through the channels; she had almost given up hope when her phone rang. Nessa had probably forgotten her key. She reached over to her bag and fished around for the phone.

'Nessa?'

'Lauren?'

'Luke!'

'You're in London!'

'Yeah, Hoxton, it's not far from you, is it?'

'No, yeah, I mean, are you doing anything?'

'Now? Eating yoghurt. On my own. How about you?'

'Look, Lauren, do you wanna come to the beach?'

Lauren could see the layer of cloud outside. It was nearly totally dark and she was cold even in socks and her jumper.

'The beach?'

'Come on! Believe me, it's a laugh.'

He called round for her fifteen minutes later. Lauren didn't have time to change but she made sure she left a message for Nessa on her phone. And she pulled on the hat she'd bought at the last minute, just in case.

'What beach are you on about?' Lauren double-locked the door carefully behind her. Luke was smiling. His hair had grown but he looked the same. He wasn't wearing beach wear, either—jeans and a heavy sweatshirt.

'Come on. You'll see.'

Nessa Then

The taxi stopped outside the house in Stivenham. It was dark and the wind coming in off the sea was freezing even in June.

'We should have gone to Rio,' Paula said. 'At least it would have been warm.'

Nessa knocked at the house next door. A light was on downstairs and almost as soon as she'd knocked the hall light came on and the door opened. From inside there was the sound of the telly, a laughter track, normalness. Nessa put a smile on.

'Hello!' She had been expecting Mrs Mullan. Not that Nessa would have been able to describe the woman exactly—old woman, grey hair, she would have said—but she couldn't remember anyone else living there at all. Never a Mr Mullan. Wait, there was a son, but he had been away every time Nessa had stayed with her grandmother; scout camp, grape picking, university, Thailand. When Nessa had stayed with Gran she could only remember glimpsing the back of his head as he left.

The young man in front of her was gorgeous, tanned, with light brown hair that had seen too much sun.

'Yes?'

'Um, the key? For next door? I'm Vanessa, Vanessa Harper.' Nessa was sort of aware that his eyes weren't on her; they were fixed somewhere else. They were fixed on Paula standing just behind her, to the right. His face changed, softened, and she bet that was Paula smiling at him. She turned back to Paula. Yes, she was smiling.

Nessa coughed.

'Oh, Mrs Harper, yes, Mum's got the keys, come in.' He looked at Paula's legs. 'You must be freezing.'

The house was like Gran's flipped back to front. In the hall were a row of cold weather boots and a photo of— what was his name?—Michael Mullan, in a mortarboard.

'Here, I think this is it.' He held the keys up for Paula to check.

'Um, *she* doesn't know.' Nessa felt as if she was some lower form of life, scrabbling about low down on the forest floor while all the interesting stuff went on up in the canopy.

She said her thanks and took the key next door. Paula caught her up. 'Maybe this place ain't so bad, did you see him? He says he's been in Lom Bok or something. Tell you the truth I wasn't listening I was just looking.'

Nessa turned the key and opened the door. It felt airless and still inside. 'We're supposed to be lying low. And you're supposed to be injured.'

'I wouldn't mind lying low with him, what was his name? Mike?'

Nessa found the electricity switch under the stairs and Paula put the kettle on. Nessa drew the curtains and counted the money in piles of a hundred pounds. She'd never seen so much cash in her life. Ten thousand pounds. Less the train fare and the money they'd spent on a pair of jeans and a jumper for Nessa.

'Ten thousand pounds!' Paula wanted to throw it up in the air or burn a roll just because they could.

'We're going to need this, Paula. We might even have to give it back.'

It wasn't until they had both gone to bed, Nessa with the sock-covered gun under her pillow, that she remembered about Helena. She imagined Helena coming home, finding her gone, and going ballistic. She tried to sleep. Paula had gone out like a light. Nessa could hear her breathing. Nessa tried to imagine Paula's life, doing those things. How could she? How could she sleep? And Mum had known all the time. Helena! Nessa remembered her mother probably worried to death, and got up.

She tiptoed downstairs to the phone in the hall. It was dead. Cut off for nearly a year since Gran died, Nessa thought. Outside on the green there was a phone box in front of the shops. Paula took the door key, put on her jumper, and went out into the night.

The night in Stivenham was a thousand times darker than a London night. It was soundless, too, and Nessa had to work hard to stop her mind racing towards the idea of Ed McKay or his henchmen hiding in the porch of the pub with baseball bats and kitchen knives. The dark swirled in front of her eyes and she almost had to shut them again to stop herself seeing things.

Nessa sprinted across to the phone box and dialled quickly, her fingers failing to find the right number the first time. It seemed to take forever to connect. London, home, seemed so far away. The moon came out from behind a cloud for a second and the phone at home started ringing. Yeah, Mum would be pissed off having the phone ring in the middle of the night. Nessa checked her watch: it was two o'clock. But she'd prefer that to a vanishing act. It was still ringing. What if Helena couldn't hear it? What if she'd been out so late the night before she was sleeping with earplugs? It still rang. Nessa felt vulnerable inside the lit-up phone booth. She turned away from the houses. The phone still rang. Then there was a click and Nessa started talking.

'Mum, it's me . . .' and stopped as the answer-machine whirred into life.

'Mum? It's me, Ness. I'm fine. Something came up.' Nessa realized she oughtn't to say where they were in case Ed McKay found out. 'I'll call again, OK? All right? I'll see you soon, Mum.' And she hung up.

She lay in bed for ages trying to get to sleep. Her mind jumped around from Helena not knowing where she was—perhaps she was out looking? Scouring the streets with Jevonka—to Paula having to do things with old men—to Ed McKay coming after his money. Why didn't they give it back? Send it through the post so he couldn't complain. That just left the car—still in the forest—and Paula's escape. How could they stop Ed being mad and coming after them? She wished she had brought that autobiography from home. She couldn't remember half of it now and the more she tried to remember anything the further away the memory slipped.

Dawn came early, not long after half past four. Nessa had already decided they would send the money back. They'd find some other way of living; she had a bank account, fifty quid saved up from Christmas. They could send the money and the gun and then maybe he'd lose interest. This wasn't gang warfare; this was a couple of girls.

Nessa thought she'd talk it through with Paula tomorrow, or rather later today. She closed her eyes and drifted, eventually, into sleep.

When she did wake up it was lunchtime and Paula was cooking bacon and sitting at the Formica kitchen table laughing with Mike Mullan. Mike's tanned skin was only a few shades lighter than Paula's. They both stopped and looked up as Nessa came in. Paula had her sunglasses on over her bruised eyes.

'Hi, Ness, I couldn't find a telly anywhere.' Paula wrinkled her nose. 'A house without a telly. Well weird.'

'I told her I didn't think Mrs Harper had one. You could borrow my mum's though, she's not back from her sister's for a week yet.' Mike Mullan talked through a mouthful of bacon sandwich.

Nessa looked at him. He looked as if he should be somewhere else, on a beach in Australia wading out of the surf, not Stivenham. His eyes were green, like open space or sea. Nessa looked down; he hardly registered she was there. She cleared her throat.

'Paula, we've got things, stuff, to do.' She tried to sound businesslike.

Paula took the frying pan off the stove and tipped the rest of the bacon onto a plate.

'It can wait, Ness, can't it?'

Nessa said nothing. Mike got up. 'I'll go then. Thanks for this.' He took the remains of the sandwich with him and let himself out.

'What d'you have to do that for, Ness? He's all right,'

'Paula! We're supposed to be on the run.'

'And what's he gonna do? He's got no idea! He's only interested in Thailand and getting into my pants.' Paula smiled at the idea and picked up a strip of bacon. 'I reckon you're jealous. Something's getting at you. You are jealous, aren't you?'

'Jealous! You are joking! Do you remember what happened to us yesterday? Have you looked in the mirror this morning? Without the sunglasses? You drove away in Ed McKay's car with ten grand and a gun. And I haven't spoken to Helena and I should be doing English Lit right now. What on earth have I got to be wound up about?'

'Sorry.'

They both sat down. Nessa pulled out the chair Mike had been sitting on. It was still warm.

'I was thinking,' Nessa said.

'Yeah?'

'We ought to give the money back. We ought to write a note, explain about the car, send the money and the gun back, stay here for a month or two, and then perhaps he'd leave you alone.'

Paula didn't laugh. Nessa thought this was a good thing at first. She sat silently picking up the edge of the Formica at the corner of the table until Nessa had to tell her to stop.

'Well, what do you think? If it works we can just go back to normal. You can get some proper modelling and I can, I don't know, do retakes, get a job.'

'Yeah, I see that. I see Ed opening a big brown envelope with his name on and sending us a little thank-you note. Not!'

'Have you got a better idea? At least if we give the stuff back, tell him where the car is, it's fair.'

'Fair? Nessa, I wonder about you, I really do. This is nothing to do with fair. He wants what's his, oh yes, granted, but more than that he wants other people to know he can't be ripped off. It's about front! Honestly, you watch enough of them cheesy movies. It's all front. What do people think when they think Ed McKay? He doesn't want his mates thinking, two teenage girls ripped him off for ten grand and you know what? That's one of them there on the cover of *Marie Claire*! This is all about how he looks. You know what he said to me? He said he owned me, said I was a dirty little slag and no one would hire me for any magazines except the top shelf ones. He could do that, he probably already has. I'll probably never get a legit job again. He's gonna try and find us, whatever. Even if we send the whole lot round tied up with blue ribbon and a bunch of flowers.' Paula looked out of the kitchen window.

'Paula, I'm sorry. I didn't think.'

'One thing though, we should try and call Helena, your mum. She was going to talk to him about me, I told you, remember?'

Nessa nodded.

'She knows what's happening, she'd help, I know it. She's really solid, your mum. Said she didn't care what I'd done I still looked right for her. She promised she'd keep me on for Hush. Said I was all right.'

'Helena! Solid? Don't say that to her face!' Nessa smiled. 'I'll call her again this morning. I tried last night but there was no one in. 'S funny 'cause there was no one in the office yesterday either; Jevonka was going up the wall!'

'So when was the last time you saw her then?' Paula's voice was nervous.

Nessa concentrated. 'Yesterday, no, night before last I think.' Nessa looked at Paula. She looked terrified. Nessa read her face and felt terrified too. Mum had gone to see McKay.

Nessa tore out of the house and across the road to the phone box and dialled the workshop.

'Jevonka!' Nessa felt a wash of relief. Jevonka was in the office, that was at least a first step to all being well in the world.

'Vanessa? Are you with Helena? Thank God! It's frantic here, I've got a hundred and one things to sort out and Fabien's as much use as a chocolate teapot! Helena seems to have vanished into thin air! I've gone through the address book. I was almost going to break down the door upstairs it's so quiet. When I came in this morning I very nearly called the police or hospitals! I thought she might be lying somewhere hit by a car! Hello? Vanessa? Are you still there? Is everything all right? Hello?'

Lauren Now

'Cool, no?'

Lauren was aware her mouth was open and shut it. She lived by the sea. She had grown up by the sea. But this was like no other beach she'd been on. They were under a bridge that went over the Thames—Lauren didn't know which one—down by the river on a thin tongue of sand. There were about thirty or forty people, not all that many, just enough. There was a bonfire and a barbecue and someone with a couple of decks and speakers with electricity leads looping up towards the embankment. Luke seemed to know quite a few people: some girls called Marcy and Nick and a boy whose name Lauren hadn't been able to hear above the music. The water looked bottomless and black and moved like oil-coloured blancmange. The lights of the city on the far side of the river were gold and yellow like a Lego city done out for Christmas. Lauren couldn't help staring.

'I know! It's gorgeous down here, innit.' Nick was standing next to Lauren, half dancing, half warming herself by the bonfire.

'I never been anywhere like this.'

''S good in the summer too. Beats Ibiza, if you ask me. Well, when it doesn't smell.'

Luke came back with some beers. Lauren almost refused—

what she really wanted was a mug of hot chocolate—but she took it anyway.

'What d'you reckon? Don't I take you all the best places?'

'You've never taken me anywhere else!'

'No, I suppose I haven't. Have to make up for it, won't I?' Luke said and Nick, overhearing, smiled at Lauren. Lauren smiled back and danced to keep herself warm.

The last dance she'd been to in Stivenham had been about as far from this as she could imagine. It was last term, before Christmas. School always had a do with St Bonaventure's. It was the first year she hadn't gone to Chloe's to get ready first. But the whole evening had been a disaster. She'd not been that drunk, just enough to feel stroppy, so when two Year Elevens from St Bon's asked for the tenth time, 'What's the air like up there?' she'd thrown the rest of her drink at them and been 'escorted off the premises'.

Chloe had come outside and talked to her. 'What's wrong? Ben likes you, you know. You didn't have to do that!'

'Yeah right! And I like him, too, that's why I threw my beer. Not. I heard them, Chlo! They were taking bets on who could get off with me, I heard them!'

Lauren looked deep into the fire and wiped the thought away. This was another world from some poxy school dance. The people were different, even in the dark; different clothes, different moves, and different colours. Like me, she thought. Just like me, the quadroon. The tune changed and it was one of her favourites, the bass bounced off the concrete underside of the bridge and filled up all the air and Lauren danced.

It was much later when she felt her phone buzzing in her back pocket. 'Lauren, where are you? I came home and the flat was empty. I've been having kittens.'

'I left a message, Ness. I came out with a friend.'

'I thought your friends were all in Stivenham?'

'I'm coming home, now, Ness. I'll get a cab.'

'Make it a black one, I don't trust mini-cabs. A black cab, promise me. I'll pay when you get here, OK?'

Luke was talking to the DJ. Standing over the desk doing that head nodding that boys do. He wasn't Thierry Martin with the dark voice and impenetrable cool, true, but he was nice. Understatement of the year, she thought to herself. And he was a laugh. In Stivenham this would have been a date. A boy calls you up and takes you out. Date. But this wasn't like that. He wasn't even looking at her. She walked over and tugged his sleeve.

'I've got to go!'

He mouthed 'What?' at her.

Lauren spoke again. Luke shook his head. Lauren leant close and spoke into his ear. She could smell him. He smelt of clean and soap with an undertone of sweat. Her lips were millimetres away from his skin.

'I'll get a cab,' she said.

'I'll come with you,' he said back.

When he spoke she could feel his breath up against her cheek, every word bouncing off her face. Her legs felt suddenly as if all the bone had been sucked out of them. She wanted to lean in close to him and had to work hard to keep herself upright. She had to move away before she keeled over.

Luke took his time saying goodbye to his mates, then

they walked up the steps to the south bank and as far as the new bridge that led to St Paul's on the north side. Lauren couldn't help smiling. There were hardly any other people about. A skateboarder rumbled south past them, a pair of lovers leant against the bridge kissing each other's faces off. London was like a backdrop painted on velvet. At the bottom of the steps on the north side of the bridge Luke stopped suddenly. He gripped Lauren's arm and put his hand to his mouth. Lauren thought, hoped, for a moment he was going to pull her close like the couple on the bridge.

'Look!' he whispered. There in front of them, crossing the main road in front of St Paul's Cathedral, was a fox. Taking its time, looking both ways and padding soundlessly through the railings on the other side. It was lit orange by the sodium light, the tip of its tail black and unquestionably foxy.

Lauren gasped. 'A fox!'

'Yeah, we get them in the bins sometimes. They're not scared at all, they just do what they want.'

Lauren thought that if she could do what she wanted she would grab Luke and kiss him. That's the beer thinking, she told herself.

It took ages to find a cab that stopped. Plenty passed by with their little yellow lights on.

'Why aren't they stopping?'

'You serious? Two kids, one with my hair, walking around the city of London after pub chucking-out time?'

'So?'

Luke just shook his head. Lauren didn't care; in fact, the longer it took them to find a cab, the longer they were together. The city was empty, it was like walking through man-made canyons of office blocks and empty Victorian buildings. Lauren felt safe. Luke was with her. The streets were theirs. Lauren stepped out into the road just as a bus rattled past. Luke reached out and pulled her back onto the pavement. She felt him behind her and caught her breath.

'I recognize this, we're at Liverpool Street!'

Luke didn't reply.

'Luke! Luke? Are you OK?'

'Um, yeah, sure, yeah. Liverpool Street.'

Lauren took his hand without thinking and walked him over to a taxi rank. Luke seemed quiet.

'You sure you're OK? I've had a brilliant time, really. Thanks.' She wished she could just kiss him. She put her hand up to her hat and almost took it off. But couldn't. She thought the best thing would be to go home quickly before something went wrong. She would have liked to kiss him but what if he laughed at her? What if he had a girlfriend? Some fine-boned urban sophisticate with plenty of her own hair?

'I can walk from here,' Luke said not meeting her eyes.

'You sure?'

'Yeah.'

'I'm going home tomorrow night.'

'Come round tomorrow. Can you?'

'Yeah. Yeah.' She got into the taxi. 'Hoxton please, Arden Street.'

The driver clicked the meter on. Lauren waved at Luke until the taxi had pulled round the corner. She slumped into the seat, her insides fizzing with hope and happiness

153

and regret. Did he think of her just as a mate? He wanted to see her, didn't he? She thought of all the time she had wasted on making Thierry walk and talk through her day-dreams.

'You OK, love?' The taxi driver looked at her in his mirror. 'Won't be long, get you home, love.' He shook his head and smiled good-naturedly. 'I dunno, I got a daughter the same age as you . . .'

Nessa Then

Nessa caught the bus to the train station five miles away. She left Paula in her grandmother's house; they both decided that would be safer. Nessa had kept her mouth shut when Paula said Mike could look after her.

Nessa sat on the train watching the landscape blur into green. She had a sort of plan: talk to Jevonka, ring round all the hospitals, then, if she still came up with nothing, try and talk to Ed. Maybe stake him out first, see if he had Helena tied up somewhere. No, that was just stupid.

Nessa hoped it wouldn't get that far. The motion of the train soon helped her catch up on the sleep she'd missed the night before, and she didn't wake up until the train braked loudly for Liverpool Street and she jolted awake.

It was the start of the rush hour; the station was filling up with workers going home. She walked down towards the tube station and that was when she saw the newspaper stand.

The London *Evening Standard* put out editions all day. The headlines changed as the news warmed up from afternoon to evening, but Nessa couldn't avoid this one. She stopped. Balled her hands into fists and felt the fingernails dig hard into her palms. The words were big black screaming capitals.

FASHION DESIGNER FOUND DEAD IN RIVER, it said.

Nessa stood still in front of it for what seemed like a long time. Commuters swirled around her and past her like shoals of fish. There was no question it was Helena. She knew that. It was more that if she could rewind time, if she could stop herself reading any more, buying a newspaper and seeing her mother's name, then maybe it would never have happened.

Helena was dead. If it was true, then why hadn't she known already? If you love people you're supposed to feel these things, aren't you? There's supposed to be a connection, isn't there? Maybe when she called last night, maybe that was it, that fear she'd felt. Nessa's insides were cold. If she could have looked at herself from the outside she'd have seen she was shaking.

A man bumped his briefcase into her and the spell was over. Nessa realized she was crying. She uncurled her hands and looked at the red marks on her palms. The tears fell effortlessly. She walked out of the station into the street past three more newspaper boards yelling the same news. FASHION DESIGNER FOUND DEAD IN RIVER.

She walked all the way home. Her head was so full. And the more she cried the more her head throbbed. She passed a phone box and thought of phoning Paula. But Paula would be freaked out. She'd probably jump on the next London train and then there'd be another body found somewhere else. Perhaps, Nessa thought, she should turn round and get the train back to Stivenham. What else could she do?

She turned the corner into her street and there was a police car outside the warehouse. If she went in they'd want to question her: she was probably a suspect. Or maybe the police already had Ed locked up safe? That sounded a little too good to be true. Nessa cursed herself for not buying the newspaper and at least trying to find out what was going on. She ducked into a phone booth and called Jevonka in the office.

But it was just the answer-machine. Nessa looked out beyond the glass. Life was normal out there. Men stopping for lunch in greasy spoons, buses passing, traffic crawling. The smell of London in summer: dirt and food and petrol fumes. All the same as when she'd left. London didn't stop because Helena was dead.

She bought herself a cup of tea and an *Evening Standard* and sat in the café in Clerkenwell Square. She had to steel herself to read it. Breathing in deeply, just like Helena sometimes late in the evenings when she couldn't wind down. She rubbed her temples in circles the way her mother did. Then she opened her eyes and read:

The body of Helena Harper, one of British fashion's leading lights, was pulled from the River Thames at Deptford last night. The designer had been missing since she left her workshop on Monday. Police are following several leads. It is understood Ms Harper's label was in financial difficulties and her perfume launch had—according to a source—'put her under an unprecedented amount of pressure'.

Nessa pushed the newspaper away. Financial difficulties? What were they on about? Mum had been fine, she'd never said anything about money. And as for pressure, Helena loved it, she would make more of her own if there wasn't enough from outside.

Nessa would have to let the police know what had happened. She would go home, talk to them and call Paula;

well, she could call Mike next door. Paula would have to know now. She pushed the hair away from her face. She felt exhausted. She thought for a second of all the other girls at school holding their pens and turning their exam papers over and she wished she was one of them. She had to stop herself crying again. She pressed her eyes with the heel of her hands to stop the tears coming. She'd talk to the police. Put them on to Ed McKay because whatever had happened he had to be behind it or under it or somehow to blame. Nessa finished her tea and stood up. The thought of Ed McKay locked up made her feel a very small bit better.

She walked up to the warehouse and took her key out. She needn't have bothered, the door was open. She wasn't sure what to expect; she'd only ever seen the police do their stuff on TV. The workshop was empty. From what she had seen she thought there'd be teams of uniformed officers sifting through the shelves.

'Hello?' She shut the door tight behind her and went upstairs. 'Hello!' She found Jevonka and Fabien sitting around the kitchen table with a uniformed policeman and a middle-aged woman. Fabien looked washed out and lost. Jevonka had aged ten years; her teeth were gritted and her hair pulled back tightly. The woman wore a dark blue suit and at first Nessa thought she must be an accountant. But the woman had a photo in her hand. One from last year in the south of France. Helena hugging Nessa to death. She had to be a policewoman.

'Vanessa? I'm Detective Inspector Porter.' She put out her hand for Nessa to shake. 'Ah, Ms Steele said you were out. With a friend, yes?'

Jevonka ignored the woman and got up and held Nessa tight. 'I'm so so sorry. Nessa, I never knew. When you called I never knew!'

Jevonka and Fabien had faces sticky and shiny with old tears. The policewoman put the picture down. 'We do realize this must be a difficult time . . .'

Nessa pulled a chair out from the kitchen table. She didn't want to sit down, she wanted to steady herself. She knew that the sooner she got all the stuff out about Ed the better. She wouldn't mention Paula at all in case they raced off to Stivenham. Just the stuff about Helena.

'I've got something to say.' Nessa realized her voice was wobbly. She breathed deeply and gripped the chair hard. 'About Helena, about Mum.' The others all looked at her. 'You remember, Jevonka, you said she went out that day, on Monday. I know where she went. She went to see that man. She went to see Ed McKay.'

Nessa thought she saw a light go on in the policewoman's eyes, but she held her gaze.

'We know all about Ms Harper's dealings with McKay. She owed him money.'

Nessa felt her mouth fall open. She looked from the policewoman to Jevonka. Jevonka didn't look surprised at all.

'Mum owed him money?'

The detective nodded. 'We know all about Mr McKay, I assure you.'

'But it had to be him—that killed her, I mean—she was seeing him on Monday, that's where she went. I know it! You should be doing a post mortem or something. It's murder, it's obvious!' Nessa was aware of her voice getting squeakier and shakier. She thought she must sound like a scared child. The adults seemed completely uninterested in this information. She sat down and Jevonka took her hand.

'Vanessa.' The detective looked concerned. 'We know this is difficult.' She looked hard at Nessa. 'Mr McKay came to see us this morning. He told us your mother had met him on Monday in Wapping.' She shifted in her seat. 'He said she was very tired and emotional.' The policewoman pushed her hair away from her face and sighed. 'Disturbed, he said. She was asking for money. Look, I don't know how to put this easily. He said she had a habit—you know, cocaine.'

There was complete silence. Nessa could feel the anger in her rising up, her face reddening. 'She wasn't an addict. She used it at parties, that's all!'

The policewoman went on, 'Vanessa, we are not treating your mother's death as suspicious. She had a fall—we think she may have had her reasons.'

Nessa thought if she opened her mouth she would scream. She stared back at the policewoman who was smiling synthetically at her.

'I'm sorry, Vanessa, but your mother had many problems, mostly connected to her business. Things weren't going well.'

Nessa still said nothing. She didn't believe a word of it. It was all wrong. They'd got it wrong. Helena was no fool. Mum was doing fine, better than fine. The new collection, the parties, the perfume. How on earth could she have got it all so wrong? She went to speak but Jevonka shushed her.

'It's all right, I put a call through to your father, Nessa.

He said he'd be here by the end of the week. We'll get you through this.'

Nessa felt the information like a blow. 'He's coming here? But he's in Kenya, on his farm.'

'It's all right, darling, I got hold of him eventually. He said he'd come as soon as poss, so don't worry, Nessa. Like I said, we'll get through this.'

Jevonka and Fabien were both smiling, those weak 'chin-up for the brave, motherless child' smiles. Nessa looked at them and then at the policewoman, all professional cool. She pulled her hand away from under Jevonka's and ran to her room.

On her desk next to a pile of school textbooks was *The London I Know*, Ed McKay's autobiography. His face grinned out smugly from under his coiffed seventies 'do on the cover. Nessa picked up her compasses and stabbed and twisted them into his eyes. Helena never owed him money, they had it all wrong. She knew Helena hadn't killed herself, that was so unlikely.

And now her dad was coming. She shuddered. Graham Bunting. The last time Nessa had met him he'd been in town with his wife Diana. They were coffee planters in Kenya—almost, but not quite, aristocracy. They lived in another world, fuelled and numbed by alcohol. Graham Bunting was perhaps the only subject that Helena and Nessa had agreed on completely. He was a prat, an aberration, a mistake. The only mistake Helena ever admitted. 'I was young, Ness, he was the brother of a girl at school. He was gorgeous, beautiful. Well, until he opened his mouth and you realized he'd left his brain at boarding school. No, darling, it wasn't *you* who was the mistake, it was me and him. I don't know what I was thinking!'

Graham Bunting coming from Africa to take her back to the farm? She wanted to run back to Stivenham and hide as soon as possible.

Nessa closed her eyes. A week ago life had been normal. Helena having a go, school like shit. All that had gone now. She lay flat on her bed and tried to cry but she had no tears left.

Lauren Now

Sometimes, Lauren thought, Nessa was unbelievable.

'Nessa, I was fine, all right. I was with Luke!'

'Luke! Luke who? I don't know a Luke. I didn't know you knew anyone in this town, let alone a Luke!'

Ian made hot chocolate and kept his mouth shut.

'And I left two messages, Nessa, two! One on your phone . . .'

'Which, of course, I left on during the recital . . .'

'You could have checked in the interval! And one here, look!' Lauren picked it up. It was written on a bit of kitchen roll, the pen smudging into the dimples. It said *Gone out don't worry back soon Lx*.

'Yeah, right. I was *so* reassured by your note. Lauren, this is not the community hall in Stivenham, this is not even a night out in Ipswich. This is London. In case you hadn't noticed. I was going up the wall.'

Nessa put her head in her hands.

Ian came through from the kitchen and put down mugs of chocolate in front of them.

'She's right,' he said. 'She was.'

'Sorry.'

'Well, I'm going to bed. Are you going to be long, Ness?'

Nessa shook her head, looked up at Ian. She put her hand out to Lauren's.

'Look, you know what I'm like.'

Lauren nodded.

'And I'm not that bad! You know it's been hard. You know I'm not your mum. But I'm trying. I was petrified. You don't know how big this town is. You don't know half of what nastiness goes on. I don't even want you to have to know. I was so scared.' Nessa sighed. 'Please don't do that to me again, yeah?'

'No, Nessa.' Lauren squeezed Nessa's hand.

They sipped their chocolate for a long time.

'So. Was it worth it?' Nessa asked.

A smile broke across Lauren's face. Nessa kissed her goodnight.

'Tell me in the morning, love.'

In the morning Lauren heard Ian leave but then fell back to sleep. He'd said yesterday he had some old girl's monkey-puzzle tree to sort out in Stowmarket. Lauren didn't wake again until Nessa knocked hard at the bedroom door and she sat up half thinking she was late for school. The bedside clock said ten thirty.

'Oh God, Ness, is the taxi here, am I late?' She threw the duvet back.

''S all right, Lauren. Work's off. It's OK. I thought you could do with a lie in, but you've got a visitor.'

'What?'

'Luke. The Luke I never knew about. He's here. He's keen.'

Lauren saw her bare, pale, twig legs uncovered and flipped the duvet back quickly. 'He's here?'

'That's what I said. He can't stay. He says he's got to work in the shop, so I'd move it if I were you.'

Lauren pulled her jeans on and stumbled, unwashed, into the kitchen. Luke looked as good as he had last night. Nessa had already sat him down and made him a coffee. His skateboard was leaning up near the front door.

'Hi.'

Luke said nothing. Nessa looked embarrassed for Luke. Then Lauren realized he was looking at her hair.

'Oh, yeah, I had a hat on last night.' She felt her head.

''S cool,' Luke said nodding slightly.

Lauren sat down. Cool. Her hair was cool. Maybe she didn't need a hat at all.

Nessa diplomatically went out to get a Sunday paper.

'Your mum said you weren't working.'

'Mmm? Oh, no, Nessa's not my mum, she's my guardian. It's a long story.'

'I'm not going anywhere.'

'No, believe me. Nessa said you were on your way to work. If I told you the story of my life you'd be here all day.'

'You could come over with me, or just come round later. Whatever. I mean, I know it's not fun exactly but it's not bad; there's the market, when I get boring. 'S probably not as well paid as modelling. You never said you were a model!'

'I'm not! Not really.'

'Your . . . er . . . Nessa said. She said you were working for Julien Isaacs!'

Lauren was sort of listening. She was watching the way his mouth moved when he spoke.

'Sorry, you've probably got plans.' He stood up. Lauren put her hand out to stop him.

'No, I'd love to, I mean, I don't know about Nessa, she might want me to do stuff, but I don't see why not.'

'Really?'

Lauren nodded.

Nessa wasn't gone long; she came back with a brown paper bag full of warm bagels. Luke had to leave to open the shop and Lauren thought she'd better have a shower first. So she washed and sat down for a coffee and a bagel with Nessa.

'He's nice,' Nessa said not looking up from her paper.

'I think so.' Lauren was already on her second bagel. 'And you don't mind if I hang out at his shop?'

'I wanted to go to Somerset House, there's an exhibition there. It's quite nice going up town on your own. Tell you what, though, I could pick you up—pack the car and meet you there.'

Lauren said nothing.

'Is that OK?'

'Yeah, Nessa, it's fine. It's not that. It's going home. School and stuff. I wish we didn't have to.'

'That, my dear, is life.' Nessa buttered a piece of bagel. 'And anyway, this weekend, this isn't life. Not really. I mean you haven't hardly had to do any work. Just swanning around in a paid-for flat. No wonder you don't want it to end.'

'You had a good time too!'

'Maybe,' Nessa said smiling.

'So. One thing before I go.'

'Yeah?'

'You always go on about London, about the mess and the dirt. But look at you, you love it. What is it about you and this place?'

'Lauren, I grew up here, I went to school here. And just talking about school is enough to put me off my bagel. It's like I said. You can't trust it all, there's things going on you can't see, you don't know about.'

'Yeah, but it's like that at home as well. Chris and those leaflets, the way people are with each other.'

'Lauren, believe me, I know what I am talking about.'

Lauren kissed Nessa goodbye and walked through Hoxton down to Spitalfields market. She thought it must be something to do with her mother, Nessa's mother, Helena. London must remind her of all that, Lauren thought, swinging her arms and catching her reflection in shop windows. The streets were punctuated by large open-fronted coffee shops. Lauren imagined her and Luke sitting in one of them. Like lovers. She smiled and stepped out across Broadgate.

The shop was swamped with a party of Japanese tourists waiting for the Jack the Ripper Walk. Lauren squeezed through the crowd who were buying up copies of cockney rhyming-slang dictionaries.

'Don't tell Dad but this is how the shop stays afloat.'

The walk leader was a young man in a suit and a top hat.

'He's an actor really,' Luke whispered. 'But he's not bad, scares some of them shitless.'

Lauren watched. The young man told the crowd about

the East End, about Victorian London and that the Ripper was never found. He also said that the bodies of the victims were laid out in the basement of the shop.

'Is that true?' Lauren asked.

'One of them was brought here. It's about all we've got that Books Etc. in Liverpool Street doesn't have.'

Lauren shivered. 'Creepy.'

'No one wants Dad's books any more. They just want gas lights and picturesque prostitutes in corsets, this lot. Dad reckons they're, like, marginally better than the other lot.'

'What d'you mean, other lot?'

Luke walked to the wall of the bookshop nearest the door. It had a hand-written sign saying London Crime in red letters. He scanned the shelves, pulling out books, then walked back to the counter and dumped the lot in front of Lauren.

'This lot.'

Lauren picked out the book on top and read.

'*The Profession of Violence*.'

'Actually that one's not bad, check the others.'

'*I'm Mad Me, the Life and Crime of Jackie "Mad" Malone*.' Lauren picked up another: '*Cockney Sparrers, The Other Side of Sixties London, From Soho to Shadwell: A Story of Gangland . . .*'

'See what I mean? Someone wanted to do a book launch here next month; Dad turned them down flat. I mean, those people, it's like a pose, a look or something. Sort of *The Italian Job* meets *Carry On Lock Stock and Robbing*. They think it's all smart suits and David Bailey snaps, not money and dead people, broken people. But when you look at it, I mean really look at it, they all went around nailing bits

168

of each other to furniture and making money selling drugs or girls or whatever.'

Lauren had got about halfway through the pile of books.

'That's the one, there, having a big do on the day his new book comes out. Sees himself as some kind of national treasure. He was on the telly, on some chat show, saying how he might have been a bad boy in the past but he's done his time. Crap! Dad said they only got him on some technicality and he only did three years. He's been living it up in Spain and Northern Cyprus, Dad said. No way was he having anything to do with it.'

Lauren turned over the book. The cover had a smiling man in his thirties with an orange perma-tan and seven-ties hair-sprayed stiff hair. '*The London I Know.*' She read the title aloud. Something made her look longer.

'Yeah, that's the one. Ed McKay. You all right?'

'Yeah, sure.' She put the book down. But on its own, not with the others. 'I think my mum knew him. Or Nessa. Or something.'

'What, your Nessa knew him? She's not that old, is she?' Luke picked up the book. 'I mean it says here he was down for that big bullion robbery in '77. She was just a baby, wasn't she?'

'Yes, I suppose so. Maybe I got it wrong.' Lauren picked it up and flicked through it. There was something about the book. She was sure she'd seen it before, but she couldn't imagine it was something Nessa would own.

'If you really want it it's yours.'

Lauren thought for a moment. 'Nah, I think it's just the hair. Now I don't have so much I must be jealous!'

'If you're gonna grow yours like that you can forget it.

I ain't going anywhere with you if you do.' Luke put the crime books back and Lauren forgot about Ed McKay.

She forgot about it all until Nessa came by to pick her up.

Clive had joined them in the shop after lunch. Luke seemed mightily pissed off at his dad turning up but Lauren liked him. She elbowed Luke in the side.

'Luke, he's nice. He's funny.'

'Yeah, you haven't heard the joke about cycle path one hundred times.'

Then Nessa arrived and it was Lauren's turn to be embarrassed.

'Lauren, this place is amazing.' She walked up to Clive. 'Clive? Vanessa.' Nessa put out her hand.

'Not one for cheek-kissing, Nessa,' Lauren whispered to Luke.

Clive showed Nessa the shop and Lauren started getting her stuff together.

'I won't leave anything this time.' She went through to the tiny stockroom and picked up her jacket and her hat, and the books Luke had said she could keep. Luke handed her a plastic bag. They could hear Nessa laughing loudly at something.

'When'll you be back?' Luke wasn't looking at her.

'I don't know.' She pulled on her jacket, and before she had said anything else Luke had manoeuvred himself up against her and was kissing her.

Lauren had hoped this would happen all day. She had tried to stand particularly close to Luke when he was sorting the local history out, but nothing had happened. Lauren had begun to tell herself that she'd been reading too much

170

into the whole situation. He was a good guy. She just hadn't come across many. Not many, any. And now he had launched himself at her and his tongue was in her mouth. She was just surprised. Terrifically surprised. She jumped backwards, almost knocking herself out on a pile of second-hand Mayhew's Guides to London Life. Luke flushed. Nessa called. Lauren left.

She sat in the car next to Nessa while Nessa went on and on about what a lovely man Clive was and how wonderful his shop was and wasn't she lucky to have come across such nice people. Luke was very good looking wasn't he and had she invited him up to Stivenham, and why didn't she?

Lauren was paralysed. All she could hear was her heart hammering inside her chest and the traffic on the motorway sliding past. All she could see was the look of hurt on Luke's face as she pulled away. What did he think of her now? She held her phone tight in her hand. She would phone him as soon as they got home and say sorry a million million times. What if he never kissed her again? What if she'd blown it completely?

It started raining as soon as Nessa turned off the motorway. 'Lauren, you're looking deathly. Are you sure you're all right?'

Nessa Then

Nessa went into her mother's room. It was tidier than Helena usually left it and there were piles of papers on the bedside table. No doubt the police-woman had stacked them like that. Nessa could see there would be nothing to help her here; the police would have taken anything away that they thought was mildly inter-esting. She pulled all the drawers out and found no revealing letters, no explanation, no suicide note. She found her own birth certificate and a pile of school reports but nothing important. Nothing that gave her any answers. She lay flat on the bed and smelt a faint trace of her mother on the duvet. Nessa closed her eyes and breathed in. The smell was a Hush prototype. Nessa remembered reading the copy for the adverts that she supposed would never happen now. *Hush, for your secret self.* Helena may have had her secret self, but Nessa knew it didn't involve cocaine mountains and owing money.

When Jevonka knocked at the door to tell her the police were leaving Nessa didn't come out. She heard the street door close and Jevonka running back upstairs. Jevonka came back to the bedroom and sat on a chair by the door. Nessa could see she felt uncomfortable but Nessa felt cold, not sympathetic. Jevonka leant forward.

'Vanessa, are you sure you're all right? I know this must

be a shock. I'm blown away. I mean, who'd have thought it, Helena!'

Nessa stopped rifling through her mother's bedside cabinet and looked Jevonka in the face. Surely Jevonka wasn't that stupid? Jevonka's hands were clasped together in her lap. She looked exhausted; she pushed the hair away from her face.

'Are you going to be OK, on your own, I mean? Is there a friend you could stay with, you know, until Graham, your dad, arrives?'

Nessa thought she might start laughing the way crazy people did in films. But she stopped herself. Stared right back.

'Jevonka, I used to think you were on the ball. I mean, you know—knew—Helena, she wouldn't have hired you if she didn't think you could do ten things at once.'

Jevonka looked bashful.

'However, I'm beginning to think I was wrong. Do I look all right? My mother has just been murdered. I know she's been murdered and you think I'm just making it up. Come on, Jevonka, you know that McKay. You've seen him. Did she really owe him money?'

'I wasn't the bookkeeper. I was a PA. You know this business, Vanessa, she could have been knee-deep in debt or coke or both. One thing you can't dispute is she was close to that man, that McKay.' Jevonka got up. 'And I was worried about you.'

'Ooh, poor little Vanessa, motherless and alone. We'd have known, Jevonka! Fabien takes more coke than Mum ever did! And who told you to phone that human slug Bunting? Go home, Jevonka.' Nessa turned back to the cupboard. 'I'll be just fine. I'm sixteen. I'm an adult. And you and Fabien can leave the keys to the workshop on your way out.'

'Vanessa, I am trying to help. Believe me I want to find out what happened to your mother as much as you do.' They looked at each other.

'Jevonka, Helena was my mother. You were the hired help. You don't know what that man was capable of. He's a killer, Jevonka. Just go home. Go back to the States, or wherever.'

'Fine! If that's what you want.' Jevonka slammed the door as she left.

Nessa felt bad immediately. She thought about running after her and saying sorry. But by the time she had made it out into the street Jevonka had gone. Nessa made herself promise she'd call her. She would need every tiny bit of help she could get.

Nessa went down into the workshop. In the floor of the main room there were traces of sand between the floorboards. That party was months ago. Another life ago. There were cuttings from newspapers and glossy magazines on the wall, colour swatches and bits of fabric, drawings and photos and pictures of Fabien's King Charles spaniels.

Nessa picked up a ball and threw it across to the other side, listening to it bounce with a hard concrete/metal sound. The street door rattled as a group of people passed and Nessa shivered. She sat down at a desk and wrote herself a list.

1. Call Graham Bunting. Put him off.
   How would she do that? Simple. Remind him the

money's all vanished. She knew he wouldn't be in a hurry to leave Kenya.

2. Call Paula.

Paula would have to know. If she found out on the news or something she'd freak. And anyway, Paula knew much more about Ed than she did. Plus Paula had the money and they'd need every penny. Plus, and she tried not to think this out loud, there was the gun.

3. Find Ed.

She crossed it out, wrote Get Ed instead but that looked just as stupid. Sort it out, she wrote at last.

Then there'd be funerals and lawyers and all the horrible paraphernalia of death. She remembered when her grandmother died. Helena had been so upset by it all she hadn't even bothered to get rid of the house in Stivenham. Nessa put her head in her hands. The only other thing she was sure of was that she didn't want to spend the night here. There was too much space and too many ghosts floating around in the high loft-style ceilings. She pulled out Helena's appointments diary from her desk. It was no help. What did she expect: *Monday—meet Ed, kill myself?* She shut it again and looked for the address book. Ed was there, his office address anyway; it was in Soho. The policewoman said Ed had met Helena in Wapping. Nessa flicked through to photographers. There was the address, the place she'd first seen McKay, the glass-roofed studio. New Providence Wharf.

Nessa checked the street door was bolted and went back upstairs to pack a bag. She looked round her bedroom, was there anything really important? She sat down on her bed and felt for her charm bracelet. That was it; the shell, the fish, the blue glass eye, the bracelet was the only thing she'd take. She smiled to herself. Paula had thought she was lucky; well, they'd both need all the luck they could get now.

Then she went up into the kitchen and made herself a herbal tea and sat down in front of the phone. Graham Bunting first, that would be easy, then Paula. She picked up the handset and dialled.

She held herself together talking to Diana Bunting. Her voice floating halfway across the world, Diana was delighted Nessa didn't want them to come.

'It'll be fine, Diana, I'm staying with friends. From school.'

'It's such an awful business, Vanessa. You know you have our deepest sympathy at this difficult time. Are you sure you'll be all right? Graham *is* rather busy at the minute.'

Yeah, right, Nessa said to herself.

But when she talked to Paula all the tears came out. Paula was quiet at first, numbed. But there was no doubt in her mind.

'Oh my God, Ness. He done it. He did, didn't he?'

'They don't believe it. They're saying she owed him money, that she was using cocaine. McKay's been to the police, pillar of the community that we all know he is. Said she was *disturbed* when she came to see him. He's just walking away. He can't do this, Paula. Can he?'

'I'm coming back, Ness, I'm coming now.'

'Don't be stupid, Paula. What if someone sees you?

What if McKay gets to finish the work he started on your face?'

'Forget it, I ain't staying here. I could be hiding for ever if we don't sort this out. I'll get the next train. We're gonna show him. And look, Ness, we'll be all right, you an' me. We're family now. We're all we've got an' he's not gonna touch us. Wait for me at Liverpool Street, I'll be there as soon as I can, all right? He's not walking away this time.'

Nessa went round the warehouse one last time. It felt as if she was saying goodbye. Not just to the building but to some part of her life. She looked a last time round the workroom, took the address book and the appointment diary with her just in case, and last of all Ed's book, jammed into the pocket of her jacket.

She walked out into the street. It was summer and the start of the rush hour. Nessa walked up past the Willow cinema and down to the main road. She could walk to Liverpool Street. It would clear her head, and Paula wouldn't get in until after eight.

She sat in a café opposite the station for a long time. The waitress must have noticed that her eyes were pinker than normal and let her be.

Nessa pulled out *The London I Know* by Ed McKay and read. By the time she'd read through 'My early years' the third time she was sure the man wasn't a nutter so much as clever: at eleven he was already running errands for local gangsters, graduating to running his own protection rackets all over London. He never got caught for anything himself, not like a lot of petty crooks; all the way up until the bullion robbery in '77 there had been other, lesser, men to take the fall, to do the time. They'd never managed to put him away for that robbery either, even though he admitted as much now. What had Paula said? Double jeopardy? It meant you couldn't be tried for the same crime twice. So even if he admitted it all over his new book, there was nothing the police could do. Ed McKay was no fool, and he liked violence, Nessa could see that.

Some time just before the big robbery he took over a pub in Hoxton, the Garland. There was a picture of him and his lovely wife at the bar. That was the start of his legit entertainment business, the cinemas and snooker halls. The time in Spain hadn't stopped him, either, he *'made contacts'* it said. What the book didn't spell out was how he really earned his money, his bread and butter. Paula knew some of it. The property deals in the early eighties financed by drug money—not just cocaine and cannabis, either, he had a healthy line in cigarette smuggling too. Nessa shut the book. They had a lot to do.

Liverpool Street station was full of commuters, floods of them heading back to Essex and East Anglia. By eight the crowds had thinned and the station just seemed big and empty. Nessa stood in front of the arrivals board as the letters and numbers clicked over. Platform 6. She turned and walked to the barrier. Paula, beautiful, recognizable, even with a baseball cap and sunglasses, stood taller than most of the other passengers and Nessa was so pleased to see her she practically flung herself at her. They stood together for a long time and it wasn't until they broke apart Nessa realized they'd both been crying.

'It's gonna be all right, Ness, I promise. God, I am so sorry for all this. If I hadn't asked Helena to talk to him . . .'

'It's done, it's done. I don't blame you.' Nessa wiped her eyes. 'Did you bring it?'

Paula nodded. 'And the money, look.' She turned around. 'See?'

'Hi.' Mike Mullan, beach boy, was standing behind Paula, carrying the holdall. He waved sheepishly at Nessa.

Nessa's mouth fell open. 'What the hell did you bring him for?'

Paula folded her arms. 'He said he wanted to help, didn't you, Mike?' Paula leant close to Nessa and whispered. 'I had to tell him, Ness, he saw the money, and anyway, he's not completely useless.'

Nessa watched Paula link arms with Mike and wished she'd never phoned her. She thought she would have been better off on her own.

Lauren Now

Luke's phone was off the hook and the bookshop was shut. Lauren looked out of her bedroom window at the rain falling in near horizontal sheets. It had been such a good weekend and now it hadn't. She couldn't imagine spending another weekend in London without feeling her insides heave, close to vomiting at the thought of what happened. He must think she was some prize idiot, some country know-nothing. Lauren squeezed her eyes shut. But that was worse because then she saw the look on his face after he kissed her. She checked her homework diary, but she couldn't even distract herself with that because she'd done it all before they'd gone to London to please Nessa.

Her bedroom seemed even smaller than she remembered it; she couldn't even pace around effectively without stooping to avoid bashing her head on the sloping ceiling. She sat down and went through the whole Sunday with Luke inside her head. Then she remembered the Ed McKay book. Hadn't Nessa said he knew Paula? She was positive she'd seen it somewhere around the house. She thought of shouting down to Nessa but she'd gone round to Ian's as soon as they'd got back, just like a lovesick teenager.

Lauren went into Nessa's bedroom. Didn't Nessa have her own copy? Perhaps she'd seen the book there.

She was scanning the shelves when the phone rang. Lauren felt her heart leap. Could it be Luke? It wasn't. Just someone for Nessa.

'Does Vanessa Harper live there by any chance?' It was a woman's voice, a bland voice, like someone off TV.

'Yes, but she's not in at the minute; can I take a message?' Lauren said, but the line had gone dead. Lauren assumed it was about piano lessons and put the phone down. The woman would call back.

Lauren looked on Nessa's bedside table. A couple of novels and a guide to open gardens in Stivenham in 1998. She stretched out for the clock and knocked the pile onto the floor—and there it was, underneath a pile of non-fiction books with one-word titles. Nessa did have it. *The London I Know* by Ed McKay. She pulled it out, piled the other books back up and took the McKay book into her room. It was exactly the same as the book shop copy, only ten times more used and dog-eared. She couldn't imagine it was Nessa's thing at all. She flipped through the pages and the book nearly fell apart in her hand. Lauren promised herself to ask Nessa about it later.

But when Nessa came in late and told her to check that she had everything for Monday at school, Lauren forgot to say anything about the phone call or the book.

She wasn't reminded until she was at school. Lauren wore a hat on the way in. No one looked twice until registration when Mrs Whelan told her to take it off. She whisked it off quickly as if she was taking a plaster off. Chloe's mouth fell open and Lucy smiled.

'Yeah, great. Really.'

Lauren felt herself flushing. Then she pulled herself

together and sat up straight so she towered over the other girls. Brave, she thought, that's what Eda said.

'Come on now, girls, settle down.' Mrs Whelan, the form teacher, looked up from the register. 'Lauren, I think your hair looks smashing.'

Lucy Marsham looked towards her and mouthed 'smashing'. Lauren felt her cool slipping away. A compliment from a teacher was as good as the kiss of death. The bell whirred for lessons and Lauren held herself tall and walked down the corridor as if she didn't care and into the comparative safety of the art room.

In art they'd been doing lino cuts. Lauren had on an overall that was far too short in the arm and only struggled past her hips. She had spent the last few weeks gouging a tiny piece of lino into a fair representation of her own finger tip, all the patterns and lines, close up. It had stopped looking much like a finger tip and Lauren thought of it more as a kind of whirlpool. Maybe whorlpool. She made a face at her own bad joke. At least she didn't have to tie her hair up out of the way any more.

Ms Thomas had set up a table for inking covered over in sheets of newspapers. Our Lady's took girls from everywhere but it was mostly the *Daily Mail* or *The Times*. Lauren held her lino square and inked it furiously with a roller. She'd only meant to go over it two or three times but it was only when Ms Thomas called over to her that she stopped.

'Lauren! I think you've got enough ink there, now.'

'Oh. Have I? Yes, sorry, Miss.'

Lauren read the paragraph one more time. The headline read: 'East End Crime Lord Set To Celebrate New Life

With Book'. There was a picture that could have been the same man as the one on *The London I Know*; only this one was much older. His hair was silver-grey although his eyebrows were still black. His whole face had sagged and dropped into heavy jowls. He looked serious, sad even; he could have been a character actor from some British film. The caption underneath the photo read '*Ed McKay seen last year at his mother's funeral in Bethnal Green.*' Lauren struggled to call back whatever it was Nessa had said. Maybe she had imagined it—no, she was sure she had mentioned the name. Didn't she say Paula knew him? Knew of him?

She'd have to get round to asking. That was the man Luke had been talking about.

Luke. He flashed up into her head and she suddenly felt sick again.

At lunchtime she went to the library and booked a computer. She wanted to e-mail Luke, but she also wanted to keep out of the way of Lucy Marsham, who had been enjoying the reaction to Lauren's hair. Lauren imagined Luke turning on his computer and reading, but she couldn't imagine his reaction.

Hi, Luke, I'm sorry, what else could she write? Kiss me again? Please? I'll get a train now if you like, right now. She couldn't write that. *I must have looked a right idiot.* Kiss me again. *Please call me, text me whatever, I'd really* (no, take the really out—too desperate) *like to see you again*. That's just cack! Couldn't she think of anything better? How about: no one I really like has ever kissed me; or, I'm going mad because I haven't talked to you and I don't know if you think I'm a total nutter. No, even more desperate. *I did try your phone but it was switched off.* True. *I had a*—wonderful?

lovely? brilliant?—*really good time with you on Saturday night. Please call, Lauren*

Lauren pressed send.

There was still another twenty minutes of lunch. Twenty minutes of finding something to do that meant she could stay inside. She looked across to where Ms Forrest the librarian was arguing with a sixth former about the state of a returned book.

Lauren clicked on to a search engine and typed Ed McKay. There were pages and pages and pages. Him by the pool of his villa in Spain. Ed outside court with his lovely wife after he'd been given a not guilty for the bullion robbery. Smiling and pulling a pint behind the bar of his pub in Hoxton. His son Ashley, it said, had had a chequered career in the music industry. He'd had a bit part in *EastEnders* and the occasional role in *The Bill* as a policeman. There was the photo of Ed at his mother's funeral, last year, when he was still serving time for fraud, handcuffed to a prison officer. And a smiling one of him with the politician who'd been put away for perjury last summer.

There were so many photos Lauren didn't notice the time. She had got on to a page of pictures of Showbiz Ed—Ed with boxers and singers and actors—when Lauren froze. There was one of a party; the clothes were ridiculous, skirts like balloons and hair solid with hairspray. Ed was surrounded by girls, skinny, pretty girls; he was holding a glass and everyone was smiling and Lauren realized she recognized the girl on Ed's left. It was Paula. Her own dead mum Paula, alive in colour. Smiling in too much make-up. She looked so young, 15, 16? Ed had his arm around her waist. You could just see his fat fingers curling around Paula's middle. The weirdest thing was that Lauren felt as if she'd seen the picture before. She pressed print as the bell went for afternoon lessons. She would be late for Biology.

Nessa Then

'None of these bloody phone boxes work!' Nessa slammed the handset down and pushed the door open. Outside the air only smelt of petrol rather than the heavy, fuzzy, smell of piss inside the phone box.

'Try this one.' Paula pushed through into the next one. Nessa had a pocket bulging with ten pence pieces.

Nessa spread the piece of paper with the number flat and dialled again. She cupped her hand over the handset. 'It's ringing!'

Paula leant close and pulled the door shut inside.

'Hello? Is that McKay Partners Investments?'

'MPI, how can I help?'

Nessa made her voice as smooth and cool as she could. 'I was wondering, is Mr McKay available?'

'Do you have an appointment?'

Nessa paused a fraction too long.

'An appointment?' the voice said again.

'Erm . . . no, I wanted to make one, to make an appointment, yes.'

'Does Mr McKay know you? If you leave your number I'll call you back tomorrow.'

Nessa put the phone down.

'What happened?'

'It's no use, Paula, we can't do it this way. Even if they

did let me speak to him, what are we going to do, wire me up with a tape recorder and get him to confess all?'

They left the phone box and walked back to their hotel.

'Couldn't we stay anywhere else?' Nessa hated it. She'd spent the night in a box-sized room on her own listening to Mike and Paula next door. Twice she'd taken the gun out and held it, opened it. A couple of times she'd imagined slipping out at night and shooting him. Or trying to. She practised holding the gun two-handed and opened it to check for bullets. It had taken a long time to figure out the mechanism. But that wasn't the answer. There had to be some other way.

Helena had always had money and all the hotels she'd stayed in before were gleamingly clean. Here she couldn't bear to use the bath, in a tiny mould-pocked room down the corridor, and the sheets were a dingy magnolia that had once been white. The ceilings were plastered in textured swirls and reminded her of a Van Gogh painting with all the colour taken off.

'I don't know if I can spend another night here, Paul.' Nessa hitched the curtain open. Outside it was a London summer, children in school uniform swung their bags at each other. 'I preferred the one by the station.'

'Yeah well, they'd have looked twice at me, I bet. And what about the bags? One stuffed full of cash money, the other with a . . .'

'Yeah, I know, I know,'

'And like you said, we don't want anyone knowing where we are. Ed's looking for me and the police are gonna notice eventually if you aren't around.'

'I'm sixteen, I'm an adult!'

'Right.'

Nessa shut her eyes and crossed her arms. Paula sighed.

'I think we should check out New Providence Wharf,' said Nessa.

'Yeah, you said that, only shouldn't we wait for Mike to come back from Fredericks Mews? He might find something.'

'Yeah, a bit of paper with *I done it*, signed E. McKay.' Nessa rubbed her eyes. 'Come on, Paula, he's useless; I bet he's still wandering down Oxford Street. I don't know why you brought him with you, he's rubbish.'

Paula smiled. 'Not entirely . . .'

Nessa walked out of the hotel and hailed a cab. 'Wapping, New Providence Wharf, please.'

'Sorry, Ness. I didn't really mean to bring him, but he was like a puppy, you know, those big green eyes. I never meant to tell him anything, but once he clapped eyes on the cash . . . I had no one to talk to, Ness, I was all on my own!'

'So was I.'

'Yeah, I know. But you're . . . Helena said, she said, *Vanessa is so self-sufficient*. I just can't keep my mouth shut. Oh, you know what I'm like, Ness, I don't mean anything bad.'

Nessa looked at Paula sitting on the far side of the cab. It rattled through the city and past Tower Bridge. Nessa, despite herself, smiled a little at Paula. Paula beamed back. 'I couldn't do this without you, Ness, you know that.'

The taxi pulled up in a narrow street that ran like a canyon between warehouses. Nessa paid and the girls got out. Even though it was a sunny day it was dark at street level and Nessa felt cold.

'This is it.' Paula walked towards the building. 'The one with the photographers.'

Nessa thought it looked different, darker than when she'd been here with Helena. There was a chain across the door and a sign, NO ENTRY. MPI PROPERTY—COMING SOON LUXURY RIVERSIDE FLATS. Ed must have made good his promise and thrown the artists out. Paula rattled the door but it was locked firm. Nessa saw a passage at the side of the building where there was a ribbon of light.

The girls walked through the alley and onto the riverfront. It was the light that Nessa noticed first. The intense grey-white light as the city opened out. There were the skyscrapers to the north-west, the Natwest Tower, and Centrepoint, the dome of St Paul's, and, spanning the river, Tower Bridge, like a pop-up picture book illustration. Then, to the east, brown and grey shadow warehouse buildings and the new blocks in docklands sticking up through them like tiger's teeth. It could have been two different countries.

'Come on!' Paula stepped out onto the concrete quay. Nessa followed. There were steps down to the river; behind them the warehouse rose up like a wall. Nessa felt scared, they were so exposed. But the place seemed to be empty. There were no other people around, not even builders. A police launch tore down the middle of the Thames like scissors through silk. Both girls stepped back and said nothing until the boat had passed. Nessa felt her feet crunching on broken glass. There were no windows low down. She looked up.

'Do you think it happened here, Paula? Do you think he did it here?' It felt so damp and cold in the shadow of the warehouse. Nessa imagined her mother, flying, falling out of the glass-roofed studio on the top floor.

Paula shook her head. 'How would we know?'

'We have to work out what happened, we have to think about it like those programmes on the telly, re-enactments and things. There'd be broken glass and . . . I don't know. Blood?'

'What's that gonna do? I hate to tell you, Ness, but unless there was someone in the room with them who saw what happened and is gonna risk having their nuts perforated by speaking out, no one's saying nothing.'

'But there's loads of glass, look. It could've happened, we can't just sit back.'

'That's not what I said.' Paula walked to the edge of the concrete and sat down, dangling her legs over the side. 'I dunno yet, but whatever we do or find, it's got to be water-tight. We've got to find some way of giving the police something.'

'But what if they ignore it, Paula? They don't believe he did anything to you and they don't believe he killed Helena, either.'

Paula smiled. 'Nessa, they're never gonna believe me. I'm 15, been on the game, been in care, wrong colour, stands to reason I'm the biggest liar on the block. Ed McKay? Reputable businessman? No contest. But they might just believe you.'

'What do you mean?'

'Remember, in the car, that policeman.'

'That was only one. And he was dazzled by your legs. The detective, the woman the other day, she didn't believe me.'

191

'Then we have to prove it. Prove it like they say on the telly, beyond all reasonable whatsit.'

'Doubt.'

'Yeah.' Paula threw a pebble down towards the water.

'OK, right. Something big. He's involved in lots of stuff, you said.'

'Yeah, it's drugs mostly, a bit of porn, a bit of protection.'

'If we give them enough the police will have to do something. Won't they?'

Paula shrugged.

Nessa said nothing. The world she'd grown up in didn't operate like this. In Nessa's world you went to a policeman if you were in trouble and it was safe. People didn't die, girls didn't get beaten up by fifty-year-old men. London was a safe place.

'I can't believe the police won't listen, Paula.'

'Look, Ness, a man like Ed McKay, he's bound to have friends everywhere, isn't he, and some of those friends will be in the police. I mean, they're just like the rest of us, and underneath, some are better than others. You know, 's nothing new. I knew this copper once when we lived in Forest Gate, he used to give me lifts home if me and Arlene were out late, and all he wanted was . . .'

'No, don't tell me, all right? I don't want to know. Do you think he might have someone working for him in the police? That'd explain a lot. But they know he's a villain, they must know the sort of man he is.'

'Think about it, Ness. Your mum, she liked him, she had him round for parties, to have pictures taken next to him, to say what a darling he was.'

'Yeah, until she found out . . . she didn't know all that stuff about you, she can't have. She was trying to help you.'

'Nessa, I'm not having a go, all right? Back off. I just mean to say, people don't see what they don't want to see. She knew some of it. They all did. Notorious, that's what Ed said he was, that's what he said people liked. The fact he'd done these nasty things.' Paula shuddered. 'It's a little sick. That's what people are like, not just your mum, the whole world. A bit of rough, a bit of sick. A bit of someone else being hurt.'

Nessa sighed. She saw that you could get up and go out in the morning and never come back and no one would care. You could tell the truth, shout the truth, and no one would listen. If you didn't have money or status or strength you were invisible.

Paula had rattled the door at the back of the warehouse but it was shut tight. Nessa felt useless. How could they prove what seemed so obvious, how would they ever find out what had happened? At the back of her mind she remembered the gun. Perhaps if they couldn't get any justice by asking . . .

Paula came back. ''S no use, Nessa. Place is locked up. Come on, Ness, we do need some proper plan. And you better do it, cause I'm rubbish at plans.' Paula smiled. Nessa rubbed at her eyes.

'Yeah. Right. A plan. A way to get some proof that is cast iron. So they have to listen.' Nessa breathed in and shuddered at the same time, and Paula rubbed her back for a long time.

Lauren Now

'Lauren, are you sure you're all right?'

Lauren sat at the kitchen table pushing the food around her plate with her fork. She imagined Luke sitting around the big comfortable kitchen of their house in Spitalfields; he'd probably brought some other girl home. She was probably kissing him now. Kissing him properly, not running off like some stupid twelve year old. He'd still not mailed or phoned.

Nessa was still talking. 'Only I can't say I've not noticed. You've been so low since we came back from London. I know it might have seemed a bit of an anticlimax, but that's what modelling's like, waiting around, jumping when they say jump. Anyway, Lauren, I thought you did very well. That man, that Isaacs guy, he thought you were really something; I think there'll be work for you if you want it.'

Lauren said nothing.

'Lauren?'

'Sorry, Ness, it's not the modelling. Honestly, it's not. I didn't mind it at all, it's not like doing double chemistry.'

'So is it school, then? Are you having trouble with that what's-her-name, Lucy thingy? Girls can be so cruel. Did they give you some grief about your hair?'

Lauren wanted to tell someone everything about Luke.

She looked into Nessa's concerned face, but her mouth wouldn't work.

'Well, I do wish you'd let me know what's eating you up. There's nothing I can do if you don't talk to me, Lauren.'

Lauren was about to speak, to change the subject and ask about the photos of Paula she'd printed out at school, when the phone went.

'It won't explode, you know!' Nessa said as Lauren dashed to pick it up.

'Hello?'

'Vanessa Harper?'

Lauren handed the phone to Nessa and looked out of the window. Stivenham was brightening up, spring had come at last and Chloe's mum was on the other side of the green chatting to Mrs Mullan and handing her a bright yellow leaflet. Poisonous, Lauren thought.

Nessa was talking on the phone, but her voice sounded icy, not like Nessa at all. Lauren could see Nessa's face had blanched. And when she put the phone down she was shaking. Really shaking.

'Are *you* all right, Nessa?'

Nessa couldn't look her in the eye. 'No, maybe not.' Nessa pushed her plate away.

'You're not eating either?'

'I don't think I can, Lauren. I feel like I've been hit on the back of the head.' She stood up. 'I think I need to talk to Ian.' Nessa picked up her jacket and her car keys. 'Now.'

'Ness! Hang on, what is it? What's up? Who was that on the phone? What's happened?'

'Lauren, I'm sorry.' Nessa rubbed Lauren's shoulder as if she was the one who needed comfort. 'I'll sort it all out in my head; I'll be back in a minute.' She was almost at the front door when she stopped.

'Lauren, love, look, don't answer the phone when I'm out. Come to think of it, do me a favour, go round to Chloe's for a bit. Please? I'll pick you up in half an hour, yeah?' Nessa's voice wavered; Lauren felt even more uncomfortable. 'Please, love?'

'Nessa, just tell me, yeah?'

'I will. I promise. I just need to . . .' Nessa raked her hand through her hair. 'I just need to get stuff straight. I just don't want you on your own, in the house. Please?'

Nessa held the door open for Lauren.

'I don't understand, Ness.'

'Just do it, OK, for me?'

Lauren took her jacket.

'I'll pick you up at Chloe's, yeah, in half an hour, an hour.'

'Yeah. Right.'

Lauren slammed out of the house. She'd been in a bad mood before and now this off-the-wall madness from Nessa. Chloe's mum took hormones or something; perhaps Nessa was heading for the menopause, but wasn't thirty-two a bit early? Maybe not.

Lauren pushed her hands into her pockets and started walking. She heard the door go again as Nessa left and the car engine turned over and Nessa drove off towards Ian's. Mrs Mullan and Chloe's mum waved. Nessa didn't wave back. Lauren thought how selfish Nessa was being, all bound up in her cosy little Ian-world; she didn't care what was happening to Lauren at all.

She'd just rounded the corner into Chloe's estate when

197

she started thinking about Paula again. Paula wouldn't have been like that; Paula would have been the glamorous friend she'd never had. Paula would have sat her down, 'What's wrong, babe?' She bet Paula would have called her babe. And she'd have been able to talk to her about Luke. Paula would probably have known exactly what to do. Paula would have had stories, too, parties, the life she'd had before. Lauren stopped outside Chloe's. The last thing she wanted to do was come apart in front of Chloe.

Nessa was off her head. Don't stay in the house on your own! How old did she think Lauren was? Lauren turned and started walking home again; she passed Chloe's mum who handed her a sunny yellow leaflet. Lauren smiled. 'D'you think I could have a few?'

'Oh, would you, Lauren? I keep asking Chloe to take some into school, but you know what she's like, only interested in one thing—well, maybe two things, but not what's going on around her; nothing important.'

Lauren took a big handful. 'Thanks.'

'Ooh, it's so good to see young people involved these days!' Mrs Mullan and Chloe's mum smiled and Lauren walked on a few steps, and then, in front of both of them, tipped the lot into the litter bin. She turned back to Chloe's mother and Mrs Mullan, who were watching open-mouthed, and smiled again.

That was for you, Eda, she thought to herself. Then she went home.

The phone was going as she put the key in the lock. Suddenly her hands were jelly hands, unable, incapable. She struggled with the lock and pushed inside, ran to the phone. 'Hello?'

'Lauren?'

'Luke!'

'I got your e-mail.'

Lauren sat down on the steps. The front door flapped open in the wind. Her heart was hammering. She thought Luke must be able to hear it down the phone.

'Luke.'

She was still on the phone when the headlights of Nessa's car swung into the road in front of the house. Lauren had to hurry Luke off the phone. The little dial on the receiver showed she'd been talking for nearly an hour. They hadn't really talked about anything. Luke said he'd had no credit for days and the computers at home had been down. He said he'd been worried he'd never see her again. Lauren glowed just remembering. *He* was worried! She felt like she could handle anything. He said he'd phone again. Just to make sure.

Then the front door opened and Nessa was there with Ian. Nessa was red-faced, furious.

'I thought I told you! I thought I said you were to go to Chloe's! I was just there, what *did* you say to her mother? Jesus, I don't ask much, Lauren! This is important!'

Lauren backed against the wall. Ian took hold of Nessa, held on to her. 'Cool down, Ness, come on. Cool down. Explain.'

'I don't want to explain now! Ian, they know where we live! I want to get out.' Nessa turned to Lauren.

'Lauren, were there any calls, anything at all, while you were here?'

Lauren shook her head. 'I was just talking to Luke. I

mean, I never—we never—meant to talk for so long, but you know . . .'

Nessa hugged Lauren so tight she thought she'd asphyxiate. 'Lauren, love, I'm sorry.'

'I don't understand, Ness.'

'We have to go.'

'Go? What are you on about?'

'Lauren, please. We just have to go, stay somewhere else for a while.'

'Nessa, are you all right?' Lauren looked at Ian. His face was grim, but not mad. Was Nessa going mad? What was it?

'Come on, Nessa, you've got to tell her.' Ian was standing in the doorway. Nessa nodded.

'Tell me what?' Lauren asked.

'Everything,' Nessa whispered, 'I'll tell you everything. But we have to go first, it's not safe. We have to go now.'

Nessa Then

Nessa and Paula were sitting in the caff round the
corner from the hotel when Mike came back from
Fredericks Mews empty handed.

'It's been cleaned out, by the looks of things, completely
empty.'

Paula sighed. 'I really loved that house.'

Mike squeezed her hand and she smiled. Nessa had tried
to stop herself feeling jealous of Paula, but it was very
hard work. The way they were with each other, so close,
so touchy-feely. She looked away. She felt very alone.

'Never mind, eh, Mike; you did your best, he did, didn't
he?'

'Yeah. I'm sure you did,' Nessa said sharply.

'Come on, Ness, we're all trying.' Paula sipped her
scummy tea.

Nessa thought she was fed up with trying. Nothing was
any use. Ed McKay had been doing his business for so
long he seemed to have everything sewn up. And Nessa's
head felt like her brain had turned into pudding. She
pushed her chair away from the table.

'We've still got the office address, you know, in Soho,'
said Paula. 'We haven't tried that yet.'

'Yeah, and I can see him letting us in and having a little
chat. Look, I'm going for a walk, OK?' Nessa stood up.

Mike was tracing his hand down Paula's beautiful cheek. 'All right?' They weren't taking this seriously at all. Paula felt fine now she had Mike to protect her; she didn't care about Helena. Well, it didn't look like it.

'See you later then, yeah?' Paula called out. 'Don't be too long or we'll worry.' Mike whispered something to Paula and she collapsed into giggles. Nessa left.

She started walking north. Parry Street, it had said in the book, that's where the pub was, Ed's pub, The Garland. It took her nearly an hour and she got lost twice. Nessa walked past furniture makers and builder's yards, derelict buildings, and knots of kids who should have been at school. I suppose, she thought to herself, that includes me.

Nessa walked past it twice. It wasn't a pub like on the telly, no hanging baskets or mirrored windows, no swinging pub sign. It had been remade, painted bright pink and black with a neon sign that glowed pink-red. If it hadn't been for a painted-over plaster relief on the wall that still read The Garland, she'd never have found it. Whispers, it was called now. Like a cut-price West End nightclub beamed down into a shabby corner of the East End. There was loud music inside. Lunchtime disco? Nessa thought that was unlikely. She paused in the doorway to read the name above the door, licensee Edward John McKay—it was the one. She pushed through the double doors.

Inside, the music was deafening. Old disco, the sort her mother liked. The walls were either black or mirrored and the air, thick with tobacco and beer, almost knocked her back. It wasn't dark outside, but inside it could have been night already. It was fairly full: men in suits. No women. There was a space between the tables and a young white girl with a long ponytail coming out from the top of her head was dancing. It was a strange, energetic-yet-bored style of dancing, disco a go-going-nowhere.

'Oi!' Nessa spun round; a man holding a tower of empty glasses was shouting at her. It wasn't Ed McKay. 'Oi, if you're next you can change in the upstairs Ladies!'

'Pardon?' Nessa shouted back but the man had gone.

She looked over at ponytail girl. She was now wearing only a shiny plastic bra, knickers, and suspenders. Nessa felt herself pale. The men were all watching the girl. Holding their pints and sipping and looking so hard as the girl took her bra off Nessa thought they might bore holes in the poor girl's skin. They were ordinary looking men. Men with shiny suits creased up at the back. Nessa stared at one man in particular: he wasn't that old, not decrepit, not grey-haired, just tired. Then she realized the man was staring back and Nessa hurried up the stairs.

The first floor hadn't been renovated. The walls were beige and shiny over textured wallpaper. Brown gloss paint on the stair-rail was thick and shiny as sauce. The carpet was worn in the middle. It was strangely quiet, too, only the thin thump of disco floated up from downstairs. Nessa reached a landing. There were four doors, two marked PRIVATE, one was the Ladies, and one unmarked.

Nessa stepped as quietly as she could to the nearest door and pushed down on the handle. The door opened and Nessa found herself in a large open room with stacks of chairs piled up at one end. She shut the door again and tried another. Cleaning equipment. She was about to try the third when she realized there were voices on the other side and she froze. Strained every bit of hearing.

'So he reckons it'll blow over, I mean the woman's a glorified dressmaker, it's not like there's any comeback. He's sold it to the bill as she's a junkie, well, stands to rights most of that lot are. Yeah, junkies or shirt lifters . . . Yeah, right, I know, he's more upset about his motor, yeah, beautiful, the blue one, yeah. Disappeared off the face of the earth! I know, yeah! That little slapper, yeah, I know, no probs, we think she's still in town, she'll regret it soon enough . . .'

Nessa found she was standing right up against the door. Suddenly there were footsteps coming up the stairs and she bolted for the Ladies. It stank. She put the lid down on one of the seats and sat down to think. It wasn't a cast-iron confession. But she had no doubt the man was talking about Helena and Paula. Perhaps she should have gone into the office. And what? she asked herself, confront him, threaten him? She put her head in her hands. She couldn't think straight at all. She could see her reflection in the mirror over the sink. It was someone else. The girl in the mirror hadn't slept properly and looked as if she could use a shower. She could hear her mother, *Darling, that look just doesn't work*. Nessa pinched her arm to stop herself crying.

Suddenly the toilet door opened and ponytail girl came in carrying a mug half full of pound coins and fifty pences and a pile of clothes. Nessa turned on the tap and splashed her face. The girl put down her clothes on the shut toilet seat and started dressing.

'Bloody hell, that lot are hard work,' she said, slipping on an Arsenal shirt. 'I hardly made enough for a taxi, the shits! If I were you I wouldn't bother, tight as a hen's arse.' She had her jeans on now and she untied her hair. 'Oh, sorry.' She looked Nessa up and down. 'You're not working, are you?'

Nessa shook her head. She felt as if she was seeing into a parallel universe. Like in books, except in books parallel worlds had wizards and magic or space flight or time travel. This world—was it the world Paula had lived in?—this world made her feel sick. They had been talking about Helena and Paula and it was nothing to them. Nothing at all.

Nessa left before ponytail girl had finished talking. She ran all the way down to Old Street where there were more people about. She didn't slow down until she reached the ticket hall of the tube station with its familiar London Transport livery. Nessa felt as if she'd just come back from visiting hell.

By the time Nessa reached Soho the rush hour was just beginning. She found the street with McKay's office quickly and walked past the building twice. She told herself she would go in the third time. And she would have, too, if she hadn't seen someone she recognized walking down the road the other way. She almost shouted and waved, but checked herself and ducked into a fabric shop doorway in time to see Jevonka Steele cross the street and ring the bell to Ed McKay's office.

Nessa couldn't believe it. There was no way out of this. Ed McKay had everything sewn up. Jevonka was working for him too? Beating up Paula was just everyday stuff, was just a kind of normal for him. Not only had he killed Helena, he'd probably got Jevonka to make her sign over everything to him. What if Jevonka had got Helena to sign over the business without her knowing? Nessa could see it: *'Helena, just sign off this order for me'*, and really it's the deeds to the business . . .

That was ridiculous, wasn't it? That didn't happen in real life.

Nessa waited for an hour in the doorway but Jevonka didn't come out. The street filled with people going to and from the theatre to restaurants, laughing and walking fast past the world they didn't want to see. It was nearly dark, Paula might be worrying. No—not worrying. In her room with Mike. Not worrying at all.

On the way back to the hotel on the tube, Nessa tried to clear her mind. But it was no use; her brain felt like soup. On the opposite wall of the carriage was a poem. It went on about candles burning at both ends and Nessa couldn't read it without thinking about Helena; she felt the prickling in her eyes and knew she was going to cry. She got off the tube a stop early so she didn't have to look at it any more.

It was dark now. The streets were empty and smelt of sick and traffic. Nessa walked with a purpose and held her keys inside her hand; if anyone tried to jump her they'd be in for a shock. She turned off the main road and it was even quieter. Somewhere a dog barked, a car passed and swept the street with light. Nessa quickened. She was sure there was someone behind her.

The hotel was in sight now. Nessa felt relief, she took her hand out of her pocket, ready ears strained to listen. But her mind must be playing tricks. There was nothing but the rattle of trains and the traffic on the main road.

Inside the hotel the man behind the desk was watching a football match. The sound was turned up and the crowd was roaring. Someone had just missed a free kick. Nessa went upstairs. Maybe Paula had thought of something. Nessa knocked at her door.

'Who is it?' It was Mike. Nessa sighed. She'd interrupted them again. She heard the key turn and the door opened a crack.

'Mike? It's only me.'

Inside he was packing, stuffing his clothes into his back-pack the way people did on the telly, hurriedly throwing things around.

'What are you doing?' And then she saw his face. Nessa gasped. It was as if the side of his face had been scraped raw. It was red and shiny, weeping slightly.

'Oh my God.'

'I got most of the blood off. Messed up the towels. They threw me out of the car. These men.' His voice was shaking.

'What men? Was it McKay?' Nessa assumed he'd been in the office in Soho.

'I don't bloody know!' He zipped the holdall up; his voice sounded on the edge of tears. 'I've had enough, Nessa. This isn't for me.' He shook his head. 'I was going to New Zealand, I thought Paula might come. Forget it. She's not that kind of girl, is she? They told me exactly what kind of girl she is.' He picked the bag up and winced.

'What happened? Please? Just tell me.'

'Look, she may be used to this but I'm not. She'd dragged me over to that mews again. I told her it was empty. But there were some men there, recognized her, didn't they. Look, if you don't mind me saying, it's her that caused your mum's death, isn't it. She's a tart! She's been on the game!'

'It wasn't like that, Mike.'

'They told me. She didn't even deny it. She's just a slag. Now, if you don't mind.' He arranged his bag on his back and opened the door. 'Jee-sus!'

It was the first time in her life Nessa had ever hit anyone. Her hand stung and she waved it trying to lose the pain. Mike, stunned, sat back down on the bed.

'You idiot! Go home. Go back to bloody Stivenham and shut your eyes. You shit! I told her you were rubbish.' Nessa's voice was so hard Mike's jaw dropped. Nessa turned away from him so he couldn't see she was shaking. 'Piss off. Go on. Piss off.'

Mike didn't move. 'Before I hit you again, all right?' Nessa turned around to face him. She had picked up the bedside lamp and she held it up like a weapon. Mike scurried out of the door. Nessa caught sight of her reflection in the mirror and put her weapon down.

She washed her face in the basin by the bed. She put on some clean clothes and had a drink from the bottle of water Mike had left. Nessa felt cold inside. She knew Mike was talking rubbish, but that was the way a lot of people would see things. A lot of stupid people. She held the bottle up and drank a toast to her mum, to Helena, for being different. They could have taken Paula anywhere, Nessa thought, the pub, the office, the warehouse, somewhere else. It would take a lot of taxi fares to find her. But she would. However long it took. No messing around now.

Nessa thought it was a relief to get back outside. The night air was cold and sharp and the orange street lights dazzled against the navy blue sky. In her jeans pocket she had a roll of twenty pound notes. In her inside jacket pocket, still wrapped in the Argyll sock, she had the gun. As Nessa walked quickly down the street towards the main road she felt it thump heavily against her chest, like a hard external heart.

Lauren Now

Lauren had only been to Ian's once. Actually no, she'd never been inside. Only outside, waiting. It seemed a nice enough flat. It was part of the converted vicarage on the road to town. They'd said nothing in the car. Lauren had sat in the back with her knees drawn up to her chest, watching Nessa's eyes for madness in her reflection in the rear-view mirror.

Ian went into the kitchen and turned the central heating on. It felt cold, as if the flat had been empty all day. She'd expected pictures of trees—the elm, mountain ash, Douglas fir—isn't that what tree surgeons would have? But Ian's walls had photographs, stone and air, pictures of space. Lauren hugged herself. Nessa tried to smile but Lauren could see she was struggling.

'So what is this?' Lauren sat down on the big worn sofa. Ian's geriatric dog Carrie roused from sleep in the kitchen and waddled up to meet them. Nessa had her hand up to her mouth as if she was afraid of what might come out. This must be something big to put the wind up Nessa like this. 'Is this to do with my mum—with Paula?'

Nessa sat down opposite Lauren and sort of shook her head for yes. 'Give me a minute, love, I have to get it straight in my head. I have to make it sound real and not like something you see on the TV.'

Ian came back from the kitchen and sat next to Nessa. He took her hand and Lauren suddenly wished he wasn't here. She wanted Nessa for herself. Nessa must have felt it too because she shook him away. They were alone. The only sound was the dog breathing and the water in the kettle gearing itself up to boil.

'You know most of it,' Nessa started. 'You know about Paula dying when she did and leaving you to me. You know about us driving out of town in McKay's car, trying to run away, coming back to London and Paula getting caught. You know we were friends. Good friends. Most of the time. You know she was inside, in jail, when you were born.' Nessa shuddered. Lauren nodded. 'The thing is, Lauren . . .'

'Yeah?'

'There's lots I haven't said.' She put her hand up to quiet Lauren. 'Most of it doesn't seem real; some of it, well, it wouldn't have done any good, the whole story's too messy, too stupid. So much happened. Helena, my mum, I never told you everything about that. But this is about Paula.' She turned her hands over and over in her lap. 'It was my fault she ended up in prison. She should never have been inside.'

'What?'

'Listen. Please, listen.' Nessa shut her eyes. She breathed in a long shuddery breath. Lauren made to speak but Nessa stopped her. 'I have to get this out. Just let me speak. I went after Ed McKay with a gun. His gun, it was. I shot him with his own gun.'

'You?'

'I shot him. Missed, of course, nearly dislocated my shoulder when it kicked back. I shot him right through

210

his bespoke hand-made shoes. And the worst thing is I could've done it properly. He was there, arms out, *go on, do it*, he goes, like I was a kid and I wouldn't, and of course he was right. I couldn't. They'd already ruined Paula's face by then, sent her nose sliding west across her face, knocked most of her teeth out—she was getting some work done in prison, you know, they could have sorted that out. But not her face. He was a nasty man, he knew what would kill her.'

'But, Nessa, I don't care if you shot anyone, well, not McKay.'

'Haven't finished.' Nessa breathed in again and spoke quickly. 'Just listen. It was above Whispers, his pub, in the function room. I'd been all over London that night looking and they were only in the pub. Upstairs in the pub!

'Anyway, upstairs wasn't clubby at all. Just pubby. The door said "private". Inside there was this man standing over her, over Paula, and he'd hit her. Blood was everywhere and these little white things on the floor, they were her teeth. Her teeth! McKay was sitting down watching. Just sitting in a chair like it was normal, like it was life, wearing his expensive coat and smoking.' Nessa wiped her face.

'See, when I shot him, when I missed him, it was almost exactly what they wanted. Poor little rich girl mad with grief goes over the edge and shoots East End businessman.'

'He wasn't a businessman!'

'I know that, love.' Nessa started again. 'As I was saying, the man who'd been hitting Paula stepped forward. I thought he was going to hit me. He wasn't wearing a jacket and his sleeves were rolled up. There were tiny polka dots of blood on the white material, I can still remember it. I pointed the gun around, you know, from him to McKay, two handed, just like on telly. McKay got up, slow, calm. He wasn't a big man but he knew how to hold himself to make you feel really small. He tells the other man to go. I shout "Don't move!" like that. Click off the safety catch the way I practised. He laughs. Paula is crying. Really quietly. I could tell even with the thump of the music coming through the ceiling. And snuffling like her nose was full of blood and snot. And there was this smell. The smell of the beer and smoke coming up from downstairs, McKay's aftershave, thick and choking, and cutting through it this high, sort of sweet smell. I think it was the blood.'

Lauren squeezed Nessa's hand.

'McKay stood up, dared me to shoot him. And I did. But I was crying too. It went through his shoe. Lace-ups, I remember, not slip-ons. And it was weird, you wouldn't believe it, seeing McKay hopping around, swearing like he'd invented it, and the guy who'd been hitting Paula was trying not to laugh. "My Lobbs!" McKay went. He was looking at his shoes. "Hand made! The kid's a nutter! Oi! Girl? Are you wanting to go the same way as your mother?" He was furious. Then he saw the other man trying not to laugh and he was too. Burst out of him, a deep laugh. Then they were both laughing. Looking at me, at the hole in the shoe, I can still see that. I couldn't believe it. As big as one of those old pennies. They just laughed.

'I moved. I was fast. I took Paula's hand and tried to get her to run. They were laughing! We went over the roof, into a builder's yard, I couldn't look at her face. I wanted to take her to casualty—she shook her head, wouldn't speak. We climbed through the chain link out of the yard into a tight cobbled street. It was dark and the cobbles shone, everything sparkled in the rain. And just when our eyes were getting used to it a light came on, like suddenly the night had flashed past and it was day, only it wasn't. It was police. They had a couple of cars there already. So quick! Paula sat down. I tried to get her up. I'd never seen her like that, no fight in her, nothing. I was petrified. I was. I'd never been that scared. When the police cars came up the street, slowly over the cobbles, I thought I was going to shit myself.

'Paula must have been more together than I thought. She burrowed her hand into my pocket, uncurled my fingers from round the gun. I was holding it so tight! First, I thought she was clinging on to me. Then I realized, well, I thought I realized, she was trying to get rid of the gun. So I let her take it. She never said what she was going to do. I didn't realize. I didn't think. I suppose I kept thinking we'd get out of it somehow like the other time, in the car. The policemen got out of the cars in slow motion and I just stood up with my hands in the air like on westerns. And the police took us away. In different cars.'

''S all right, Ness. Look, I know it was horrible. But what does this have to do with now? Why did we have to run away?'

Nessa pulled her hand away. 'Lauren, don't you understand? Paula went down for me. *She* took the gun! *She* let me off. It should have been me inside, not her. Don't you see? Paula should never have gone to prison. She'd done nothing. It had all been done *to* her.'

Lauren looked at Nessa.

'Paula went to prison and I didn't! She protected me, Lauren. She took the gun out of my hand, and took it away. I told the police it was me over and over, honestly I did, but they never believed me. They thought Paula had corrupted me, they thought they knew what she was. One time, I tried to talk to the brief—lawyer—they'd set up for her. He was so busy he couldn't care less. I kept telling him, I kept on at him, she did it in self defence! But that didn't fit their script. She had a record, she'd been on enough at-risk registers to paper the walls. They took one look at her and thought, prison fodder. She was right. I didn't know how lucky I was.'

Lauren sat still and alone. Nessa's face was like a theatrical mask for tragedy, all pulled down and grim with small sad eyes.

'I don't understand, Nessa. If you told the police why didn't they believe you? If you said it loud enough or clear enough, they would have believed you. Didn't McKay tell the police what happened?'

Nessa was shaking her head. Her voice came out very quiet. 'I tried. I tried and tried. Even after you were born. Even after Paula was dead. I wrote letters, so many letters. McKay vanished—he went to Northern Cyprus. He came back a few years ago and served three years for fraud. Financial irregularities. They've never got anything big on him. Not ever. McKay wanted to hurt Paula any way he could. He put her inside. And I couldn't have stopped it.'

'I don't believe it.' Lauren pulled her hand away from Nessa's. 'I can't believe you let her down. You let her down. She wouldn't have killed herself if she hadn't been inside.'

Lauren could feel the pain rising inside her. She looked

at Nessa, pink eyed, face shiny with tears. She looked at her hands knotted together in her lap and then at Ian, hovering in the kitchen doorway, pretending not to listen.

'Lauren, I'm so sorry. That's just half of it. That's only the start.' Nessa shifted on the sofa. 'We have to get away.'

Nessa put her hand out to touch Lauren's hair. Lauren veered away.

Lauren felt the tears coming and held them back. She wanted to get out of here now. Go—go where? Home, away, anywhere. She stood up. Picked up her jacket.

'I have to have a walk, get some air. Have a think,' she said, keeping her voice as reasonable and measured as she could. She wanted to scream. She couldn't think at all because her brain seemed to have reduced down to mush.

'Lauren, don't be long, please. I haven't finished, there's more, there's other stuff. I don't want you wandering around. It's not safe.'

Lauren turned as she reached the door.

'No. No more "stuff", Nessa, not now. And this is Stivenham, nothing's going to happen to me, is it?' Lauren walked quietly out of the house into the night. She was aware of Nessa calling after her, an edge of hysteria in her voice, and Ian holding her back, calming her down.

Lauren folded her arms across her body and started walking, not stopping, looking down at the segment of pavement directly in front of her feet. It was quiet. In the dark an aeroplane broke through the cloud above, traffic passed somewhere unseen, and on the other side of town a train pulled out of the station. Lauren felt down in her pocket. There, rolled up against the seam was a note—a fiver, a tenner? She couldn't tell what it was by touch and she didn't bother looking; however much she had on her she was going to need more.

Lauren walked past houses with lights on and curtains drawn, past snatches of sounds, TV, music, a door banging. She felt as if she'd fallen down between the cracks. In another life—someone else's, perhaps—she had thought she was on the way to being a model, to having a way out of thinking about life. Now she couldn't escape thinking about Paula and Nessa; everything was wrong, the way she'd imagined them, the people she thought they were. She put her head down and walked as fast as she could.

Outside the house everything looked the same. The chip shop across the green was lit up and open. A girl Lauren recognized from school walked past and smiled. Nessa must be mad, Lauren thought. The house was fine. There weren't cars with blacked out windows full of men in too-small suits waiting for them. It had to be some guilt thing. Lauren felt in her back pocket for the keys.

'Lauren.'

Lauren jumped. The keys fell out of her shaking hand and onto the step.

'Chloe! My God!'

Chloe was behind her on the pavement holding a bag of chips. 'You're white as a sheet! I never meant to scare you . . . Lauren?'

Lauren picked up the keys and opened the door. She thought that if she looked at Chloe she would start crying.

'Are you all right? Was it Mum? She was furious! Had me and Jack wiping down her precious leaflets, said you'd binned them. Did she have a go?'

Lauren shook her head.

216

'I don't blame you, though. I wish I'd thought of dumping them. The woman's obsessed.'

'I'm all right, Chlo,' Lauren said keeping her voice still. Lauren smelt the warm chip smell and listened as Chloe went on about Lucy and Lucy's new boyfriend, Tom, and how Lucy had fixed her up with Tom's mate to go to the cinema and how his breath smelt of cigarettes when she kissed him and now she wished she hadn't because in the daylight he had more spots than skin and . . .

Lauren stood in the doorway. She almost started talking over her about Nessa and Paula but listening to Chloe, plugged into real life, it sounded all too ridiculous.

'You're sure you're OK then?' Chloe asked.

Lauren looked at her. Old Chloe would have seen she wasn't. Chloe held out her bag of chips. Lauren shook her head.

'Your loss! Lucy asked me over but Tom's there and I'll be in the way.'

Lauren watched her go; she almost shouted after her, but kept her mouth shut and closed the front door behind her. In the dark of the hall the red answer-machine light flickered anxiously on and off. She had made up her mind. She'd pick up the twenty-pound note in her bedroom and go to Luke's. Just for a few days. If Luke wouldn't let her stay maybe Minty would. Just to get out of the way, just to let Nessa know how pissed off she was.

Lauren went up the stairs without turning the light on and went into the bathroom. She sat down on the loo seat and relaxed. Shut her eyes. Nessa wouldn't really have let Paula down? All those stories about best mates, all those tales of two girls against the world? Lauren pulled the flush and remembered that Rain were selling her as the new English Rose. Lauren looked at her face in the mirror over the sink. 'English Rose, my arse!' she said aloud. Her skin was paler than anyone she'd ever met but did that mean she was English? Hybrid Tea, perhaps.

Lauren looked hard at her face. There was one thing she wanted to ask Nessa. She had asked her once, after a barbecue at Chloe's. Watching Chloe's dad flip burgers. Nessa had said she didn't know. She'd said Paula had never told her who it was. Lauren had accepted it at the time, but maybe Nessa just didn't want to say. There were tests. Lauren had read about it, DNA, blood. Surely Nessa could have found out if she'd wanted to?

'Bitch,' Lauren said aloud.

Outside a car door slammed, loud and sharp, and then another. Like two full stops. Too loud and too quick to be customers for the chippy. Or Mrs Mullan's visitors. Lauren turned the landing light off and looked out of her bedroom window.

Her heart thumped tiny pattering mouse-like beats that made it hard to breathe. Two men had wandered off some TV film—she could tell, how? The way they moved, their expensive casual clothes, not suits, and glasses. Sunglasses? At night? Lauren watched one man fold his and put them in his trouser pocket, she could almost hear the noise they'd make if he sat down on them.

They didn't know where they were, they looked up and down to check their bearings. But Lauren knew they were coming here. Nessa wasn't mad. She may have let Paula down but she wasn't mad. Lauren slid herself under the bed. It smelt of dust. She screwed up her eyes as if she could magic herself away, as if she was a five year old playing games. Lauren heard the faint crack of splintering wood as the front door gave way and they came inside. She heard them swear, heavy London swearing, as they tripped over the pile of shoes in the hall. She didn't hear them come up the stairs. Perhaps if she stayed completely still they'd go away again. She thought she'd sneeze. Nothing happened. Maybe they were just burglars. Ordinary burglars. She listened hard. Nothing. She held herself still for what seemed like hours. Hours and hours.

Slowly she uncurled her legs, then she rolled over. It was going to be all right. They must have gone by now. Phone, money, Luke. Maybe it was a bit late now, but she didn't fancy staying here, not with the door all bust up.

Then a hard, bright light was on her face and a hand closed tight as a vice around her ankle and suddenly Lauren couldn't breathe at all.

Nessa Now

Nessa splashed her face with cold water and looked at her reflection in the mirror over the bathroom basin. Her eyes were red around the rim but otherwise it was the same face. Twice the age she'd been when this had all started, but she didn't feel older, didn't feel grown-up, just felt tired. Had she ever been an adult? She had thought she was when she was sixteen, but what made an adult? Someone who took risks, or the woman she'd become, chugging along in the music library?

Nessa towelled her face dry. She had no choices now. The past was all rushing back and if she did nothing what would happen? What if Lauren didn't come back? What had the woman on the phone said? *'You must stop harassing my client.'*

What did McKay think she'd been doing? Nessa looked herself in the eye. She had to find Lauren, explain properly, explain how something had snapped inside Paula, must have done, and that Ed McKay had killed both their mothers.

Nessa sighed. She knew she shouldn't have let her out of the house. Ian had talked to her, told her it would be all right. But it wasn't. Nessa looked at her watch. Lauren had been gone two hours. Ian had no idea. This wasn't Ian's real, ordinary world. Ian's normal encompassed bark diseases and root rot and dealing with difficult trees. His normal didn't run to gangland violence and murder. Ian said she should wait. She'd phoned Chloe and Luke and still he said wait. Then they had shouted at each other. Loud shouting like a TV soap. Nessa hadn't felt so alone for a long time. She breathed a couple of deep breaths, trying to make herself stronger, and felt for her car keys in her pocket. She walked through the sitting room and out of the flat.

Stivenham at night was dead quiet. Nessa put her headlights on dip and drove home. All the lights in all the houses were off. She parked the car away from the house and sat still for a minute. She knew something bad had happened, she knew she would find out in a little while. She got out of the car.

In the dark Nessa could hear the sea coming and going along the beach. Her footsteps sounded terribly loud and her lips felt dry in the salt wind.

She could see the front door was open. Not so much wide open as not shut. A crack of a different darkness at the side. If Nessa had been watching herself on the telly she'd have shouted at the screen, 'Don't go in there!'—it was asking for trouble. But Lauren had vanished. Where else was there? Nessa closed her hand around her phone. Should she call the police? That was what you did when people went missing or your house was broken into. But the phone call earlier had told her this wasn't ordinary life. The woman had said she was Ed McKay's PA. Paula would have killed herself laughing. 'PA? That's a new name for it!' Nessa locked the car door and crossed the road.

She stood on the threshold of the house then stepped inside. She stood still in the hall and tried to listen. 'Lauren?' she whispered. Nothing. The house was empty.

The answer-machine flashed its red light like a tiny beacon.

For a long minute Nessa stood rooted to the ground. She pictured Lauren lying out on the floor upstairs looking like she was asleep but not asleep. Then what if she was only, truly, asleep? But the door, the wood, was splintered and cracked; it had been forced.

She went upstairs treading on the edge of the steps so they didn't creak, just like she had when Lauren was a baby. Upstairs. The curtains were open and the yellow light came in from the street. Lauren's bedroom door was open. Nessa looked inside.

It felt as if the air had been kicked out of her chest. Nessa staggered and put out her arm to steady herself against the wall. Lauren's bed was turned over. Completely turned over. Nessa gritted her teeth and prodded the duvet with her foot. But there was nothing there. Nessa closed her eyes and turned away. Lauren was gone.

She ran out of the house and sat in the car. She almost called the police again but stopped herself. She left a long message on Ian's voicemail, trying to explain what she was going to do, even though she had to admit she wasn't too clear herself.

'Ian? I'm going to London. I don't know where Lauren is but I can imagine. Ian, McKay thinks I've got something on him but I haven't. The PA said something about proof, about handing it over, but I don't know what she's on about. Please, Ian, I know this sounds like something on TV to you, but it's not, this is all real. I'm going to London. I know she's there somewhere. I'm not calling the police yet. They won't find her before me. And McKay might hurt her. He might hurt her.'

Nessa bit her lip and clicked the phone off. She held

the steering wheel in both hands and wept. 'Sorry, Paula; sorry, Paula, I'm so sorry.' She opened her eyes, almost expecting an angry ghost, but there was nothing. Just the orange brown light of the village at night and the murmuring of the sea. Lauren wasn't here. Nessa wiped her eyes. She picked up the phone and called Luke again, but there was only a message. Nessa held herself together and as calmly and as evenly as she could asked Luke to get in touch if he heard from Lauren.

'Please, if you hear anything.' She could hear her own desperation. Nessa breathed deeply and sat up. What did McKay want now, after all these years; hadn't he taken enough?

She put the car key into the lock and twisted it. The engine turned over and Nessa drove away. She turned the radio on and stabbed at the buttons . . . the fishing news, a boy band, a choir singing madrigals. Nessa turned it off again. Her mind was racing. What if Lauren had got in touch with McKay? After all, she'd kicked off this modelling thing, how did she know what else was going on in Lauren's life? What if—the thought made her insides rollercoaster—what if she'd written to him, what if she thought he was her father? Nessa had to brake suddenly and the phone shot off the car seat and into the footwell under the dashboard. A red light at an empty junction. Nessa's hands were sweaty on the wheel.

What if he *was* her father? When she had found out Paula was pregnant Nessa had made charts, tried to work backwards and forwards to see if she could work out if Lauren was Mike's. The dates didn't fit. Maybe something had happened with Ed in the pub, that last night? Nessa felt suddenly sick and sweaty, she pulled over onto the hard shoulder of the motorway and waited for her heart rate to slow to normal.

*   *   *

It was three whole months before Nessa saw Paula again. By then Paula was in a Young Offenders' unit outside London and when Nessa visited she could see Paula was at least five months gone. Every visit she asked who the father was but Paula wouldn't tell, even after Lauren was born. 'Don't ask, Ness. I never ever want to think about it. All right?' she said and stared hard at Nessa.

The baby was beautiful, and as Paula said, 'She is mine, the one thing that's mine in the world, Ness. No one else's. Ever.'

Paula held Lauren close and hugged her tight but she wouldn't tell. Even the last time, when Nessa took Lauren home for the weekend. Lauren was seven months old and babies couldn't stay with their mothers after eight months. Paula made her promise she'd take her, be her guardian—she'd sorted the forms out in prison, and it was only until the sentence finished, only a few more months. She made Nessa promise to stay in Stivenham with her.

'Bring her up in the country, by the sea.'

'They'll let you out in three months, you said. And you said Stivenham was a dump.'

'That was different. I wasn't thinking like a mother, was I?'

'What am I going to do there?'

'I dunno, but the air's clean, it's fresh, not like London.'

'Suppose so.'

'You promise, treat her right, Nessa.'

'Of course I will.'

'I know you will, you love her too, don't you? I mean, what's

not to love?' Paula held Lauren up and she smiled. Nessa put
out her arms and took the baby.

Nessa held her close. 'It's not rocket science.' She nuzzled her
face into the baby's neck and smelt talc. Paula watched and smiled.

'I know you'll do, Auntie Ness. Now give us her back, Ness,
just for a sec, just to say goodbye.'

'Course.' Nessa handed her over. 'Anyway, Paula, like I was
saying, you've still not told me who the dad is. Was it Mike? Is
that why you want me to take her to Stivenham?'

'Mike? Are you mad? He's nothing to do with it!' Lauren wrig-
gled in her lap and Paula started singing some pop song Nessa
half recognized; she sang it breathily, quietly. Nessa leant forward
across the table in the prison visiting room.

'Was it one of your . . . you know . . . clients?'

Paula didn't take her eyes off Lauren for a second. She just
kept on singing.

'Paula! Listen!'

'Ness, it doesn't matter. Look at her, look! She's gorgeous, she's
so new. She's perfect.' Paula stopped, looked into Nessa's eyes.
'She doesn't live in that world. She doesn't have anything to do
with them people. Any of them. Right? Take her into your world,
give her that. Make her lucky, yeah.'

'Yeah.'

Nessa looked from the baby to Paula. The baby waved its tiny
hands.

'Look at her, Nessa, look at her fingers.' Paula kissed them
one by one. 'I don't want that for her, none of that. Promise you
won't let me down?'

'Promise.'

*   *   *

226

On the far side of the motorway a double-sized articulated lorry rumbled east. There was no other traffic. Nessa picked the phone off the floor of the car and checked for messages. Nothing. Then she turned the car key and pulled out across the motorway into the fast lane.

Lauren Then

The smell was disinfectant. Hard and germ-free but sort of lemony. And there was noise, sounds that bounced off hard walls. Keys, of course, and babies crying. Laughing, singing; doors, locking, unlocking, locking. And my mum talking to me, whispering close in my ears, telling me stuff, all sorts of stuff. She smells of cocoa butter, sweet and creamy, she says, 'She'll look after you, Auntie Nessa. You'll have a home and she'll be cool, you'll see. She's a laugh, yeah. You'll be better off with her. It'll work out this way, honest.'

A kiss. I feel it on my forehead, a cigarette-flavoured kiss that makes me turn away first. But then I smile because I like the feel of it and I want it again. A lip-soft, skin-soft kiss, and her arms around me closing around me so I smile more. Then she speaks again, 'Gotta go, later, yeah. Be good.' And I shut my eyes tight.

Next time I open them I know the air is different. Salt and cold, stinging my eyes. The light is so hard grey-white I keep my eyes half shut. The air slices past my lips and they are hard and dry. The kiss on my cheek is salty, too, and I forget the smell of cocoa butter for lavender and soap.

And this voice is half singing, half crying. I want to tell her not to cry, but I can't make the words with my mouth. I wave my hands and smile. And in the end—is it a week, a month? I can't tell if it's years or hours—she stops.

Lauren Now

Lauren opened her eyes. She'd never had dreams like that before. So vivid, colours and smells and everything. Perhaps there had been something in the water she'd been given last night. She turned over and realized her whole body ached. Her head throbbed; her mouth felt bristly as a doormat and tasted of metal. She sat up slowly and opened her eyes; perhaps the whole kidnapping thing had been some kind of dream too. A dream that started with Nessa responsible for Paula's death and ended with what?—abduction? No, she had the bruises and the marks on her wrist where they'd tied her in the car.

What did they want from her? Or was this more to do with Nessa, the phone call, the other 'stuff' she'd promised to tell? Lauren cursed herself for walking out, cursed herself for not listening to Nessa.

Of course it wasn't a dream. This place was real, wherever she was. Outside she could hear what sounded like children singing, a playground, but she couldn't see it. There was traffic noise, heavy traffic, buses and lorries, but there was no sign of that outside the window either, just a small Hollywood-London mews street. Pastel-coloured toy-town houses with square windows and neat front doors. She looked hard, trying to commit it all to memory, imagining herself on *Crimewatch* being congratulated on escaping and being brave under pressure. Except, of course, at the moment she didn't feel brave at all.

It had to do with McKay, it must do. She remembered Nessa after the phone call white as a sheet and shaking. And what had Luke said? *The man's a nutter.*

Was this his house?

The room was small, just big enough for a three-quarter-sized bed, but it was clean and the walls were dazzlingly white. A comfortable cell. She looked out over the little cobbled street. Was anyone looking for her? She felt for her phone, but they must have been through her pockets. What if she never saw Nessa again? Lauren sniffed back the tears and told herself not to be so pathetic.

Down in the street below two black-veiled women glided past and out of sight. From a house across the road a brown-haired woman in a grey tracksuit locked the door as she jogged. Lauren banged on the window. The double-glazing muffled the sound. She banged harder, took off a shoe and banged with that; then the woman looked up for a second and Lauren waved at her—maybe too man-ically—because she turned and jogged away. Lauren watched the jogger go, head down, taking no notice. God, people in London were useless! Lauren screamed at the top of her voice but she didn't look round. The jogging woman ran out of sight and Lauren's heart sank. Walking back towards the house were the men she'd met last night. They carried takeaway coffees and sandwich bags and smoked as they walked. As Lauren watched, a large saloon car with dark-tinted windows pulled up alongside them. The men looked nervous and threw their cigarettes down as if they were Year Eights caught by the Head smoking at the bus stop. The car door opened and a man got out of the back seat. He stood up and smoothed his trousers down. He smiled up at the house and Lauren pulled back from the window. She slid to the floor. Her head throbbed louder. She knew the man from the book jacket. It was Ed McKay. And right now he was downstairs.

Nessa Now

Nessa got to London at around four-thirty in the morning. She went to the twenty-four-hour bagel shop at the top end of Brick Lane and bought a dozen hot rolls. But she couldn't eat any. She parked her car opposite the Finers' house and waited for any signs of life. The smell of the bagels and the steam fugged up the inside of her car and even with the radio turned up she couldn't stop her mind racing. More than anything she wanted Lauren to be in there behind that brick wall, angry with her, furious, but safe. If she wasn't what was she going to do?

At seven fifteen the hall light winked on and Nessa leapt out of the car and knocked hard.

'I've brought you bagels.'

Luke answered the door in a T-shirt and boxers. 'Morning.'

Nessa nodded. 'Vanessa Harper, Lauren's guardian, you remember?' Luke opened the door wider. Nessa realized she must look like a mad woman to him, excited hair and no sleep.

'Could I come in? Have you heard anything? From Lauren? She's not here? She's vanished. Have you checked your mobile?'

Luke let her in and Nessa put the bag of bagels down on the kitchen table.

Luke hadn't heard anything, he said, and Nessa had to go to the loo and cry where no one could see. Judy eventually talked her out and sat her down with a hot cup of tea.

'I think this is a matter for the police, Vanessa.' Judy pulled her coat on and picked up her bag. Her hair was brushed back and she looked normal. Nessa realized that next to her she looked like a bag-lady, like a madwoman. She felt powerless. She felt like a sixteen year old all over again.

'Look, Vanessa, you finish your tea. Luke will look after you for a minute. But, Luke, you're off to college in . . .' She looked at her watch. '. . . half an hour. Call the police if she's gone missing, but check her friends first, she could be anywhere. Believe me, I do know what it's like. Clare gave me hell for two years at least. I've got to get to work, third year ceramicists.' She put her hand over Nessa's briefly. 'I'm sorry I can't do more. Let us know as soon as you find her.'

The front door banged shut and Nessa was left on her own in the kitchen with Luke. Nessa sniffed and rubbed her eyes.

'Sorry, Luke. Lauren'll kill me for bothering you.'

'I will let you know, yeah, if she turns up.'

'I know.'

'She probably went round one of her mates' houses or something.'

'Yeah probably. You know Lauren, loads of mates.' They looked at each other and Nessa could see he was thinking what she was thinking.

'And she wouldn't have wanted to stick around at home

236

when there'd just been a break in, now would she?' Nessa
went on.

'Your house has been broken into? Last night? I don't
understand. I know you reckon the police might be hostile
but maybe you should call them, yeah.'

Suddenly Nessa's phone rang. Nessa picked it out of her
pocket, handling it like a hot potato, almost dropping it in
her haste to answer.

'Hello! Hello?' Nessa couldn't believe her ears, 'Jevonka?
Jevonka Steele? You're in London?' Jevonka sounded as
wired as Nessa felt. She sounded exactly the same as all
those years ago, businesslike, American.

'Vanessa, thank God I've found you, you haven't been
at home.'

'No, it's difficult . . .'

'I know, I know. Listen, I know what he wants, what
McKay wants. He thinks you're the one with the proof.'

'What proof? What proof are you on about? Are you
in this with McKay? Have you got Lauren?'

'Of course not! He has. Meet me. We're finishing this
now. We can do it together, Nessa. I'll see you in town.
At Patisserie Valerie's in Soho?'

'Yes, when?'

'Eleven thirty.'

'Eleven thirty. I'll be there.' Nessa clicked her phone off.
Nessa got up. She could see Luke looking at her the
same way Judy had looked at her before she'd left for
work, as if he was sure she was a total nutter too. Nessa
felt her nerves jangling. Jevonka Steele in London. The
last time Nessa had seen her it was going into McKay's
office. Oh, she'd seen her in the papers since; well, read

her name anyway. Jevonka had worked her way to the top in New York working for the biggest names in American fashion. What was she doing here, whose side was she on? Nessa supposed she'd find out.

'I'm sorry for . . . for making such a fool of myself.' Nessa drained her tea cup.

''S all right.' Luke was watching her. 'Are you sure you're OK? Was that call about Lauren?'

Nessa nodded. 'You wouldn't believe me if I tried to explain.'

'Maybe I would,' Luke said. 'Try me.'

Nessa shook her head. 'It'd take too long. I need to find Lauren. Just promise to let me know if she calls.' She scribbled the number down on a piece of paper. Luke picked it up and walked with her to the front door.

'You sure I can't help? I could be useful, you know.'

Nessa smiled at him. Maybe he didn't think she was so mad now. And Nessa felt better, she had something to go on, she was in a hurry to leave.

'I'll find her, Luke, don't worry.' Nessa stepped out into the street and Luke closed the door behind her. She raked a hand through her hair and crossed the road towards her car. It wasn't until she had crossed the road that she registered the triangular yellow shoe around the back tyre. She'd been clamped.

Lauren Now

'L auren? Is it? Of course! Even prettier than the pictures!' The door was open and the man was smiling at her. Who did he think it would be? Lauren thought to herself; he'd kidnapped her, he'd brought her here. He didn't look like a kidnapper though. His suit was expensive, and he wore what could easily have been a cashmere polo-neck underneath. He put out his hand; it was big and wide. As his jacket moved Lauren smelt some aftershave, vaguely woody and citrussy. His eyes were grey and steely and his skin was tanned and leathery. Luke had said he'd been in Northern Cyprus again, recuperating after his time inside and finishing his book. Lauren shook his hand automatically and he held hers firm and tight.

'Sorry about the lads. Jesus, you'd think people could be a little more considerate. You're feeling all right now though, yeah? Good. Hungry? Come down, I think they're trained well enough to do breakfast.' He shook his head. 'I didn't want it to be like this, you know, our first meeting.'

Lauren felt like a rabbit trapped in a particularly bright light. She had never met anyone famous but she was sure this is what it would feel like. He was still shaking her hand and he looked her up and down quite openly.

'You're the stamp of your mother, you know that?' He

239

went on without waiting for an answer, 'I know your face; well, there's some differences, and you look like you grew up under a pot, you're so pale! But look at you, she didn't half spit you out, didn't she!'

Lauren didn't know what to say. Only yesterday, last night, Nessa had said she'd gone after this man with a gun. And shot him. She glanced down at his shoes. Of course they were intact. What did she expect? The man would wear fifteen-year-old bullet-holed shoes?

'Come on, babe, me an' you have got some catching up to do.'

He called her babe. Lauren didn't know what else to do so she followed him downstairs. There was no sign of a limp. His foot seemed fine. Maybe Nessa had never shot him at all. After all, she'd believed Nessa for fifteen years but now it seemed that some of it—most of it?—was lies.

Just when she had her situation sorted—kidnapped by evil gangster—it had changed again. Maybe he wasn't so evil, maybe he wanted something else. He didn't seem so bad. And breakfast smelt good. Lauren realized she was starving and she followed the smell of croissants and coffee downstairs.

Ed McKay pulled a chair out for her to sit down; the two henchmen had disappeared and Lauren was grateful for that. She did think of making a dash for the door, but that could wait, there were pains aux chocolat and almond croissants and cappuccinos with proper grated chocolate flakes. She'd eat first.

'I'd been looking everywhere for you, babes.' He was very smooth, very charming. What had Lauren expected? Some kind of Dick Dastardly made flesh? The man didn't seem threatening, more like a larger sized Bob Hoskins. He twinkled.

'What, you've been watching me?'

'Not like that, don't get me wrong. When I saw those photos, you could have knocked me down with a feather. I'd been looking on and off for years, an' there you were looking at me, gorgeous! Quite the up and coming. Beautiful! Your mum'd be so proud.'

Lauren wiped her mouth. 'She would?'

'Too right, she was never in your sort of league, Paula.'

Lauren had meant to ask how he knew about the photos—as far as she knew they weren't published yet—but she wanted to ask more about Paula. She wiped her mouth.

'Did you know her well?'

Ed McKay smiled broadly. 'More than most, love, and in the biblical sense, of course.'

'Excuse me?'

Ed ignored the question. 'She lived here, you know, a year and a bit, she lived right here. She was one special girl, your mother. One in a million. She loved this house, too, loved living here, she did.'

'She lived here? In this house? Was she doing modelling when she was here?'

'Yeah, but like I said, it was different for her, you know, she never had the really high class look, your mother, too exotic, ahead of her time. I told her, I said she should have stuck to what she knew best.'

'And what was that then?'

Ed coughed. 'Hospitality. That was what your mother excelled at.'

'Hospitality?'

'Yeah, you know, standing around looking gorgeous, being hospitable.' McKay smiled and dabbed his mouth with a napkin. He looked at her, stared right at her. It wasn't like having your picture taken, not that kind of attention, Lauren had almost got used to that. No, this was different, he looked so hard she felt it all over, and Lauren couldn't help blushing.

'Nessa, Vanessa, Vanessa Harper, my guardian, she said Paula could have been a brilliant model.'

'Yeah, well, she was wrong about a lot of things, that one. Vanessa Harper? Short girl, thighs like a shot putter, turned your mother's head. Now, I'm not being rude or nothing, but what does a Doris like Vanessa Harper know about looking good? The girl was off her head. I reckon she had no friends, you know, latched on to Paula. Always wanted to come round, hang about. Paula was always having to put her off.' He laughed.

Lauren put her croissant down. 'What did you call her? A doris?'

'Ain't you heard the word, love? Doris, someone who's been touched by the ugly stick? Come on, I'm not telling you anything you don't know. Or did she save up and have plastic surgery?' He laughed some more and Lauren shifted in her seat. It was one thing for Lauren to slag off Nessa herself, but she didn't like to hear other people doing it.

'Sorry, Lauren. But you can't blame me if I don't warm to Vanessa Harper, now can you? Did she tell you? Did she? About my foot? Hmm?' He looked away. 'Anyway, that was years ago. I'm not a man to hold a grudge, life's too short! I don't want to be talking about her. You know what I think?' He leant back in his chair. 'I think your mother would still be alive if it wasn't for that woman. I know it was a shock, last night, but you know Vanessa Harper, she'd never have let you even talk to me.'

Lauren sipped her coffee. He was right, she wouldn't.

'So, let's not mention her, not even talk about her.' He dabbed his mouth again. 'I'm not interested in her. I just want to know about you, all about you, yeah.' He put his hand across the table and took hers. Lauren resisted pulling it away quickly. 'I know who you are.' He leant forward and Lauren smelt his aftershave over her coffee. His voice was low, almost whispered. 'I know everything about you, I know because you're mine. We're blood, flesh and blood. That woman stole you away, but you don't have to go back. Not if you don't want to.'

Lauren looked down at her plate. Her heart was thumping and the crumbs of croissant suddenly felt like sawdust in her mouth. She stared hard at the crumbs, half expecting them to rearrange themselves into some kind of message.

'Are you my dad?' was all she could manage.

'Looks like it, babe, looks well like it.' He rubbed the back of her hand with his large white thumb. Lauren noticed the fingernail was bitten down below the quick and she felt a sudden rush of sickness.

'I think I might just have a lie down.' She stood up.

Ed McKay smiled. 'You do that, babes, you do that. But hold up a minute.' He was patting his pockets, looking for something. He pulled out Lauren's phone and passed it to her across the table. 'The boys said it fell out of your pocket in the car. You've probably been going frantic looking for it. I know what girls your age are like, you live with it welded to your ears near enough.'

Lauren was dumbfounded. He was giving her the phone back. 'Yeah, thanks.'

'It's like I said, babes, get to know me, yeah? Don't believe the hype.' He leant forward. 'You can walk out any time you like, but give me some time, yeah, before you make up your mind. Now, don't let me stop you if you want some shut-eye. I know this hasn't been the best of starts, yeah, but I'm not like other dads. You'll see. I've got a job tonight and you can help me out.'

Lauren's face must have registered shock; Ed started laughing. 'Your face! Not that kind of job—what's that woman been saying to you about me!' He shook his head. 'Look at me! I loved Paula. In my own way, granted, but I'd never make you do anything you don't wanna do. It's promotion, the job, nothing else; my book, you must have heard of it, yeah? I'm on *Late Night London*, the recording's tonight. Come with us. If you like. Help your old dad out in his hour of need, so to speak. I've asked my Ash but he's in Los Angeles, so go on, say yes.'

Lauren couldn't think of anything to say. She hadn't expected this, he was kind, not vicious; well, except about Nessa, and Lauren thought it must be hard to be chari-table about someone who'd shot at you.

Lauren nodded at McKay and went upstairs. Why didn't she walk out, get away? He was her dad? She needed some thinking time. What had Nessa done? Lauren went to the window and saw the jogging woman jogging back and running on the spot on her doorstep while she looked in her pockets for her door keys. She looked up to Lauren and Lauren pulled away quickly.

What she'd really like, she thought, was to talk to Luke. She had her phone now, what was stopping her? She could talk it out with Luke—maybe go round, she was in London after all—and maybe her thoughts would stop racing.

She took the phone in her hand and started dialling the number. Then she stopped. Luke thought that Ed McKay was a monster; a criminal, a murderer. So did Nessa. But this McKay was charming, a little creepy in the way that old blokes who fancy themselves a bit are, but not major creepy. What if prison had changed him? And anyway, all murderers are supposed to have freaky eyes; McKay just used too much aftershave. And he was her father, her true father, and she'd never met any of her blood relatives before. Flesh and blood, like he said.

Luke wasn't going to like that at all, was he? Was he? Lauren lay flat out on the white cotton duvet and stared into the gleaming whiteness of the ceiling. Paula had lived here in this house. She held on to that. It made her feel closer, safer. Paula had known Ed McKay, he can't have been that bad surely, not as bad as Nessa and Luke wanted him to be? She made up her mind. She'd give him a day, one day. See what happened. After all, like Ed said, she could leave whenever she liked and she had her phone. Lauren turned over, she was exhausted. Nessa would be frantic, though, she would have phoned the whole of Stivenham ten times. Nessa always thought the worst, always thought of Lauren as an overgrown eight year old. Lauren smiled.

She heard people arriving downstairs. Her head still felt heavy and she closed her eyes. She'd leave it for now, Nessa would have to wait, and if Nessa had taken her from a father who really wanted her, didn't she deserve to wait?

Nessa Now

Nessa tore the 'Do not attempt to move this car' sign from the windscreen. It would take ages for the unclampers to come. She felt for her wallet and her credit card, perhaps she could sort it over the phone. She felt a wave of panic as she realized she didn't have her wallet. She opened the car and checked the glove compartment. Nothing.

Then she remembered, it was sitting on the coffee table in Ian's flat. She had no money at all. She'd spent her parking change on bagels. Nessa scrabbled around on the floor of the car; she put her hand down the backs of the seats and in the storage in the doors. She found one pound seventy. She looked at her watch; she was supposed to meet Jevonka in an hour and a half. She would just have to walk.

As she got out of the car and locked the door she wasn't sure if someone was watching her—a flick of a curtain in the Finer house. Would Luke lend her some money? She dismissed the idea, he really would think she was nuts, driving all the way up to London skint.

Nessa pulled her jacket close and started walking. She reckoned if she cut through the Barbican and across Holborn viaduct it wouldn't take too long. And she needed to be fully awake, to be in control. The walk might help.

Nessa stepped out across Shoreditch High Street and headed west. The area had changed so much, Nessa thought, since she'd lived in London. The place was full of retro furniture shops, coffee shops, and boutiques selling clothes with asymmetric hems in colours and ironic prints that only worked on pretty young girls. Helena would have loved it, she'd been right, as usual.

She half thought of taking a detour, of walking past her old home, but that might make her late. She walked fast, her feet making a regular rhythm on the pavement. What proof could Jevonka have? Proof Ed had killed Helena all these years later? Why should Jevonka care? Nessa reminded herself to be careful, after all Ed had destroyed Paula, taken her self respect, her face, any kind of future she'd had, and he'd threatened to do the same to her. She clasped her arms tight around her body as she walked and remembered.

*   *   *

Nessa had only been kept in the police cell overnight. Someone from social services had sat with her and a duty solicitor during the interview but Nessa only repeated her story. Paula had done nothing, she was the one with the gun. But when they asked her where the gun was, she had no answer. She wasn't sure what Paula would say and she didn't want to ruin things for her.

The woman from social services seemed happy enough when Nessa spun her a line in her best posh voice about GCSEs and her dad coming over from Kenya, but no one would let on where Paula was. She walked back to the warehouse—she couldn't think where else to go—and went inside. She was exhausted, she'd hardly slept in the cell and she was worrying about Paula;

surely they would have taken her to a hospital. Maybe she could find her that way.

It was quiet in the large empty building. Nessa dragged herself upstairs and into the kitchen.

'Hello, Vanessa.'

Ed McKay was sitting at the kitchen table. Just sitting there in his expensive suit, smiling. He pointed at his foot: it was bandaged. Nessa felt her heart thumping. She could run faster than him, she was sure. He must have seen it.

'Don't bother, Vanessa.' He sounded bored. 'My people are outside. They'll pick you up. Now, I know you're sorry for what you did, sincerely sorry, a girl like you, a nice girl.' He looked at her and she knew he was evil. Paula wasn't a person to him, just a thing he could rent out, a thing he could own. Nessa wasn't sorry at all. She walked to the kettle and switched it on.

'Like I said, I know you're sorry. Paula is, truly sorry, she told me before you interrupted us last night. That was a mistake.'

'Yeah, I was aiming at your head.'

Ed McKay laughed.

'Oh, Vanessa, Vanessa.' He shook his head and wiped his hand across his face. 'This is grown-up stuff. You want to forget all about Paula and me. You want to go back to school and grow up and get a job teaching kiddies crochet or something.'

'Paula's my friend.'

'Ah, now there's where you're wrong. You and a girl like that? A working girl? A girl who shot the only man who was good to her.'

'It wasn't her, it was me. I shot you.'

'Yeah, but Paula knows how it works, she'll do her time . . .'

'Do her time? In prison?'

'I'm not talking about boarding school, am I?'

'But she didn't do nothing!'

'Dear, dear, your poor dead mother will be spinning in her grave hearing you talk like that. This is the way of the world; girls like you shouldn't have to deal with girls like Paula. She goes inside, you go to university, that's how it is.'

The kettle clicked but Nessa was frozen. She stared at him. This was the man who'd killed her mother and he was talking about Paula being locked up.

'You can't do that. She's innocent.'

'Oh, but I can. Angry, are we? Hope you haven't got another shooter, I don't want to be hobbling about on two bandaged feet.'

Nessa picked up the kettle. She could feel the heat of the water inside; she wanted to pour it over his head. She unplugged the jug and held it up for an instant. She hoped her face didn't give her away. Suddenly McKay pushed himself up from the table. He seemed massive.

'Listen.' It was just one word, but suddenly Nessa was frozen. 'You can do two things. Your ex-friend Paula is of no concern to you. You've had a nasty shock, what with your mother dying so suddenly and all. It would be best for you if you disappeared.'

'But you killed her, and I saw what you did to Paula. I'll tell someone. I'll get you put away.' Nessa could hear her voice shaking; the water slopped inside the kettle; she put it down.

'You know that's not true. Did the police listen? You think anyone else is going to? You can walk away from me now, I'm letting you. You don't know how lucky you are.'

Nessa felt tears coming behind her eyes. He was right. No one would listen.

'Why are you doing this?'

'Paula was special, but she was ungrateful. I don't like my girls being ungrateful, forgetting who's in charge. I can't let that go, now, can I? Can I? I've got to think of my reputation.'

'I hate you. You killed Helena.'

Ed McKay smiled. 'Course you hate me, darling, now piss off.'

Nessa didn't move. She tried to stare him out, held her head up and tossed the hair back out of her face. McKay's grin only widened and Nessa saw herself in the reflection in the oven door. She didn't look brave. Just ridiculous.

McKay held the door open for her but she didn't move.

'Come on, we haven't got all day.'

He went to the top of the stairs and shouted and Nessa heard him coming back with two men. They were bigger than he was and the kitchen suddenly seemed much smaller.

'I said you could choose. You want to know what it'll be like if you get annoying?' McKay nodded to one of the men and turned to leave. 'Not where it'll show, lads, and don't make it lasting.' He smiled at them. 'This time.'

Nessa gripped the kettle as the two men came towards her from either side of the kitchen table. The one on the right was closer and she threw the thing at him. The lid flew off, hitting him in the face, and the boiling water sprayed out behind it. He jumped back. 'Jesus Christ.'

The other man grabbed her wrist. She swung the empty kettle at him but he blocked it and punched her hard in the stomach. She felt the breath knocked out of her and the pressure around her wrist as he dragged her down the stairs.

It wasn't until later she realized her charm bracelet had come off in the fight.

*   *   *

Nessa looked up. She'd reached Cambridge Circus without realizing it. The grey morning had brought some rain and

251

the West End looked tired and dirty. Nessa smiled. It felt like home.

Jevonka was sitting at the front by the window dressed head to foot in black with a slash of chalky red lipstick. Nessa was surprised; she looked younger than she remembered. Nessa saw her own reflection in the shop window and saw how scruffy and old she looked. She may have felt as confused as she did at sixteen but she looked like an advert for anti-depressants—the harassed, not-so-young mother. Nessa pushed the door open and the smell of coffee and pastries made her head swim.

'Vanessa.' Jevonka pushed her chair back as she stood up and lunged at her. Nessa didn't know what was happening, and leant back and Jevonka ended up kissing thin air. Nessa offered her hand to shake and sat down, embarrassed. She didn't live in a cheek-kissing world any more.

Jevonka ordered her a coffee. Nessa saw the marzipan animals behind the glass counter and thought of Helena talking loudly, making sure the whole place knew she was important.

'It's taken me this long,' Jevonka said, grinning like a cat. 'I always felt I'd let you down. You and Helena. And Helena helped me so much, I wouldn't be where I am today without her. I felt I owed her, and you, much more. Sixteen years, I talked to everyone, every-one.' Jevonka took a sip from a tiny cup of black coffee. 'Last year, I was still in New York, doing the shows, and I ran into Denise.'

'Denise?'

'Denise Konuralp, Turkish, beautiful, hard as nails. She worked for Ed, Paula knew her. She was like Paula but did the weird stuff, the difficult clients. She had a confession! Said it was her insurance. She lives in Manhattan now, runs a dungeon for businessmen.'

Nessa ran her hand across her forehead. 'I really don't know what you're on about, and frankly at the moment I'm not sure I care. Where's Lauren?'

'He's got her.'

Nessa stood up. 'Well, then we'd better go and get her,' she hissed. 'Now.'

'Vanessa.' Jevonka caught her arm. 'Listen, we'll get her out of there, but we need the police. We need to nail McKay for Helena's murder.'

'Yeah, and peace and love throughout the world would be nice, too, but I don't have for ever.'

'Sit down. Come on, here's your coffee.'

Nessa sat down slowly. 'You don't understand. What'll he do to her?'

'He won't have long enough to do anything. Anyway, the guy thinks he's her dad.' Jevonka's face registered surprise. 'You know that, don't you?'

'Him?'

'He reckons she's his.'

'How did he ever get that idea?'

'You know what he's like. It's a good story. Lauren is the beautiful daughter he always wanted, Paula is conveniently dead, and you've done all the hard work. He thinks she is his. He won't touch her.'

Nessa thought about this. Jevonka was right. McKay always wanted a girl.

'I still don't like it. How can you be sure what you're saying is true? The last time I saw you, you were walking into his offices in Berwick Street. This might be some kind of, I don't know, some bluff. You were working for him, weren't you?'

Jevonka was unruffled. 'Whatever gave you that idea? I went to face him out. Knowing what I do now I guess it was lucky for me he wasn't there. Read this.' She pushed a tatty blue folder towards Nessa. She folded her arms and grinned. 'That's my copy of the transcript.'

'Transcript of what?' Nessa was unimpressed.

'Denise's insurance!' She waved a cassette tape. 'See? McKay admits Helena Harper saw him that night. That she never owed him one penny and that she was making things difficult for him with Paula. Paula could have been the face of Hush but Ed wasn't having it. He thought Paula belonged to him.'

'I know that. But does he say he killed Helena?'

Jevonka nodded. 'Read it. The police have theirs, delivered it this morning after my run. And the way things are looking, today's the start of a different life for Mr McKay.'

'He'll get out of it, he always does. The man's the Teflon don, for God's sake.'

'Not any more.' Jevonka drained her cup.

Nessa took the file and pulled out a sheaf of papers. The black words seemed to be swimming on the white paper.

'I can't take any of it in,' Nessa said leaning back in her chair. 'Just tell it to me. Please.'

Lauren Now

When Lauren woke again there was a dress hanging up on the back of the door of her room. It was swathed in see-through plastic and Lauren could see it was not her thing at all. It was deep dark red, not brown enough to be real blood, more the darkest red wine she'd ever seen.

She went to the door. It was unlocked. The dress was velvet, she could see that now, close up, and it had a large piece of paper spiked over the coat hanger with SAMPLE written on it. She flipped it over. Julien Isaacs Couture was printed on the back. She touched the fabric. It wasn't like any other velvet she'd ever touched, not like that syntheticky stuff made into an overshirt that Mrs Harris the geography teacher wore for Founder's Day, or the thick heavy curtain material on the hall windows at school; this felt like nothing on earth. It slipped between her fingers and just touching it made her catch her breath. She thought about trying it on.

Downstairs there was talking. She slipped quietly out of the room and to the white-tiled bathroom. She turned on the tap and took her phone out of her pocket and called Luke. His phone was off.

'Call me back,' she said quietly, 'please.'

She tried Nessa. Nessa picked it up straight away.

'Lauren, oh, thank God, thank God, are you all right?'

'Nessa, I'm fine.' Lauren got up off the loo and turned the tap on harder. Just in case.

'Did they hurt you? Did he touch you?'

'Nessa, Nessa, calm down.' Lauren thought Nessa sounded on the edge of hysteria. 'I'm OK. Nothing's happened.'

'I'll come and get you, take you home. Just tell me where you are, OK? I'll be there right away. Listen, you can't stay with that man a moment longer. He's dangerous, all right? All right?'

The water had heated up and the mirror over the sink was steamy. Lauren wiped a hole in the centre of the mist and looked at herself. Why couldn't Nessa let her make her own decisions? Why hadn't she told her everything? She'd had years. The man downstairs only wanted to get to know her. What was so wrong with that?

'Nessa, please. It's cool, OK?'

'Cool! Lauren, please! The man's a creep.'

'Nessa, he's not a creep, OK?' She tried to stop herself getting angry. 'He's my dad, Nessa, my family.' Lauren sighed. 'And he's telling me a few home truths, so leave me alone, all right?' And Lauren clicked the phone off so she didn't have to hear Nessa freak out any more.

She went back to the bedroom and looked at the dress. She took the plastic cover off it and held it up against her. First of all she thought it had a deep plunging waistline but then she realized it was back to front. It was entirely backless, cut high and straight across at the front. And maybe the colour wouldn't be so bad on her after all. It would make her look, if possible, even paler and her freckles even frecklier. Yeah, it would look good; she slipped her jeans off and tried it on.

The TV recording was in a studio on the other side of London. Ed sat next to Lauren in the back of his car and they drove through the city just as it was getting dark. Lauren loved the feel of the material; Ed said it was made for her.

'I got one of the guys to pick something up. I told him, Julien, that is, I said it was for you. He picked it out himself.'

'You know him?'

'I know everyone, babe, everyone.' He patted her arm.

The shoes were less of a success, but Lauren hadn't wanted to say anything. They were high heeled, strappy, and too bright red against the dress. Her size eights slipped and slid about in them. Lauren hoped she would be sitting down most of the time.

Ed had been so kind, so charming, definitely not a thug. She was sure Luke must have got it wrong about him, and that Nessa had her own reasons for hating him. He'd taken her out for tea at Fortnum and Mason's. She'd asked about Paula, but that was a bit of a disappointment. He didn't know half of what Nessa knew, about Paula's life in care, or how she'd lived all over the place. She did begin to think that maybe he wasn't as knowledgeable as he made out. But he said he loved her, said he was her dad.

She had also searched his face for likeness. But although his grey eyes and Paula's dark brown ones could easily add up to her own hazel, he didn't have half the nose she had.

The car pulled off the main road and ran alongside a dark canal. On the other side of the road there was a high brick wall and Lauren could just see what looked like old fridges stacked up on the other side. Ed was lost in his own world. 'Takes me back this does. See there, where the Limehouse Cut goes down to the river, we used to play in there. All these yards, I knew the faces who ran every one. Happy days.' Ed smiled. 'Bloody hell, I near enough forgot. Last surprise of the night, here.' He pulled a box out of his pocket. 'Belonged to your mother, it did. It'll go with the frock.'

Lauren opened it. It was a charm bracelet. A thick silver chain with an enamel heart and a blue glass eye. Something about it seemed incredibly familiar and she supposed she'd seen it in a photo on her mother's wrist.

'It's lucky, that is,' Ed said, smiling at her. 'Dead lucky.'

They pulled into the studio and got out of the car. It had started to rain and a man with an umbrella stood by the door as they got out. Lauren thought maybe she could get used to this kind of treatment. The man followed them inside and shook the umbrella and a few spots of rain got on her dress. Lauren brushed them off, but Ed was furious, he swore viciously at the doorman.

'No, Ed, it's fine really. Please!' Lauren had to pull him away. 'It's not a problem.'

'The man's an idiot, can't even hold an umbrella! He's probably just fallen off of a lorry!'

Lauren coaxed Ed away and down the corridor; he had a short fuse, it was nerves, that was all.

'*Joseph Lloyd presents* Late and Live *with our special guests: actor Henry Munro; soap-star Paige Edwards opening in her West End musical debut; and one of London's most notorious sons Ed*

McKay! Now here's everyone's favourite boy next door, Joseph Lloyd!'

The voice-over guy had to read it out three times before it was right. Ed and Lauren were waiting in what somebody called 'the green room' along with the West End girl who kept spritzing her throat with some spray like it was on fire, and Henry Munro whose girlfriend kept looking at Lauren jealously.

Ed was deep in conversation with Munro. He was telling him how films these days had no idea; they needed someone like him as consultant, he said, make sure everything was authentic. There was a photographer snapping pictures of Ed holding his new book, and Ed with Henry and Paige Whatsit smiling a neon-strength smile.

'Here, Lol, Lauren, come over here.' Lauren stood up. Lol? No one called her that. Ed manoeuvred her in between himself and Henry Munro. Henry smiled at her and Lauren felt like a piece of meat in a frock. She felt his hand in the small of her back and she shrugged it off. Ed was oblivious.

'Smile, babes.' Lauren did. The camera flashed and for an instant Lauren was out of her body and looking down on herself. She saw a girl, a too-tall schoolgirl with bony hips, in a beautiful dress that was cut almost down to her bum at the back standing next to a creepy old bloke with bitten nails and a lech of an actor. She'd seen Henry Munro on the telly. Chloe had oohed over him when she was fourteen, but close up he was like the others, like all of them, terminally creepy and old.

Lauren thought of the picture she'd seen on the computer. She was just like her mum. Made up and dollied up for what? To make old men look good. The Lauren on the ground smiled but it looked like a grimace. Why did she think this was a good idea? The man didn't know her at all. She was just a girl in a dress.

Maybe Nessa was right, she thought, and wished she could just float out of herself and the studio and back to wherever Nessa was now.

Ed McKay gave her a squeeze, his bitten-nailed hands pressing into her middle. She'd never had a father. Is this what they did? Lauren felt herself dropping back to earth. She fiddled with the bracelet, pulling the blue glass eye round and round. The blue glass eye was solid and blobby and when she looked down it stared back at her the way Nessa did. The enamel heart was just one half-shade lighter than her frock. Nessa! That's where she'd seen it before: in one of those old photos of Paula and Nessa goofing around in a photo booth. It wasn't Paula's bracelet it was Nessa's. She opened her mouth to tell Ed and shut it again. Either he didn't know at all, or he did know and he hadn't told her. She closed her hand around it and remembered Nessa telling her about it. Paula had given it to her. She'd lost it, she said, just before she moved out to Stivenham. Nessa always said it was the nicest thing she ever owned.

There was a call for the show to start and Lauren excused herself and found the Ladies. She could hear the crowd outside cheering as Joseph Lloyd skipped through the large double doors and kicked off the show. Lauren wiped where her mascara had run and wished she had her phone. She would make it up to Nessa, of course, but first she wanted to talk to Luke.

Lauren washed the rest of the mascara off. She wiped the jammy dark red lipstick away. She looked like a ghost girl, pale and willowy and slightly underfed. She slipped her feet out of the high-heeled shoes; her toes were already pinched up. The thin carpet wasn't that cold. Now all she needed was a phone. She walked as far as the artists' entrance where a security guard was reading a newspaper.

'Is there a phone I can use, please?'

The guard didn't see her at first, then looked up and smiled at her as if she was a four year old in her mother's dressing-up box.

'You can use this one, if you like.' He turned around the phone on the desk. She tapped in Luke's number and waited. There was a draught from outside and her upper arm bristled with goosepimples. The man was still watching her, smiling. Lauren turned away.

'Luke, it's me.'

'Lauren? Where are you? Nessa is freaked.'

'Bow Studios, it's called, east London, I think. It's a recording of *Late and Live* with Joseph Lloyd. I've made a mistake, come and get me. Please? I'll be at the stage door, all right?'

'I'll be there in half an hour. Don't move, OK?'

'OK.'

Next to the guard there was a monitor that showed Joseph Lloyd sitting in a cowhide armchair asking Ed about his new book. Lauren stood watching it. On screen, Ed soaked up the attention.

'So, can I call you Ed? You can call me Joe! Don't want any part of me nailed to the chair, now, do I?' Joseph Lloyd looked pantomime scared and the crowd laughed. 'Now, Ed, you're an old-fashioned villain, wouldn't you say? Old school, a great British tradition.'

Lauren looked away. The security guard must have thought she was freezing because he offered her his jacket. Lauren smiled but shook her head even though she was starting to feel the cold. She checked the clock. Luke would be twenty-five minutes. Outside it looked as if it had started to rain.

'It's filthy out there, love, I hope you're not thinking of going out with nothing on your feet.' He was trying to be nice and Lauren smiled at him but shook her head.

'I'm waiting for my friend.'

'Tell you what, love, you go an' sit back in the warm. I'll get someone to tell you when he arrives. All right?'

Lauren thanked him and walked barefoot back to the green room.

There was a monitor in here, too, and now Paige Edwards had joined Joseph Lloyd and Ed. She was talking about her new musical, based on the songs of pop singer Magdalena Richards, and she was wearing the actual conical satin bra she wore for the show's finale.

Lauren rested her head in her hands. Henry Munro's girlfriend looked bored and smiled. She wasn't as pretty as Eda, but she wasn't bad looking, and she didn't seem much older than Lauren. Lauren smiled back.

'I'm Emily,' the girl said in an accent that could cut glass. 'Haven't I seen you before? Were you in *The Bill* last month?'

'I'm not an actress.'

'I'm so useless with people, everyone starts looking the same after a while. I'm Emily, Em-i-ly.' She looked Lauren over. 'That looks like a Julien Isaacs? Are you a model then?' Lauren could see from her eyes that she was drunk.

'Sort of.'

'Oh-h, you were with Ed McKay? I remember! What's he like then? Really?'

Lauren didn't know what to say. She had no idea. She'd only met him this morning.

'Nice dress, very nice.' Emily nodded and almost slid off her chair.

Lauren looked at the clock on the wall; the minute hand seemed to be crawling around the dial. She wished Luke was here now.

Back on the monitor Paige Edwards was performing the finale from the musical. The character she played, Bernardette, had earned enough money as a lap dancer to buy a new kidney for her baby brother and now the surgeon had asked her to marry him.

Lauren wanted to laugh out loud. She was sitting back-stage at a recording of a top TV show wearing the most beautiful dress in the world but she wished she was some-where else. Nessa would have been killing herself laughing at the woman on stage.

She got up. The applause for Henry Munro was so loud it sounded unnatural. She was worried the show would end and Ed would come back and she'd still be here, waiting. She wanted to have vanished. Lauren pushed through the door and looked up and down the corridor.

The artists' entrance was busy now. The security guard was dealing with two large men, one in a suit that was a little too small, the other in a leather coat that he must have thought was more *Matrix* than *EastEnders*. The guard was shouting down the intercom and looked flustered. Lauren went to the door and looked out. There was some kind of motorway intersection just half a mile away and although it was evening the traffic noise was still loud.

Leather-coat man leant towards the security guard. 'Look, we'll wait here. Just as soon as Mr McKay comes off stage we'd like a word. Please.' He flashed a card and a smile. 'Metropolitan police.'

Nessa Now

Nessa's hips were killing her. She was squashed into the back of Jevonka's smart two-seater. Every time Jevonka took a bend Nessa was thrown against the side of the car.

'It's not far.' Jevonka flashed her a sorry look in the car mirror and Nessa tried to get herself a little comfier.

'Thanks, Luke, for calling us.'

Luke shrugged. 'No probs. I knew it would be quicker than getting a bus.'

'Did she sound OK?'

'Quiet, not like her.'

'Don't worry, Vanessa.' Jevonka pulled the car off a main road and onto a dark cobbled street. 'The police will be picking McKay up.' She checked the clock on the dashboard. 'Any minute now.'

Nessa hugged her knees and shut her eyes. 'And you're sure these guys will do the right thing?'

'Surely. Vanessa, this is the twenty-first century and these guys are pros. It's nothing like the old days, believe me.'

Nessa swallowed. She tried not to think about shoot-outs or mistaken identity or Lauren spending the night in a cell.

'There!' Luke had spotted the sign. 'Bow Studios!'

The rain was still coming down in sheets. Nessa wondered how Luke had been able to see out of the windows. Jevonka pulled into the car park.

'The artists' entrance; she said she'd be there.'

Although Luke was out of the car first, Nessa surprised herself with her ability to uncurl and run through the rain to the side door. There was a buzzer on the wall; she spoke into it.

'We're here to pick up Lauren Bogle?' Nessa held herself close to the wall to keep out of the rain. Nothing happened. She made a face at Luke and tried again. Luke walked along to the door, it was blackened glass, but there was a small see-through panel. He beckoned Nessa.

Inside was a knot of people. Nessa stood on tiptoe and saw the actor she liked who'd been Mr Rochester in the new telly adaptation talking to a man in a leather coat. From the other man's stance she'd bet money on it that he was a policeman. There was something going on in there but she couldn't see Lauren at all. Luke had his hand up to knock on the glass when Nessa reached up and stopped him.

'My God!' Nessa recognized him straight away. He was older, a lot older, and slightly less chunky than she remembered. His hair was completely grey but his skin was permatan orange. Nessa felt her stomach churning. Luke's hand stopped, frozen in mid-knock. He was talking so loudly that they could both hear every word.

'Gentlemen, gentlemen!' McKay had his hands up in surrender. 'I'm not going to cause trouble, am I? For God's sake, I'm a pensioner.' He looked at one of the policemen. 'You're younger than my Ashley. Getting younger every bloody day, coppers!' He smiled and Nessa had to look away. 'I said I'll come down to the station and I will. I know the drill, I've done it enough. But do me a favour, boys, just let me walk away, quietly, nicely. I ain't done nothing. I'm just an old man trying to flog a book. The papers are going to tear me apart tomorrow as it is. Probably say it's a publicity stunt or something.' He laughed and even the policemen smiled with him.

The leather-coated policeman held open the door and nodded at McKay. Nessa jumped back. She was terrified he would see her, and like the Ed-shaped monster in her dreams chase her and chase her until she was so out of breath her heart burst. She looked for Jevonka, but couldn't see her or Luke. Her heart was already speeding up.

'Get him into the bloody car,' she muttered under her breath.

The two policemen walked either side of him into the car park. Leather-coat had his hand over his head to stop the worst of the rain. Nessa hoped McKay wasn't looking and stepped into the light of the open artists' entrance to look for Lauren. It was over, she told herself. Lauren would be all right and she'd never see that man ever again.

She scanned the room. Jevonka was making a call, leaning up against the wall. She was grinning broadly. Luke was embracing an impossibly tall, thin woman in a quite beautiful dark-red dress. It was like watching a dance and as they swung round, Nessa realized the dress was backless and the woman was so pale and cold-looking she looked as if she needed warming up . . .

'Lauren?'

It was. They stared at each other and Nessa knew she was crying.

'Lauren.'

Lauren unwrapped herself and ran to Nessa. Hugged her tight. 'I'm sorry, Ness, I'm sorry I'm sorry I'm sorry.'

'Me too. I thought I'd never see you again,' Nessa said. 'I was so scared in case I never saw you again. There's so much I never said.'

'I shouldn't have said those things I said to you. You know I never meant it. You're more than family, Ness, you know that.'

Nessa wiped her eyes.

'You've got no shoes!' Nessa pointed down to Lauren's feet.

'I know. It was the heels. They were killing me. But look, look, Ness, I got this back.'

Lauren held up her arm. The bracelet fell down to her elbow, then she shook it off.

'My bracelet! Paula gave it me.' Nessa wiped her eyes. 'It's lucky.'

'I know. It's yours. Here.'

Nessa took it and knitted her fingers in tight with Lauren's. They began walking towards Jevonka's sports car. Nessa thought her chest would burst; she breathed in deeply, tried to relax. It was all right.

'Take my coat. You'll catch your death.' Nessa took her old wax jacket off and Lauren put it on.

Nessa wiped away the wet hair that was stuck to her face. It was dark in the car park and in that one second she thought there was a movement behind her or in front of her. Somewhere close. The rain cut the dark into bars and Nessa couldn't see. Lauren screamed or the brakes of a lorry squealed.

She heard a shout, a loud, 'Oi!' and she turned towards it. There were the policemen, one running towards her in the rain, the other just behind talking into a phone or a radio as he ran. When she turned back to Lauren she had vanished.

'Miss! Miss! Did you see anything?'

Nessa's heart had started hammering up to top speed inside her chest. She couldn't speak. She shook her head, eventually squeezed one word out, 'Lauren!' and they were off in between the lines of cars ducking and running like TV cops.

'Lauren!' Nessa yelled, but the rain and the dark and the motorway traffic cancelled it out. Luke ambled over, hands in pockets.

'Whassup? Lauren in the car?' Her face must have told him everything. 'Come on! Come on, Nessa, we've got to look.' Something in the desperation in his voice snapped her into life. 'He's an old guy! He can't have got far.'

Then she was on her own again. She could see Luke bobbing and weaving through the cars. The audience were spilling out of the main studio doors; a few cars had already left the car park but one of the policemen was now stationed at the barrier not letting anyone else out.

Nessa was soaking. In the rain the lights in the car park blurred into orange and made it almost impossible to see. She leant against Jevonka's car. Useless. She couldn't save Paula then and she couldn't save Lauren now. She was useless. In her pocket she felt the charm bracelet, she could feel the heart and the eye and the shell tight in her hand.

Nessa felt the rain hammering down on her face. She had promised to keep Lauren safe, she'd promised. She couldn't just cave in, not now.

Nessa stood up and wiped the rain out of her eyes.

Lauren Now

Lauren held the old wax jacket out and smelt home, Nessa, and the sea, and warmth. She had shimmied her hands into the armholes when something bundled into her back and she was on the ground. The dress must be ruined and she wondered how on earth she would explain when the time came to give it back. Nessa must have bumped into her but then through the smell of cars and oil on the ground she smelt something woody and citrussy. There was a large hand over her mouth and nose.

'Don't make a sound,' Ed McKay hissed into her ear. There was whisky on his breath and tobacco. He was so close Lauren could feel the warm moistness of his breath. She tried to turn away but she was pinned, arms inside the jacket. He took something from an inner pocket.

'Sorry, babes.' Something clicked near Lauren's head. It was hard to keep her eyes open. The rain was coming down hard and making her blink. She felt the weight of him pushing down on her back. Half her face was slammed into the tarmac. She tried to move slightly, but then there was more pressure.

'Keep down. I'm not ready.'

From her viewpoint on the ground Lauren could see between the cars, people running. Luke! Her heart leapt when she saw his waterlogged Converses passing just a car away.

'Right, Lauren. I need your help.' He sat her up. Her feet were numb with cold. 'You're gonna stand up—not yet—with me, slow, and cool. Now don't think about shouting or running. I'm right here.'

He took the hand from her mouth. 'Remember. Quiet.' And they both stood up. He had a hand around her wrist so hard it hurt and the other was pressing something hard into her neck. 'This is a gun, babes, it's for them, all right, for the police, yeah. You be a good girl and no one will get hurt. Now start walking.'

There was a lot of confusion, one of the policemen was at the car park exit, the other was talking into something, then shouting at the crowd to get back. The crowd were grumbling: they wanted to go home.

They shuffled like entrants in a three-legged race to the canal at the far side of the car park. Everything glittered black and orange and it was raining so hard Lauren thought she couldn't breathe.

Then they were seen. Leather-coat man was running towards them and the crowd had all turned to look. Ed stopped. He kept hold of Lauren's wrist; she felt the bones in it cracking together. He took the gun and held it in the air. Lauren thought he was going to shout at the policeman—he was still coming towards them.

Something sounded so loud Lauren thought the sky had cracked open.

The policeman stopped. Stepped back.

Ed McKay whispered into her ear. 'There's still life in this old dog.'

He kissed her on the forehead. Her wrist was still held tight. 'Come on, babes.'

He pulled her onto the towpath. 'Come on, I can get the boys to pick us up. If we can get up to Carpenters Road we'll be out of here before they know it.'

Lauren thought the man was mad. There'd be police everywhere any second. But she didn't want to be the one to tell him. He seemed driven and rejuvenated and Lauren felt herself half dragged along. She trod over slime and broken hard things and things she couldn't even begin to imagine. The rain still fell and she was soaked head to foot even in Nessa's jacket. The rain washed down her neck, her back, and her legs.

In the distance the grey shape of the policeman followed. In the sky a helicopter chopped up the night sky. Lauren could see the searchlight coming closer.

'In here.' Through a gap in the brick wall and they were in a scrapyard. Lauren made out a Portakabin and a pick-up truck on its knees and a mountain of white fridges. Ed put the gun back into his jacket. Lauren caught a glimpse: it was tiny and metal. She tried to shake him off but his grip on her wrist remained.

'Let me go. Please.'

'Sorry, babes.' His teeth were very white. 'Life or death.'

A wall of fridges loomed up in front of them, as the helicopter swerved. Ed pulled her out of the light. With his free hand Ed reached for his phone.

Lauren pulled away as hard as she could and ran. She ran towards the fridges and clambered up and onto them, slipping and slipping and bruising every inch of herself. Ed was shouting. She heard the gun go off again but she moved fast. Slipping between crevasses of white goods still greasy from filthy kitchens.

The helicopter throbbed and the searchlight danced around the scrapyard.

Nessa Now

The gunshot jolted Nessa. She imagined Lauren lying in a pool of blood that matched her dress. The thought that maybe that hadn't happened yet shook her, and before she could think herself out of it she ran, slipping and squelching in her wet shoes, after the policeman. Luke was way ahead. Nessa was small and not built for speed.

Behind her she could hear a choir of differently tuned police sirens coming closer. The canal was pitted with raindrops.

Up ahead she could see the policeman scanning the path, still speaking into his radio. Nessa stopped on a bench, out of breath, and looked up the canal. She saw what looked like Luke's shadow vanish through a gap in the wall. She got up and waved to the policeman, and he waved back at her. She knew what he meant. Stay back. Leave it to us. Nessa knew what had happened the last time she'd left it to the police. She stepped through into the yard.

The helicopter was overhead and its searchlight lit up a pick-up truck with no wheels. Piles of tyres and a sea of fridges and freezers about eight or ten high stretched into the distance. Luke had started climbing up. Every so often the light swept around and Nessa felt giddy watching.

There was a pile of car exhausts stacked up against the

wall like tortured organ pipes. Nessa thought she could see or feel something moving through the bars of the rain in the dark. What she needed was a weapon.

She crouched by the pick-up truck. If she'd been a man on TV she would have wrenched the bumper off and used that. The searchlight stopped over Luke, Afro flattened, scaling the fridge mountain like Chris Bonnington. She couldn't see Lauren or Ed. She turned away from the light and looked into the dark again. It took a few seconds to see anything. There. By the Portakabin. Someone passed in front of it.

Nessa crouched around the truck. What could she do? Five foot nothing. Arms enfeebled by years in the music library. The helicopter buzzed lower and Luke was standing, hands up, in a pool of light on top of the fridges. Nessa was aware of a voice coming through a loudspeaker from the helicopter. She felt as if this was *The Wizard of Oz*. Maybe Lauren had been taken by flying monkeys. In her pocket she felt the charm bracelet pressing into her leg. She pulled it out gently and put it on; she could do with some luck. She fiddled the eye round and round. In the light on the fridge mountain she saw Lauren emerge from a freezer. Luke pulled her out. Nessa felt dizzy with relief.

Then an Ed-shaped shadow moved somewhere to the right. Nessa knew there were police around, swarms of them soon. But what if they let him go? What if they missed him and it all happened again? Paula. She'd only killed herself because of him. And Helena—now there was proof that had been him. If he walked away who knew what he might do to Lauren; the drip of lies and half lies— she wasn't going to let that happen.

Nessa darted from the cover of the pick-up towards the Portakabin. There was a pile of what—metal pipes?—she thought they were more car exhausts, but they were smaller. She lifted one; not heavy. She gripped it tightly and scuttled along the wall. Something was there. She swallowed and swung hard. This was for Paula.

Nothing.

She swung again and again and again in the dark and the rain. She heard a gun go off again and imagined the air that passed her face had been a bullet. Nessa smiled.

'You missed! You're old and crap and you missed!'

The light swung round and she saw him. The gun was pointing at her head. There was more loudspeaker babble but Nessa could only hear her heartbeat and the blood pumping inside her head. The helicopter hovered directly overhead. She swung out again, heard the gunshot, a loud, heavy crack that burst inside her head. Nessa shut her eyes and swung again, hard. She felt the pipe connect with something solid. Flesh? She looked hard into the dark: Ed McKay lay on the floor.

Later

Lauren jiggled the key in the door. She still hadn't got used to the lock and she was tired. The flight from Milan had been OK but the journey from the airport had taken for ever. That would be the last job until the New Year and she was glad of it. There was only so much standing around in clothes she could take. It was the first day back at college tomorrow and she felt so knackered she wasn't sure if she'd make it. The key turned and Lauren went in. The heating had come on by itself and inside was warm and homely. Lauren had no problems with a flat. The Barbican was heaven, near to everywhere, and she felt safe surrounded by hundreds of people in identical flats all stacked up on top of each other.

There were messages from Luke, but she'd already spoken to him on the train on the way down. One from Eda, and another for Ness from Ian. There was a final one from Jevonka but Lauren fast-forwarded through it. It was not quite a year and a half since the night that Ed McKay was arrested and Lauren still found her stomach turning over if she thought about it for too long.

The flat was quiet. Nessa was still at work. Lauren didn't turn the light on; she went to the window in the living room and looked out. The view was perfect. There was the city spread out to the west, all the way from Crystal

Palace in the south to Hampstead in the north. The tower blocks of the city huddled together like penguins looking for warmth. Lauren thought the best thing about working away was coming home. Coming home to Luke and to Nessa and just coming home.

Lauren flicked on the telly and the news was on. Lauren looked at her watch: Nessa was usually back by now. Her new job was in the music school to the north of the Barbican so it wasn't far. She pulled her college stuff out of her bag; she had catch-up to do for English and Film Studies but that wasn't so bad.

On the telly the newsreader warned of impending rail strikes, of failing schools, and measures to combat heart disease. Lauren went into the kitchen and clicked on the kettle. She didn't believe her ears at first: *'Ed McKay has died in Belmarsh prison where he was on remand awaiting trial for the murder of fashion designer Helena Harper in 1989.'*

Lauren sat down open-mouthed. She was still sitting there when Nessa came in.

'McKay is dead. Heart attack.'

'I heard, Jevonka called me at work. How do you feel?'

Lauren shrugged and shifted up on the sofa to make room for Nessa. 'I feel like I should be sad. I mean he was my dad.'

'Paula didn't want him to be your dad. She wanted your dad to be George Peppard in *Breakfast at Tiffany's* or someone like that . . .' Nessa trailed off. They sat together on the sofa for a long time, the flickering telly light casting shadows on the walls behind them.

'Thanks, Nessa.'

'What for?'

'For taking me in. For looking after me. For not telling me every day that I was a total idiot to think I knew him better than you.'

Nessa looked at her. 'The man could turn on the charm; not that he ever bothered for me.'

'Charmed Paula though.'

'She was fourteen when she first met him. And I know she did a lot of things, but inside, you know, she was very young. We both were.'

'Yeah. I'll go up there tomorrow after college, to the cemetery.'

'You do that, love.' Nessa patted her on the leg. 'I still miss her, you know. Paula was much more than a pretty face, she was a real laugh. She was the best friend I ever had.' Lauren saw Nessa's eyes going glassy. On the TV the camera swooped over the Thames as the *EastEnders* theme tune started up. Nessa reached for the remote and clicked the TV off. 'She'd be so proud of you. You know that. A levels! Everything.'

'I know. We're all right, aren't we?' Lauren squeezed Nessa's hand.

'Yeah, Lauren, we are.'

Lauren stood up. 'I'm going to make some tea, and there's a film I've got to watch for college, yeah. It's over there by the DVD player.'

Nessa reached across and pulled out the box. 'I hope it's not scary. I couldn't take anything scary, not now.'

'Don't worry, Ness, I'm doing "The Rise of the American Musical". We can forget about Ed completely and wallow in good old-fashioned schmaltz overkill.' Lauren shouted through from the kitchen. 'It's Judy Garland. You've probably seen it a dozen times; you and Paula liked them, didn't you? It's *Meet Me In St Somewhere*; we can just fast-forward the boring bits.'

'Louis, it's St Louis,' Nessa said quietly. 'And there are always boring bits in musicals, that's why they're like life.'

Nessa sat in the dark and clicked the telly back on. The music started and Lauren came through with tea and marble cake and Nessa turned the sound up loud.

Catherine Johnson was brought up in North London. Her parents are from Wales and Jamaica. Catherine studied film at St Martin's School of Art where her final piece was a remake of 'Rapunzel'. Catherine has worked as a horse wrangler, as writer-in-residence at Holloway Prison, and was reader-in-residence at the Royal Festival Hall. She also writes for film and TV. Catherine now lives in London Fields and has two children.